KILLING WEST

A Novel
By

Lee Gimenez

RRP
River Ridge Press

Killing West
by
Lee Gimenez

This is a work of fiction. The characters, incidents, and dialogues are products of the author's imaginations and are not to be construed as real. Any resemblance to actual persons, living or dead, is entirely coincidental.

Printed in the United States of America.
Published by River Ridge Press.

First edition.

Cover photo: Copyright by Kiselev Velerich; used under license from Shutterstock, Inc.
Cover design: Judith Gimenez

ISBN-13: 978-0692245873

ISBN-10: 0692245871

Other Novels by Lee Gimenez

The Washington Ultimatum

Blacksnow Zero

The Sigma Conspiracy

The Nanotech Murders

Death on Zanath

Virtual Thoughtstream

Azul 7

Terralus 4

The Tomorrow Solution

KILLING WEST

Chapter 1

June 5
Shanghai, China

"And if he won't talk?" Rachel West asked.

Her CIA field officer, Jason Taylor, took off his wire-frame glasses and began cleaning them. "In that case, Rachel, you kill him."

The two were standing in an empty room on the 81st floor of an office tower overlooking the Huangpu River. She glanced away from him and out toward the nighttime skyline of the Pudong District. Ultra-modern skyscrapers surrounded them with a kaleidoscope of neon light. She turned back to Taylor. "Seems extreme. When I was briefed at Langley, I was told this was a fact-finding operation."

"Things have changed," Taylor replied.

Rachel studied the mousy-looking man in front of her. Thin and balding, he had the appearance of an accountant, not a field officer. "How so?"

"We just found out Zhao Deng is secretly trying to buy Sincore Technologies. That would make it his fourth purchase of a large American tech company. The Agency now considers Zhao a national security threat."

Rachel realized the significance. Sincore was one of the crown jewels, rivaling Microsoft, Intel, and Apple in size. "I understand. How do I proceed?"

Taylor handed her a large manila envelope. "It's all in here. We've been tracking Zhao for weeks. His whereabouts, itinerary, contacts." He pointed out the window to one of the towers in the distance. "Primarily he works out of his corporate office over there."

Opening the envelope, she skimmed the contents. "He's a billionaire – probably has top-notch security."

"That he does, Rachel. It won't be easy."

"One question."

"Yes?"

"Why me? Why was I assigned to this? Looks like you've already got other people on the ground."

The man smiled. "That should be obvious. First, you speak fluent Mandarin. And two, Zhao likes beautiful Western women. You fit the bill on both counts. We figured you'd be able to get close to him, get his guard down."

"I'm not a whore," she snapped, "if that's what you expect."

He held up his palms in front of him. "Sorry if I gave that impression. It's just you have assets that may become useful."

"Fine, as long as we understand each other. You'll be my main contact here in Shanghai?"

"That's right," he said, as he handed her a cell phone. "Any problems or questions, call me on this. It's a special phone – can't be traced by Zhao or anyone else."

"How does the Chinese government fit into all this?"

"They don't, Rachel. This operation is strictly black ops. Their government doesn't even know we're here."

She nodded. This was standard procedure for her branch of the CIA. "I couldn't bring my usual tools on the flight over. I'll need a few things."

"No problem. I booked you a room at the Fairmont Peace Hotel. Just let me know what you need and I'll have it delivered there. Any other questions?"

"Not right now."

"In that case," he said, "I'll be on my way. I suggest you check in at the hotel and get some rest before you start. You look tired."

Rachel thought about the fatiguing fourteen-hour flight she had taken into Pudong International. "Good idea."

The balding man turned to go, then faced her again. "One more thing. For security reasons, from now on we won't be meeting in person."

"I understand."

Taylor left the room and she gazed out the windows at the riot of neon lights illuminating the nighttime sky. From this vantage point it was easy to see that Shanghai was China's largest city. It had a population of over 19 million, and was the country's business and financial center.

She tensed as she thought about the upcoming mission. Taylor was right – it wasn't going to be easy.

***

Rachel West peered through the high-powered telescope pointed down toward street level.

She was on an upper floor of a vacant, under-construction office building, across from the skyscraper housing Zhao's headquarters. Focusing the scope for a tighter look of his building, she clearly saw the activity below. Although it was nighttime, the area was well-lit, allowing a full view of the security guards manning the building's entrance. Most of the workers had already left the skyscraper, but the sidewalks were still crowded. Yincheng Road, which fronted the building, was choked with vehicles.

She was crouched behind a low wall, dressed in black slacks and a black T-shirt. It was dark and stifling hot, the concrete floor still radiating the daytime heat. Her clothes were beginning to cling. The only sounds were the hum of vehicle traffic from below and the occasional whine of commercial jets flying overhead. The building's construction work gave off an acrid smell.

Windows hadn't been installed yet, and a gust of wind blew in, swirling her long hair. She tucked more of it under her watch cap. But she relished the breeze, a welcome change to the sweltering summer heat.

Rachel had been monitoring Zhao's movements for four days, and the man had a routine that didn't vary. At 8 a.m., a pearl-gray Bentley stopped in front of his building. He exited, flanked by two muscular bodyguards, and went inside. Then at approximately 8 p.m., the same car returned to pick him up along with his bodyguards. Zhao was always escorted.

She had also done surveillance of his walled estate in the outskirts of the city. The palatial home, like his headquarters, was a virtual fortress with armed guards and high-tech security everywhere.

Glancing at her watch, she noted it was almost 8 p.m. now.

She watched as, like clockwork, the Bentley pulled to the curb and Zhao and his bodyguards climbed in. A moment later the large car disappeared into traffic.

Standing, she began breaking down the telescope and stuffing it into her backpack. As she did so, her thoughts turned to tomorrow.

Another day of surveillance? she wondered. *Or move ahead with my plan?*

Realizing she had learned all she could by observing Zhao, she decided to put the operation into action.

***

Although it was only 7:50 a.m., Yincheng Road was already packed with slow-moving vehicles – cars, trucks, mopeds, and hordes of bicycles. Rachel waited for the light to change, then crossed the street and stood at the corner.

After scanning the skyscraper's entrance, she began walking towards it. The sidewalk was crowded with pedestrians. Striding close to the curb, she kept an eye out for the gray Bentley. The cacophony of noise in the area was almost deafening – the blaring of car horns, the screeching of brakes, the snatches of conversation, and scuffing of shoes. And although it was early morning, it was already brutally hot, the heat accentuating the body odors from the mass of people all around her.

Rachel wore a short, red dress, her long blonde hair flowing past her shoulders. A slender, yet curvaceous woman, she was in her mid-thirties. Considering she was tall and one of the few Westerners in the crowd of Chinese, she felt she would stand out. Or so she hoped.

Moments later she spotted the large sedan pull up to the curb. Picking up her pace, she reached the Bentley as the doors opened and the men exited the car.

On purpose, she bumped into one of the bodyguards. The bulky man whirled around and confronted her, a scowl on his face, as his hand reached into his jacket.

"*Baogian! Duibugi*," Rachel said in Mandarin, which meant: *I'm sorry! Excuse me.*

Zhao's face lit up when he saw her. Placing a hand on the guard's shoulder, he smiled at her and said, "*Zaoshang Hao.*"

"*Zaoshang Hao*," she replied, returning the smile. *Good morning.*

Then, with a flip of her long hair, she turned and walked away.

***

Returning to the building's entrance the next day at the same time, Rachel managed to walk by as Zhao exited the Bentley once again. She made eye contact and gave him a small wave before striding past.

She repeated the process on the following day as well, this time giving Zhao a wide smile. He returned it and began speaking to one of his bodyguards.

Rachel slowed her pace as she continued down the crowded sidewalk. Reaching the corner, she glanced back. As she had hoped, one of the guards was following her. Crossing the street, she walked several more blocks until she reached Riverside Park. There she bought a ticket for one of the ferries that were constantly crossing the Huangpu River.

While keeping a covert eye on the guard to make sure he was still tailing her, she leisurely boarded the ferry, giving the man plenty of time to get on.

The commuter boat crossed the river and she disembarked, then strode along Zhongshan Road the two blocks to the Fairmont Hotel. Entering the marbled lobby of the famed hotel, she made her way to the elevator and up to her room to wait.

***

There was knock on her hotel room door at 6 p.m. that evening.

Rachel had expected it would come sooner, but Zhao, being a wealthy and cautious man, had obviously been scrutinizing her credentials.

After checking the eyehole, she opened the door to a white-haired Asian man. He was dressed in a black suit and tie and looked to be in his sixties.

"*Wei?*" she said. *Yes?*

"*Wo Jiao Yang*," he said, handing her a card. *My name is Yang.*

He gave her a small bow. "I am Mr. Zhao's personal assistant. Are you Eve Lewis?"

"Yes, that's right," she replied. Lewis was her cover name.

"Mr. Zhao would like to meet with you."

"I don't believe I know him."

The white-haired man smiled. "He's seen you by his building several times. He's a distinguished, heavy-set man accompanied by bodyguards."

She feigned surprise at first. "Of course. I remember him now." She laughed. "He must be very rich, since he has a Bentley."

"That he is, Miss. I understand you're a financial advisor. Mr. Zhao is always making investments and is interested in retaining your services."

Rachel grinned. "I'm always looking for new clients. Does he want me to visit him at his office?"

"Actually, no. He'd rather discuss things over dinner. On his yacht."

She knew Zhao had an attractive American wife and three children. She also knew faithfulness was not one of his strong points. It wasn't hard to figure out why he wanted to meet on his boat. "How lovely. When?"

"If it's convenient, tomorrow night at seven. A limo will pick you up then."

"Shall I bring my laptop? I have financial spreadsheets I like to review with prospective clients."

"You won't need that, Miss. Good day." He bowed again, turned and left.

***

Rachel lifted the large suitcase and placed it on her hotel room's bed. One of Taylor's men had dropped it off earlier.

She opened the case and studied the contents, satisfied the field officer had been able to obtain all the tools she'd requested. In the case were four items: An MP-5 short-barreled machine pistol; a break-apart Sig Sauer snipers rifle with scope; a Glock 42 handgun with a sound suppressor; and one last item, a thin and lightweight, but very deadly, carbon knife.

Unfortunately for tonight's dinner with Zhao, she wouldn't be able to utilize most of the items in the case – his security was too good.

She selected the Glock 42 from the suitcase and wrapped her hand around its small size. The weapon was easy to carry and conceal, but still fired a lethal .380 round. A compact version of the regular size Glock 17, the 42 was her favorite tool. Lightweight and accurate, it fit into the smallest of handbags. But probably still too bulky for tonight.

Putting the pistol back in the case, she then picked up the carbon knife and lightly touched the tip. It was razor sharp. Bending down, she took off one of her four-inch heels and inserted the knife into the custom-made slit on the sidewall inside the shoe. The Louboutin shoes were constructed just for her and she always packed them in her bags when on assignment. She hadn't used them often, but it was comforting to know they were there. Putting the shoe back on, she closed the case and stored it in the closet.

Next she went to the room's full-length mirror and studied her appearance. Rachel was wearing a white, form-fitting, low-cut dress with spaghetti straps. She hated wearing dresses, always had. Much preferred jeans or slacks; anything but dresses. But tonight wasn't about what she wanted – it was all about Zhao and what he wanted.

Satisfied with her appearance, she picked up her small purse and glanced at her watch. It was almost time. Leaving the room, she made her way down to the lobby and outside to the hotel entrance.

The stretch Mercedes limousine was already there, waiting for her. The limo driver opened the rear door and she eased back onto the leather seat.

She had expected the limo would take Zhongshan Road toward the port of Shanghai, but instead they went south for a short distance to a helipad by the river. Waiting on the pad was a large passenger helicopter, with Zhao's company logo painted on the fuselage. The man was full of surprises, she thought.

Rachel climbed into the helicopter, the jet engines whined on, and the craft lifted off. Moments later it was cruising high over the city. Unlike most helicopters, this one was whisper quiet. The rich aroma of the leather seats filled the cabin. Besides her and the pilot, no one else was on board.

As she settled back on the seat, she gazed at the lights of the city, trying to calm her nerves. Tonight would be difficult. She had been in tough situations many times before as an agent, but this was different. Zhao's security was first class. Getting in would be easy. It was getting out alive that worried her.

Pushing those thoughts aside, she went back to staring at the lights below. The helicopter flew north along the coast, then headed out over the open waters of the Yellow Sea. Twenty minutes later she spotted it, a large white yacht, its multiple decks well-lit in sharp contrast to the nighttime blackness of the sea.

The helicopter circled the yacht once, then descended to the helipad at the rear of the ship. The craft powered down and a minute later the door to the helicopter opened.

Yang, Zhao's assistant, stood there. "Miss Lewis," he said, "welcome aboard. I'll show you inside."

Climbing out, Rachel followed the man across the wide deck. The yacht was immense, she noted, over 200 feet long. She also noticed the tight security – six armed men were posted on the deck.

She was led into a teak-outfitted corridor, past several plush sitting rooms, a dining room, and a theatre. All of the rooms were unoccupied. At the end of the hallway they reached a closed door, flanked by a large, beefy Asian man. She recognized him as one of the bodyguards who had been with Zhao. He was built like a bodybuilder and his suit fit him tightly around the shoulders and chest. The guard raised a hand.

"*Ting Zhu*," he said. *Stop*.

He motioned to Rachel's purse and she handed it to him. The guard searched it and gave it back to her. Taking a wand-like device from his pocket, he activated it. The device hummed to life and he waved it along her torso, legs and arms.

Obviously satisfied she was unarmed, he turned off the device and stepped aside.

Yang, who had stood next to her quietly while this was going on, shrugged. "*Baogian*," he said. *I'm sorry.*

Then Yang opened the door and stepped inside. She followed him into the large, luxuriously appointed room. It was a study, with floor-to-ceiling bookcases along two of its walls. Expensive-looking Chinese artwork hung on the other walls. The floor was made of intricately-carved tiles and plush leather couches were at the center of the room. There was no one in the study.

"Would you like something to drink, Miss?" Yang asked. "We have a well-stocked bar."

"No, thank you."

"In that case, I'll take my leave. Mr. Zhao will be with you in a moment." He bowed, turned, and left the room. He didn't close the door though, and she noticed the bodyguard was still outside, flanking the entrance.

She scanned the study quickly, looking for other doors or windows. But there were none, not even portholes. Walking around the spacious room, she surveyed the contents, looking for anything she could use as a weapon, but before she had time to open cabinets or drawers she heard voices from the corridor.

Zhao stepped into the room and closed the door behind him. The short, heavy-set man flashed a wide smile. "*Miss Lewis, ni hao ma*?" He extended his hand. *Miss Lewis, how are you?*

She walked over and bowed slightly. "*Gaoxing jiandao*," she replied, shaking his hand. *Pleased to meet you.*

He motioned toward the sofas. "Please, have a seat," he said, continuing in Mandarin. "I'll get us a drink. What would you like? I prefer scotch myself."

"I usually don't drink during business meetings."

Zhao laughed. "You're amusing and beautiful. A charming combination." He turned and went to a teak cabinet. Opening it, he began pouring from a cut-glass decanter.

Sitting on one of the couches, she studied the man, who was dressed in an obviously expensive suit that concealed his portly frame, but couldn't hide the heavy jowls of his fleshy face. He appeared to be in his early fifties, and had a shiny, bald head and thick hands.

A minute later he handed her a drink and sat across from her.

"Mr. Zhao," she said, "I understand you're interested in retaining me as a financial advisor?"

The man laughed again. "Please call me Deng. No reason to be formal here." He took a sip from his scotch. "And I am interested in you. Very interested. I've read your background, Eve. Impressive credentials. MBA from Harvard. Seven years with one of the largest brokerage firms in New York. Now a financial advisor on your own. You make good money."

She realized he had been thorough in researching her cover story.

He took another sip from his drink. "As I said, you make good money, but I also know you enjoy gambling, and that you owe a lot of money." He waved a hand in the air. "What if I could make all those debts go away?" He snapped his fingers. "Just like that, you'd be debt free. On top of that, you'd be paid a very generous salary. Much more than you make now."

"And what would I have to do to earn it?"

Zhao smiled. "We're both adults here. I think you know. But there is one thing we need to take care of, before I could commit to such a generous arrangement."

"What's that, Deng?"

The man smiled again, and this time it was cold, calculating grin. "You have to show me how skilled you are. As you Americans would say, I need a test drive." Leaning back on the sofa, he unbuckled his belt and unzipped his pants.

"You don't waste much time, do you?"

"I don't have much time to waste, Eve."

She forced a smile and stood, then approached him and caressed his fleshy face with her palm. His skin was sweaty and she was repulsed by the touch. The obese man stank of alcohol and cigars.

"I'll just go and check the door," she said, "make sure it's locked. I wouldn't want anyone to disturb us. Then I'll take care of you."

Smiling seductively, she turned and went to the closed door and found it already locked. Then, steeling herself for what was to happen next, she went back to the sofa.

Rachel sat down next to him. "You're going to enjoy this," she purred. Just lean back and let me do all the work."

Zhao's eyes were bright with anticipation. He took a long pull from his drink and while he was doing so, she kicked off her high heels. Her heart racing, she bent over, picked up one of the shoes and removed the knife hidden there. She quickly brought the sharp tip of the knife to the man's throat.

"One false move and you're dead," she hissed.

A confused look crossed Zhao's face. "What is this? A joke?"

She jabbed the knife, pricking his skin. He flinched, and a small trickle of blood dribbled down his throat.

"This is no joke. You're dead unless you do what I say."

His expression changed from confusion to anger. "All I have to do is yell out, and my guards will come in and kill you."

She stabbed him again, this time cutting deeper into his skin. "Do that, Zhao, and you're history. If my guess is correct, this room is well insulated for sound. I'm sure this isn't your first tryst here. I doubt your guards would hear you."

Making a fist with her free hand, she punched him hard in his exposed groin. The obese man groaned and doubled over in pain.

When he recovered a minute later, his eyes were wide, and he edged away from her on the couch.

She thrust the bloody tip of the knife so it almost touched one of his eyeballs. "If you don't cooperate, I'll gouge your eyes out. Then I'll slash your throat and cut off your balls for good measure. Understood?"

Whatever bravado he had left evaporated. He cringed away from the knife. "I have money, Miss Lewis. Lots of money. How much do you want? I'll give it to you! Just leave me alone, you crazy bitch."

"Where do you store your weapon?" she hissed.

"What weapon?"

"Your gun, Zhao. You're a thorough man. I'm sure you keep a handgun in this room."

"Over there, in that cabinet."

She motioned with the knife. "We're going to stand up, you and I, and we're going to go over there and get it. You yell out, you die."

"Yes ... yes ... can I at least close my pants?" he whimpered.

She glanced down at his crotch. "Go ahead." She smiled, in spite of the tension she felt. "Looks like that thing's wilted anyway."

He zipped up and buckled his belt.

Holding the knife to his throat, she led him to the cabinet, which he opened. Resting on one of the shelves was a Beretta semi-automatic handgun. She picked it up and was going to put it in a pocket, when she remembered the garment she wore had none.

"Damn dresses," she muttered. "Lie on the floor, Zhao," she ordered, "face down."

"What do you want? I offered you money."

"Shut up and do what I say!"

The man complied, lowering himself to the floor.

Putting the gun and knife down on a side table, she rummaged through the cabinet and found a computer cord. Grabbing the man's hands behind his back, she tied him up.

"I'm bleeding," he groaned. "I need help."

Rachel kicked him hard in the kidneys and he grunted. "I told you to shut up, Zhao."

When she was done tying him up, she stood and picked up the handgun. Ejecting the clip, she saw that it was full and reinserted it. Then she racked the slide on the Beretta and said, "Okay, Zhao, sit up and lean against the wall. And no false moves."

The man did as he was told, and she crouched down across from him, leveling the pistol at his face.

His eyes went wide again. "Please ... don't shoot me ... I'll pay whatever you want."

"It's not about money, Zhao. I want information."

"What? What are you talking about?"

"This is how it's going to work. I ask the questions, you answer them. It's that simple."

The man nodded. "Yes. But at least lower your gun – it could go off by accident."

Rachel grinned. "That *would* be tragic." She lowered the gun a fraction.

"I'm bleeding," he pleaded. "I could die! Could you please bandage my throat first?"

She stared at the bald man sitting in front of her. It was true; a steady stream of blood was seeping from his wound.

"Five minutes ago," she spat out, "you wanted me on my knees sucking your cock. I *should* let you bleed to death."

A panicked look crossed his face. "I'm sorry about that. I meant no disrespect."

"Bullshit. But I do need you alive."

Standing, she went to the cabinet and grabbed a cloth napkin. Walking back, she wrapped it around his neck and tied it. The crude bandage would do for now. Crouching in front of him, she held the pistol to his forehead. "Now. You talk, or by God I will kill you."

"What do you want to know?"

"Why are you buying American tech companies?"

"I'm an investor. It's what I do."

She slapped him hard across the face, leaving a bright red mark.

"I told you ... the truth," Zhao blurted.

"Not the whole truth. You're buying them in secret, through dummy corporations."

"I ... I ..." he stammered, as if he didn't know how to respond.

"Why are trying to buy Sincore Technologies, Zhao?"

"Like I said, I'm an investor."

She whacked the handgun across his face, striking his mouth. He groaned as a trickle of blood ran down his lip.

"We could do this all day, Zhao. Now, no more bullshit. Why are you secretly buying American tech companies?"

His shoulders slumped and a look of resignation crossed his face. "I guess ... I have no choice. But they'll kill me if they find out I talked ...."

She pressed the muzzle of the Beretta to his forehead. "I'll kill you if you don't."

"Okay, okay. I'll tell you!"

"Do it!"

"I'm the front man."

"For what, Zhao?"

"For the group."

"What group?'

His eyes darted nervously around the room; it was clear the man was still afraid to tell the truth.

"It's complicated," he whispered.

She cocked the pistol. "My patience has run out."

"I'm part of a group of businessmen," he said in a rush. "Called Prism."

"Where is this group based?"

"We meet in Helsinki ..."

Rachel heard something behind her. Turning her head, she saw the room's door fly open and Zhao's bodyguard burst in, brandishing a handgun.

Then it all happened at once in a blur of motion.

She ducked for cover behind a couch and heard the roar of shots. But instead of being aimed her way, the bullets struck Zhao, making ragged holes on his forehead. His head snapped back, slamming against the wall, and his body sagged. Blood and brain matter covered the wall, and the odor of cordite filled the room.

Raising the Beretta, she peered around the sofa and fired off three quick rounds. At the same instant she saw the muzzle flash as the bodyguard fired back.

Rachel felt a blinding pain and everything went black.

Chapter 2

Langley, Virginia

Alex Miller was in his nondescript office reading reports when his desk phone rang. Picking up the receiver, he listened a moment and hung up.

Pushing aside the stack of reports, Miller opened a desk drawer and pulled out a folder labeled, *Rachel S. West*; the CIA logo and the word *Confidential* were printed on the bottom of the cover.

He opened the file and scanned the dossier to refresh his memory. West had been a good operative, with a host of commendations.

An orphan, she grew up in Atlanta in a series of foster homes. Some dark chapters there due to an abusive foster father. Highly intelligent, West had received a scholarship to Georgia Tech, graduating with a degree in computer science. She had also been in ROTC, and after college she went into DCIS, the criminal investigative arm of the U.S. Department of Defense. After that she transferred to the Agency. She had worked for Miller for the last two years.

He closed the dossier, and gazed out the window. It was an overcast day, and from his vantage point, all he could see was the parking lot, a high fence and a stand of scraggly trees. The two-story building where he was located was constructed of gray cinderblock – it was squat, ugly, and devoid of any architectural features. There was no sign, only a street number. Except for the razor-wire topped fence that surrounded the place, and the security cameras everywhere, it looked like any other warehouse. Known as the 'Factory' in Agency circles, the building housed one hundred people – agents like West, and various support staff and technicians.

Located four miles from the CIA's gleaming glass-and-chrome Headquarters building, the Factory was responsible for doing the Agency's dirty work. Black ops, wet-work, the sharp point of the spear. Assassination, if necessary, was part of it – although it was euphemistically called 'termination with extreme prejudice'. Miller headed up the Factory and although his official title was Director of Special Operations, most days he saw himself and his group as the people who took out the trash. But his job paid well, and he knew that no matter how many downsizings the CIA went through (and there had been many), the top brass always needed someone to take out the trash.

Turning away from the window, Miller stood and walked out of his office. Making his way past rows of industrial-looking cubicles occupied by mostly male agents, he reached the elevator and took it down to the basement level.

Stepping out, he strode down a long corridor. Worn linoleum covered the floor, the walls needed paint, and the fluorescent tubes overhead popped and flickered. But he had worked here so long, he was oblivious to all that. He stopped at the last door in the hallway, opened it and stepped inside.

The small, white room resembled a hospital. And in fact, the bare-bones medical facility that occupied half this floor was staffed by in-house personnel who cared for injured field agents. A medicinal smell pervaded the room.

Lying on the hospital-type bed was Rachel West, her eyes closed. She was dressed in a white gown, with a blanket draped over her legs. An IV tube was connected to her arm.

Miller pulled up a chair by the bed and sat down. A heavy bandage covered one side of her head and her face was pale. Considering all she'd been through, the woman still looked very attractive, he thought.

"Rachel," he said softly. "Can you hear me?"

She opened her eyes, turned his way and gave him a glazed look.

"How do you feel, Rachel?"

After a moment her eyes focused and she shrugged. "I'll live."

"They treating you okay?"

"The doc's fine, but the nurse is a real bitch."

Miller chuckled. "So I've heard. Sorry I couldn't come see you sooner, but the doctor had you heavily sedated."

She glanced around the room. "How long have I been here?"

"Three days."

"What the hell happened? All I remember was being on Zhao's yacht and I got into a shootout with one of his bodyguards. It's all a blur after that."

"You killed the bodyguard, but one of his rounds grazed the side of your head. You're lucky to be alive."

She lifted a hand and gingerly touched the bandages on her head. "Guess I am lucky. But it still hurts like hell."

"After the shootout," he continued, "the yacht came back to Shanghai, the crew called the cops, and they took you to the hospital there. Later the Chinese police contacted the U.S. Embassy and they got a hold of us."

She nodded.

"I have good news for you, Rachel. Headquarters called me this morning. You'll be receiving a Distinguished Service Medal for your actions. Bravery in the line of fire, wounded in action, and all that. It's a big honor."

"I'll be sure to frame it," she replied sarcastically.

Miller rolled his eyes. "I see you haven't changed one bit."

He leaned forward in the chair. "Rachel, can you tell me exactly what happened during the shootout? Zhao's dead, but the Chinese authorities wouldn't give us any details. One of our agents in Shanghai did some investigating, heard rumors from the crew that Zhao was killed by one of his own guards."

"It was strange, Alex. While I was interrogating Zhao, one of his bodyguards burst in and instead of shooting me, kills his boss, then fires at me."

"You're sure about that?"

"Absolutely."

"So the bodyguard betrayed him."

"No question about it."

Miller considered this a minute. "Something else has happened that's troubling."

"What's that, Alex?"

"The CIA field officer in Shanghai, Jason Taylor, has vanished. Our agents there can't locate him."

"You think Zhao's people killed him?"

"It's possible. But after what you just told me about the bodyguard, maybe Taylor was turned. Gone to the other side, whoever that may be."

She nodded.

"From now on, Rachel, I'm keeping this operation totally in-house. We may have a mole at the Agency."

"You're cutting HQ out of the loop?"

"That's right. I want to run this strictly with Factory personnel." He paused a moment. "Were you able to pump any information out of Zhao before the shooting?'

The pretty woman chuckled. "Not the kind of pumping he wanted, but yes, I got him to talk."

"What did you find out?"

"Zhao admitted he had been buying American tech companies. And he was about to purchase Sincore."

"For what purpose?"

"I don't know. But he did say he was only the front man."

"The front man?"

"That's right. He told me he was part of a group."

"What group?"

"He called it Prism."

"What does that mean?"

"I don't know, Alex."

"Where is this group?"

"Zhao said they meet in Helsinki."

"Helsinki, Finland?"

"I assume so, but before I was able to get more out of him, the bodyguard came in and all hell broke loose."

Miller leaned back in the chair, processing what she'd told him.

She waved a hand in the air. "How soon before I can get out of here?"

"The doctor said two more days. Why?"

"I need to get back to the field."

"You have a plan, Rachel?"

"I'm working on it."

Chapter 3

Shanghai, China

Rachel West slowed the rented sedan and pulled it to the curb in front of the house. Yang's home was a small, modest one-story located on Yongjia Road, in the city's south side. The neighborhood was upper middle-class, the houses sandwiched together tightly, as she would have expected in a crowded place like Shanghai.

Rachel had decided it would be easier to approach Zhao's assistant at his home, rather than trying to get through the multiple layers of security at the dead billionaire's corporate building.

It was 8 in the evening, and she hoped the man was home.

Climbing out of the car, she strode to the front door and rang the buzzer. Rachel was dressed in her usual attire – slacks, a blouse, and sports jacket.

A moment later Yang opened the door. "*Wei?*" the elderly, white-haired man said.

"*Wo Jiao Eve Lewis,*" Rachel replied. *I'm Eve Lewis.*

A perplexed look crossed his face, then a flash of recognition. "Miss Lewis, of course. Please come in." He stood aside and she went into the small living room.

"I'm sorry for your loss," she said.

"It's a difficult time," he replied, his tone sad. "Mr. Zhao was my boss, but I also considered him a friend. Please have a seat. May I get you a cup of tea?"

She sat in one of the armchairs. "Yes, thank you."

Yang left the room and came back a minute later. He handed her a cup and sat across from her.

"I'm surprised to see you, Ms. Lewis. I knew you'd been taken to the hospital ... are you okay?"

She absentmindedly touched the side of her head, winced from the pain. Her long hair covered the bandage underneath. "Good as new."

The man nodded. "I'm still not over the shock. Not just that Mr. Zhao was murdered, but that one of his bodyguards did it."

"Have the police given you any details?"

"No. But Chinese authorities are not known for their openness."

She smiled. "So I've heard. Although I didn't know Mr. Zhao long, I feel connected to him. That's why I'm here."

The elderly man arched his brows.

"Mr. Yang, I want to find out why he was killed."

Yang looked skeptical. "You're a financial planner, Miss."

"That's true. But I was almost killed too."

"I see your point. How can I help?"

"As Mr. Zhao's personal assistant, you probably knew more than most about his business dealings."

"That's right, Miss."

"Recently he was involved in purchasing American tech companies."

Yang raised a palm. "He kept that very private. In fact, he handled that project all on his own."

"Isn't that unusual?"

"Yes, it was. Usually I assisted him with all large transactions."

"I see." She took a sip of the hot tea, which was excellent – slightly bitter, with a hint of mint. "Mr. Zhao told me he was part of a group. He called it Prism."

The man shrugged. "I'm sorry, Miss. He never said anything to me about that."

Rachel studied the man's face. He seemed to be telling the truth. She tried a different approach. "Did Mr. Zhao ever visit Finland?"

"Yes. He went there several times."

"What was the purpose of his trips?"

"He never said – I surmised the trips were of a personal nature."

"Oh? He took his wife along?"

Yang smiled. "No. I believe he had a friend in Helsinki."

"A woman?"

"Yes, Miss. He told me her name was Erica."

"What was her last name?"

"He never said."

Rachel took another sip of tea. "Can you tell me anything else about her?"

"Mr. Zhao always enjoyed the company of beautiful women." He cleared his throat. "Women like yourself. My guess is that Erica fit that profile."

"Do you know where they met?"

"I believe she has a home in Helsinki, but they met at a hotel."

"Which one?"

"The Belle Epoque."

Chapter 4

San Francisco, California

The Sincore Technologies building was a glass-and-steel tower overlooking San Francisco Bay. Located in the Embarcadero area, the sixty-story structure was nestled between several other high-rise office buildings, and was only blocks away from the Transamerica Pyramid, one of the city's most visible landmarks.

It was after eleven in the evening and most of the company's employees had already gone home.

Zach Stevens, the CEO of Sincore, had just finished a disturbing phone call. What he heard made him wary, even frightened. *Why in hell did I ever get involved with such an insane plan?* he thought. It was something that had nagged him for weeks. *But it's too late now. I'm in too deep.*

Stevens gulped the rest of the scotch he'd been sipping during the call, poured himself another, and tossed it back.

Tired from the long day, the man got up from behind his desk and left his penthouse level office. Taking the elevator to the building's underground parking lot, he made his way to his car.

Getting into his black Lexus, Stevens started the engine and exited the lot. He took Montgomery Street and headed north, his thoughts focused on the alarming phone call. There wasn't much nighttime traffic and it didn't take him long to drive to his Pacific Heights mansion on Webster Street.

Pulling into the driveway of the elegant Victorian home, he turned off the engine. Built in 1881, the home had the same architectural touches as the rest of the mansions in the exclusive neighborhood. Arched stone doorways, French doors, and tall windows decorated with intricately carved filigree. Doric columns supported the portico.

Stevens stared at the home. All the lights were off, save the portico lights, meaning his wife had already gone to bed. For a moment he visualized her sleeping peacefully on the four poster bed. They had been married for ten years and he treasured those years as the best of his life.

As he grabbed his briefcase from the passenger seat, he heard an odd clicking noise. Puzzled, he glanced at the dash and confirmed the car was indeed shut off.

In that split-second that it took for him to inspect the dash, the twenty pounds of Semtex attached to the underside of the Lexus detonated.

The blast from the plastic explosive lifted the 4,700 pound sedan several feet off the ground, creating a massive fireball that instantly vaporized Stevens, the car, and the nearby shrubbery. The echo from the explosion was heard as far away as Fisherman's Wharf.

Chapter 5

Helsinki, Finland

The SAS Airbus 300 touched down at Vantaa Airport, rolled down the length of the runway, then began taxing to the gate. Rachel West glanced out the plane's oval window, watched as other commercial jets took off and landed.

The Airbus reached the terminal building and the passengers began to deplane. Rachel grabbed her sport jacket and carry-on bag from the overhead bin and made her way into the terminal.

After clearing customs, she rented a car and exited the building. Although it was June, it was cool out, typical for Finland. She had been in the area before as an operative and was familiar with the place. Breathing in the crisp, fresh air, she relished the refreshing contrast to the dank environment in Shanghai.

She located the Volvo in the rental lot fronting the terminal and got in. After consulting the car's GPS nav, she drove the twelve miles to downtown Helsinki.

Cruising past the exclusive Belle Epoque Hotel, she pulled into the parking lot of small inn she'd stayed at before. The inn was a couple of blocks from the hotel, and a lot less costly. Even the Agency had to watch expenses, her boss at Langley was constantly reminding her.

Rachel checked-in, showered, and changed into fresh clothes.

Although she was wearing her usual attire – slacks, simple blouse, navy jacket, and flats – she felt naked without her Glock. But getting through European customs with the pistol was nearly impossible. Normally she would have met with a local CIA field officer who would supply her with any necessary tools; but since this was a Factory-only operation, she'd be on her own. Hopefully she wouldn't need the Glock. And if she did, she'd have to improvise, a standard part of her job.

She grabbed a quick meal at the inn's restaurant and walked the short distance to the Epoque. Located across from Esplanade Park, the elegant red-stone building was originally built as a palace in the 19th century and later turned into a hotel.

Walking into the marbled lobby, she scanned the scene. It was mid-morning, and the front desk was busy with customers.

Bypassing that area, she strode to the concierge's station. Behind the elaborate teak desk sat a distinguished-looking, silver-haired man wearing a gray, pinstripe suit. Pulling her cred pack from her from her jacket and flashing it at the man, she said, "I'm Rachel West with Interpol, and I need your help with a case I'm working." Interpol was Europe's version of the FBI and she had used that cover on previous assignments. She spoke in English because her Finnish was crap. She also knew most people in Scandinavian countries were fluent in English.

The concierge seemed startled by her statement, took the wallet-like cred pack and inspected the contents carefully. The Factory tech guys were master forgers and the I.D. and badge in the pack were almost identical to the real thing.

After a moment the man handed back the pack. "Of course, Miss. My name is Mr. Shubert. How may I be of service?"

Rachel sat in one of the brocade, wingback armchairs that fronted the desk.

"I'm investigating the murder of a frequent guest at your hotel," she said. "A Chinese businessman by the name of Zhao Deng."

A flash of recognition crossed the man's face, but he said nothing.

"Do you know him, Mr. Shubert?"

The concierge shook his head and appeared nervous. "No, I don't believe I do."

"Maybe this will help," she said, pulling out a photo of Zhao and sliding it across the desk.

Shubert studied the picture. "I'm sorry. I don't know him."

The concierge was starting to piss her off. By his demeanor it was clear he knew Zhao, but was afraid to talk.

"Listen, Shubert. I know you have a cushy job at a fancy hotel, and you're used to dealing with rich businessmen, but this is a murder investigation." She leaned forward and hardened her voice. "If you impede Interpol, I'll make your life a living hell."

The man straightened his shoulders. "The privacy of our guests is paramount. It's a trademark of our hotel."

Her face flushed in anger. "If your hotel's manager knew you were providing prostitutes, he probably wouldn't be happy." Picking up a pencil that was resting on the desk, she snapped it in two and threw them at his chest.

Startled, he pulled away from her by rolling back his chair. After a moment, he shrugged and pulled the chair back toward the desk. "Perhaps I may be able to help. What would you like to know?"

"Zhao was a guest here, correct?" she demanded.

"Yes."

"How often?"

"Many times."

"Why didn't you say so in the first place?"

"Mr. Zhao is a generous man. Very generous. He is also a very private man. Wants to remain as anonymous as possible. You said he was murdered?"

"Yes, that's right."

"How tragic," he said sadly. "He'll be missed."

"You mean you'll miss his tips." She lowered her voice. "Zhao was part of a group of businessmen. Tell me about them."

"I know nothing about any group."

"He never met with other businessmen here?"

"No, never."

She studied the man closely for any 'tells', signs that he was lying. He appeared to be telling the truth. "Okay. But he met with a woman?"

"Yes, that's right."

"What's her name?"

The concierge opened a desk drawer, took out a thick, leather-bound book and flipped through it. Running his fingers down a page, he said, "Erica."

That fit what Yang had told her in Shanghai. "What's her full name?"

"Erica Anheim."

"Tell me about her."

He flashed a sly smile. "A beautiful girl."

"I figured that. What else?"

"She's a woman who makes friends easily."

"A call-girl."

He shook his head. "Nothing so common. She's a companion."

Rachel rolled her eyes. "Spare me. Erica is a high-end hooker."

"In a matter of speaking."

She waved a hand in the air. "A lot of wealthy businessmen stay at this hotel. Being the concierge here, you probably line up 'companions' for them. Is Erica one of your go-to girls?"

A worried look crossed his face. "I don't do anything illegal. I provide companionship for consenting adults."

She gave him a wry smile. "Sure. What's her address?"

Shubert glanced at his book and read it off.

"Where's that?" she asked.

"Just outside Helsinki, not far from here."

"Convenient."

The man nodded.

"Okay Shubert. You've been helpful. I may have other questions, but that should do it for now." She reached across the desk, picked up one of the broken pieces of the pencil. Pointing it at him, she said, "Let's keep this conversation private. I'd hate for you to get into any trouble."

Dropping the pencil on the desk, she stood and flashed a smile. "Have a nice day."

***

Rachel West pulled into the driveway of the upscale townhouse and shut off the Volvo. The two-story home was constructed of steel and opaque glass and spoke of money. Erica must be very good at her job, Rachel mused.

The agent climbed out of the car, strode to the front door, and after pulling out her cred pack, rang the bell.

A moment later an attractive brunette in her early-twenties opened it. She was wearing a long, white bathrobe.

"*Joo?*" the woman said.

"I'm Rachel West with Interpol," Rachel replied in English, while holding open her cred pack.

"What's wrong? Am I in trouble?"

Trying to put her at ease, Rachel said, "No, you're not. Are you Erica Anheim?"

"Yes."

"May I come in, Miss Anheim?"

The young woman opened the door fully and stepped aside.

Rachel walked into the large, tastefully decorated living room. Sleek wood furniture sat on gleaming hardwood floors. It reminded her of the Nordic modern look found at an Ikea store, but more expensive.

"Have a seat, please," Erica said.

"Thank you."

They sat across from each other and Rachel studied the brunette. Like Shubert had said, she was stunning. Long straight hair, blue eyes, classic high cheekbones. It appeared she was wearing nothing underneath her robe.

"You're with Interpol. What's this about?" Erica asked, tension in her voice.

"I'm investigating the murder of someone you know."

"Murder? Oh, my God, who?"

"Zhao Deng."

"Oh, no! That dear man." She seemed genuinely distraught.

"You knew him long, Miss Anheim?"

"Over a year."

"You knew him professionally, isn't that right?"

"He was a good friend."

"I've talked to Shubert, I already know what you do for a living."

Erica shrugged. "So? I considered Deng a good friend. One of my favorites." She waved a hand in the air. "He helped me buy this place."

"Generous of him."

"He was like that. Always buying me things. You said he was murdered. How horrible. What happened?"

"I'll ask the questions. Now, tell me about your relationship with him."

"Like I said, I've known Deng for over a year. Shubert introduced us. We meet at the hotel whenever he comes to Helsinki."

"Who was with him?"

"His bodyguards. They were always with us – when we went out to dinner, or shopping, they never left his side except when we were in the room, of course."

"I see. Zhao was part of a group. He called it 'Prism'. What do you know about it?"

The young woman looked perplexed. "Prism? I never heard of it."

"You're sure? It's very important."

Erica went quiet, and her face creased in concentration. "I'm sorry, but no, Deng never told me about Prism."

Frustrated from the lack of progress, Rachel growled, "Maybe I should arrest you for withholding evidence."

"Please, I don't know anything about this group! I swear. You've got to believe me."

Rachel leaned back in the seat, tried a different approach. "Did Zhao ever talk about his business?"

"No, not really. He was only interested in the sex."

"I'm sure. Why did he come to Helsinki? Just to visit you?"

Erica chuckled. "I'm good, but not that good. No, Deng would go to meetings."

"At the hotel?"

"No. He said it was an hour's drive."

"But he would come back the same day?"

"Yes, he'd go out in the morning and be back in the evening, to spend time with me."

Finally Rachel felt like she was getting somewhere. "He drove to these meetings – so they were most likely outside of Helsinki."

"I guess."

Rachel visualized a map of Finland. Much of it was rural. "Did he drive to another city in Finland?"

"No. He said he went to an estate in the countryside."

"Whose estate?"

"He told me one time it was owned by a Russian man – that's all I know ..."

"That's good, Erica. What else can you tell me?"

"I can tell you what kind of sex Deng liked."

"That won't be necessary. Is there anything else you know about his business dealings?"

Erica shook her head. "I'm sorry. I've told you everything."

"Okay."

The young woman yawned.

"Long night last night?" Rachel asked.

"They're all long. Comes with the job. Most of the time I sleep during the day and work at night."

That would explain the bathrobe in the middle of the day, Rachel thought.

"Would you like some coffee?" Erica asked. "I just made some."

"Sure."

The brunette got up and went to a counter that separated the living room and the kitchen, and began pouring from a carafe. While she waited, Rachel glanced out the window at the skyline of the city in the distance. She could make out the green cupolas of the Helsinki Cathedral and the tower of the Finnish National Museum.

The brunette returned a moment later carrying two steaming mugs. She handed one to Rachel and sat back down.

The operative took a sip – the coffee was hot and strong. She savored the slightly bitter taste. It was much better than the weak stuff they'd served on the flight over.

"What happens now?" Erica asked.

Rachel rested the cup on the coffee table. "I keep investigating."

"Are you going to arrest me?"

"Did you kill Zhao Deng?"

"Of course not!"

Rachel grinned, sure that Erica was no felon. "Then I won't arrest you."

The young woman seemed to relax. "That's good. I need to keep working. Especially now that Deng is dead. I still can't believe it. Can I ask how it happened?"

"He was shot by one of his own bodyguards."

"Oh, God. How horrible."

"Erica, did you ever suspect any of his guards would turn on Zhao?"

"No. Never. They kept him well protected, wherever he went. They were all the same – big, muscular Asian men who never spoke. Where was Deng killed?"

"In China, on his yacht."

"Deng told me about his boat once, said he wanted me to see it one day ...."

"Did you ever visit him in China?"

"Never. I know all about his wife...."

Rachel nodded.

"Can I call you by your first name, Miss West?"

"Sure."

Erica grinned. "Thanks. Can I ask you a personal question, Rachel?"

"Yes."

"How did get into police work?"

"It's a long story."

"You seem too pretty to be a police officer."

Rachel didn't respond, not sure if that was a compliment or a criticism.

Erica flashed a suggestive smile, then loosened the sash of her white robe. Rachel could now clearly see the woman's voluptuous nude body.

"I go both ways," Erica whispered.

The agent was caught off guard. "I ... don't ... anyway, I could never afford you."

Erica giggled and flipped her hair. "I like you. No charge."

Rachel stood. "Thanks, but no thanks. I'll be on my way."

"Would you like more coffee?" Erica asked, as she pulled her robe closed.

"I think I had enough,"

"Will you be back, Rachel?"

"Depends on the case."

"Well, if you need anything else, anything at all," Erica said with a chuckle, "please come visit. You know where to find me."

***

Rachel West climbed in the Volvo, started it up, and began to retrace her route back to central Helsinki.

As she drove, she considered what Erica had told her. Once again she visualized a map of Finland. An hour's drive outside of the city would put you in the towns of Forssa, or Rauma, or Jamsa. But the young woman said the meetings took place in the countryside.

Rachel was driving on a lightly-trafficked two-lane road, and out of habit she scanned the rearview mirror. Behind her was a black, late-model BMW sedan with heavily-tinted windows.
She had noticed the car earlier, during the drive over to Erica's home. But now, seeing it twice was too much of a coincidence.

Stepping on the gas, she kept an eye on the rearview mirror. The Volvo surged forward, but the BMW kept pace, staying about three car lengths behind.

She reached in her jacket for her Glock 42 only to remember she had no weapon. Cursing, she stepped on the gas again, cruised around a bend in the road and looked back. The BMW was still there, glued to her tail. But the black sedan was closer now, just one length behind.

Rachel floored the accelerator, but the underpowered Volvo was no match for the powerful German car. With her heart pounding, she glanced back once again. The BMW had closed the distance between the two cars, swerved into the opposite lane and shot forward, coming alongside the Volvo.

The BMW's passenger's side window slid down and she saw the barrel of a large handgun. Jerking the steering wheel hard left, Rachel steered the Volvo into the other car.

Then everything happened in a split second.

She felt the shock and impact of the cars colliding, heard the crunching of metal, smelled the burning of rubber, and saw the BMW surge forward. In a blast of speed, the black sedan, now dented on the side, flew past her, veered back into the proper lane and receded in size as it sped away on the road.

Her own car continued swerving left, the steering wheel bucking in her hands. With her adrenaline pumping, she fought the wheel to regain control.

But it was too late, the Volvo veered off the road, slid on the grassy shoulder and spun around in a dizzying 360 degree turn.

The last thing she saw was the trunk of a large tree rushing towards her.

Chapter 6

Langley, Virginia

Alex Miller was on the second floor of the Factory building, walking down the corridor to his office when he spotted a man in coveralls standing on the steps of a ladder. A large bucket was sitting by the wall.

Reaching the spot, Miller looked up at the heavy-set man on the ladder. "What's wrong, Tom?"

Tom, the building's maintenance man, shook his head slowly and pointed at the ceiling. "It rained last night. We got another leak, boss."

Miller heard it now, the plops of water dripping into the bucket.

Tom climbed down the ladder. "Sir, we need to replace the roof. We should have done it years ago."

"Sounds expensive."

"It will be, boss. But we can't postpone it forever."

Miller considered this, quickly running the budget numbers in his mind. "Patch the hole."

The maintenance man nodded. "You got it. But I bet the guys in HQ don't put up with leaky roofs at the glass palace."

"Good thing we have you, huh?" Miller said with a grin. He continued to his office, opened the door and stepped inside.

Going behind his desk, he sat down. After checking his emails on his encrypted laptop, he picked up the receiver on his desk phone and dialed a number from memory.

As he waited for the other side to pick up, he glanced out his office window. It was a cloudy, gray day, and the barren trees by the high fence looked like tired, thin soldiers on sentry duty.

After a long time, Miller heard Rachel West's voice on the other end.

"Hello," she said, her voice harried.

"It's Alex. Everything okay, Rachel?"

"I guess so ..."

He heard the high-low wail of European police sirens in the background of the call. "What's going on?" he asked.

"I was in a car accident ... the police just showed up."

"Hopefully you didn't show them the Interpol badge."

She sighed. "Give me a little credit, Alex."

"Sorry. What happened?"

"I was driving back to Helsinki and this car pulls alongside me and started shooting. Make a long story short, I got away, but so did the perp."

"Get a license number?"

"Happened too fast. It was a black BMW."

"You know how many of those there are?"

"Yeah, I know," she replied, frustration in her voice. "It all happened in an instant."

"Don't worry about it ... are you okay, Rachel? Are you hurt?"

"I got a hell of a headache, but otherwise I'm fine."

"Good to hear."

"There's one thing you won't like, Alex."

"What's that?"

"The rental Volvo I was driving ... it's totaled."

"Did you get the extra insurance?"

"You always told me not to – too expensive, remember?"

Miller recalled telling all his operatives the same thing – don't get the extra insurance. Damn budget cuts, he fumed to himself. "Yes, I remember. I'm just glad you're okay. Now tell me exactly what happened. Who do you think was driving the BMW?"

"No way to know. I was working a lead and afterward the Bimmer driver pulls a gun and tries to blow me away."

"Tell me about the lead."

"Nothing concrete, but it looks like 'Prism' meets somewhere outside of Helsinki, about an hour from there."

"Okay. That'll have to wait a while. Something's happened in the States. I need you to work on it."

"What is it, Alex?"

"The CEO of Sincore was murdered in San Francisco. His car was blown up."

"Jesus. Any leads?"

"That's were you come in. The local cops and the FBI are already investigating, but I want you to go to San Fran and check it out. It's your case and you're the best person to handle it."

"The CIA doesn't do domestic, Alex. We're not allowed to investigate in the U.S."

"Don't worry about that. I'll take care of it from my end."

"Whatever you say. You're the boss. What's my cover?"

"Get on the next plane to San Francisco. I'll text you the details."

There was a pause on the other end. Then, "Alex, I need to stop back home first. Check on my mom. The nursing home called me; she's taken a turn for the worse. It'll only take a day."

Miller remembered Rachel's foster mother, who had suffered a stroke and was now in a nursing home. "Okay. But one day only. I need you in San Fran ASAP."

"Yes, sir."

Chapter 7

Langley, Virginia

Rachel West spoke to the receptionist, signed the log book, and walked down the corridor of the nursing home to her mother's room. As usual, the place smelled of cleaning solvent and the underlying scent of human decay. With its white walls and scuffed white linoleum floors, the home reminded her of a hospital, only smaller. That image was reinforced by the scores of elderly patients in wheelchairs who lined the corridors, propelling themselves to and fro, sometimes aimlessly.

The head nurse was coming out of her mother's room just as Rachel reached it. "How's she doing?" the agent asked.

"As well as can be expected," the matronly nurse replied with a sad smile. "She's sleeping now."

Rachel went into the small room and sat on a metal chair by the hospital bed her mother was resting on. The frail, emaciated woman appeared much older than her seventy years. Her closed eyes were shrunk into the sockets, and her wrinkled face was pale, almost as white as the sheet that covered her. The left part of her mouth drooped, a result of multiple strokes.

She took one of her mother's hands and held it in her own. The old woman's fingers felt cold and stiff. Still, it comforted Rachel to hold her hand. Although Alice was only her foster mother, she considered her a flesh-and-blood relative, one of the few people in the world she cared about. Rachel remembered Alice as the only one who had treated her like a real daughter. Alice had protected the teen from her abusive husband, to her own detriment. After her initial stroke a year ago, Rachel had moved her from Atlanta so she could be near and take care of her.

Rachel squeezed her hand. "Hi, Mom. How're you feeling?"

Alice's eyes fluttered open. "Hi, dear ... I'm glad ... you came ...." Her words were slurred, another result of the strokes.

"They treating you okay, Mom?"

Alice gave her a vacant stare, as if she didn't understand the question. "I'm glad ... you came ...."

Rachel's eyes brimmed with tears. Years ago, Alice had been a robust, spunky woman, full of life. It was difficult seeing her this way. "I would have come sooner, but I was traveling."

"Traveling ... what's that, dear ...?"

She squeezed her hand again. "I love you, mom."

"I ... love you ... too ...."

Then Alice's eyes lost focus and fluttered closed.

Rachel stayed there for another hour while Alice slept. Wiping away tears, she said one last silent prayer for her mother.

She leaned over and gently stroked her hair. Then she gave the frail woman a kiss on the cheek.

Standing, Rachel turned and left the room.

Chapter 8

Finnish countryside, northeast of Helsinki

Ivan Illych Petrov stood ramrod-straight as he stared at the short, wiry man in front of him. They were in the study of Petrov's large estate.

"Did she get away?" Petrov demanded.

"I don't think so, sir."

"But you're not sure?"

Arsi Lendel took a moment before speaking. "No, Mr. Petrov. I saw her car crash. But I can't say for certain that she's dead."

Petrov gritted his teeth and clenched his fists in an effort to control his emotions. Losing his temper and lashing out at his trusted aide was not productive, he told himself. "It probably doesn't matter anyway," Petrov said. "The real problem is Interpol is sniffing around. You trust the source of your information?"

"Yes, sir. I've known the concierge for years."

"And he said the female agent was with Interpol?"

"Yes. Her name is Rachel West."

"I see." Petrov clasped his hands behind his back, standing at parade rest. It was a familiar position for him, the result of twenty years in the Russian Army. But he wasn't a colonel in the army now. He was a private citizen and a businessman. A businessman with an operation in peril. "Now that Zhao Deng is dead, everything is more complicated. We can't tolerate any more problems." He shook his head slowly. "My American partner is not pleased. And he's the key."

"Yes, sir."

Petrov turned away from Lendel and stared out the floor-to-ceiling window of the study. Beyond the wide, grassy slope was a stand of lush evergreens and beyond that the shimmering blue water of Lake Saimaa. Petrov loved this home, the desolate peacefulness of the place. It was a welcome contrast to the traffic and noise back in Russia. After a time, he turned back to the other man.

"It's clear to me, Lendel, that Prism can no longer meet here. It's too dangerous."

"What do you want me to do, sir?"

"Pack up the files and the computers. We'll take them with us."

"Anything else, Mr. Petrov?"

"Yes. After you pack, burn the house to the ground."

Chapter 9

San Francisco, California

Rachel West rang the doorbell of the Victorian mansion and waited. Standing under the wide portico, she silently rehearsed her cover story.

A young Hispanic woman dressed in a maid's uniform opened the front door a moment later. "May I help you?" the maid asked.

Rachel held open the cred pack. "I'm Agent West with the FBI. I need to speak with Mrs. Stevens."

The maid nodded, as if she was used to the drill. After the bombing that killed the Sincore CEO, other police officers had obviously visited the home several times. She stepped aside and the operative walked into the high-ceiling foyer.

"I'll show you to the den," the maid said, "and I'll go get her."

Rachel followed her to an elaborately furnished den and sat on a deeply-cushioned embroidered sofa. As she waited, she glanced around the room. Large oil paintings depicting 19th century San Francisco scenes hung in gilt frames. The parquet floors gleamed as if they had been recently buffed, and the aroma of wood polish filled the air.

A middle-aged woman in a black, knee-length Versace dress stepped into the den. The attractive woman had short, curly dark hair and a regal bearing, which Rachel assumed came from living in a Pacific Heights mansion and being part of high society. She offered her hand and Rachel stood and shook it.

"I'm Eleanor Stevens. You're with the police?"

"Thank you for seeing me, Mrs. Stevens," she replied, handing the woman her open cred pack. "I'm Rachel West, FBI."

The widow took the pack and examined it closely as both women sat down on facing sofas. "It says here you're in the Special Operations section of the FBI. I've talked to a lot of police and FBI people since my husband, Zach ... died ...." she paused and cleared her throat, tears welling up in her eyes. After a moment she tapped on the ID. "But I never saw this before."

"Our department, Special Ops, deals with national security issues." It was true, there was such a department at the Bureau, but her ID was an excellent forgery, thanks once again to the Factory's tech geeks.

The woman handed back the pack and leaned back on the sofa. "I don't know what I can tell you that I didn't tell the other agents," she snapped, irritation in her voice. "Don't you people talk to each other?"

Rachel gave her a pleasant smile. "I'm sorry about that, Mrs. Stevens. We do share information, but we want to cover every angle."

"Fine. But let's make this quick. I have a charity event I'm hosting in two hours."

"Of course," Rachel replied calmly, suppressing her own urge to put the woman in her place. But the last thing she wanted was to have the widow contact the FBI and complain. The Factory provided good covers, but even they had limitations. "This won't take long. I just need to check on a few things."

Mrs. Stevens glanced at her watch, a gold and diamond Piaget. "Go ahead then."

"The night your husband was killed, you were home?"

The widow's expression changed from one of irritation to sorrow. "Yes ... that's right. I was sleeping ..."

"Was there anyone else in the house?"

"Only the maid, Consuelo."

"Of course. You and Zach Stevens had been married for ten years, correct?"

"Yes. Ten wonderful years," she said, a catch in her voice. It appeared the woman was genuinely sad.

"Any problems in the marriage?"

The widow's expression quickly changed to anger. "What are you implying?"

"Just a routine question, ma'am. We always ask that."

The woman absentmindedly touched the strand of pearls hanging from her throat. "We were close ... very close ... he treated me like a queen ... we had our disagreements sometimes, every couple does ... are you married, Miss West?"

"No, ma'am."

"Well, even in a perfect marriage, there's always minor things ..."

"Of course. When you married your husband, he was already with Sincore Technologies, isn't that right?"

"Yes, after college he and a group of other engineers started the company from scratch, built it into what it is today. He wasn't the CEO when we met, but he was the most ambitious of the group, a real go-getter. Being CEO was his dream job."

"I see. Since you were close, he would have mentioned if he had any conflicts at work. Any enemies that you know of?"

"Everybody loved Zach."

"I guess not everybody."

The widow shook her head. "I don't think anyone at Sincore was responsible. They are a very successful company, one of the largest in their industry. Zach was key in making that happen."

"Okay. How about competitors? Other companies?"

"I wouldn't know about that," the woman said with a shrug. "He didn't talk about it."

"Was he ever involved with a group called 'Prism'?"

"Prism? No."

"Did he travel often?"

"Yes. It was part of his job."

"To where?"

"All over. Sincore has divisions all across the U.S, in Europe and Asia."

"Did he ever visit Shanghai?"

The woman pondered a moment. "I don't think so. I know he went to Beijing once. You'd have to check with his office on that."

"That's my next stop. What about Finland? Did he ever go there?"

"I know Zach was in France, and England, but I don't remember him going to Finland."

"Okay. What was Mr. Stevens' demeanor the last couple of months?"

"Zach was extremely preoccupied with Sincore's pending sale."

Rachel leaned forward in the seat. "Tell me more about that."

"I know it was mostly his idea."

"To sell the company?"

"That's right," the widow replied, playing with the pearls again. "As you probably know, Sincore is a privately held company and Zach held a large number of shares."

"Why did he want to sell?"

"We talked about it – he said it would be very lucrative for us. We would be extremely wealthy."

"Looks to me like you already have plenty of money."

"You can never have enough," the woman said haughtily.

"I guess. So, for the last couple of months ... you said he was preoccupied?"

"Yes. He spent a lot of time at the office, much more than usual. I didn't like it, and I told him so in no uncertain terms."

"How did he respond?"

"He said the money was worth it, that I would see." She shrugged, then her shoulders slumped as if a heavy weight was pressed on them. "Now he's gone ... and I'm all alone ..."

"My condolences, ma'am."

The widow looked at her watch, her imperious manner returning. "Are we finished? I've got to get ready."

"One last question. Do you think the pending sale of the company had anything to do with his murder?"

The woman's lips pressed into a thin line and an annoyed look crossed her face. "How would I know? You're the FBI. That's your job to find out." She pointed a stern finger at Rachel. "Looks to me you're just as incompetent as the rest of the police I've talked with!"

Rachel suppressed the urge to slap the bitchy woman. She took a deep breath and said, "Yes, ma'am. That is my job and I intend to do it." She stood. "We're done here, ma'am."

"Well, it's about time."

***

Rachel stepped outside the Victorian mansion and scanned the wide expanse of front yard. Part of the manicured grass was scorched, a result of the explosion. The long, sloping driveway likewise showed damage. Although new concrete had already been poured in the cavity created by the blast, blackened portions of the original driveway had yet to be sanded down.

She visualized in her mind what had happened, the Lexus sedan being shredded into fragments, with Stevens in it. It must have been a gruesome scene, she thought. Luckily for the CEO, the large quantity of plastic explosive vaporized the car in a split-second, sparing the man a long, painful death.

Her thoughts turned back to the haughty widow. It was clear the woman was saddened by her husband's death and appeared to have no role in it. Still, Rachel resented her arrogant attitude. But in the agent's line of work, she constantly came into contact with people she didn't like, or trust. It was part of the job.

Pushing those thoughts aside, she strode over to her rental vehicle, parked on the driveway. The Honda 750 cc motorcycle shone in the mid-day sun. At the airport's Hertz kiosk, she'd been offered two choices, both underpowered sedans. With her recent experience in Helsinki so fresh in her mind, she wanted something with some guts. She berated the rental agent until he had grudgingly located the powerful Honda in the lot. After signing the multi-page agreement, she had been presented with the keys.

Motorcycles were her favorite ride: ultra-fast, carefree, liberating.

She climbed on the bike, strapped on the helmet, and turned on the machine. It throbbed to life with a growl, the vibration from the large engine running up her legs and thighs. It felt good.

Kicking back the kickstand, she steered the heavy bike around, glided down the driveway and roared onto Webster Street.

Fifteen minutes later she found Montgomery Street, turned south past the Transamerica building, and then took a left on California. Soon she was cruising in the Embarcadero area, the Bay to her right. The deep blue water was choppy and shimmered from the sun. She spotted the Sincore tower a moment later, downshifted, and descended into the building's underground lot.

Rachel found an empty slot, parked, removed her helmet, and climbed off. She straightened her sports jacket, smoothed down her slacks, and ran her fingers through her long, blonde hair. Glancing at her image in the motorcycle's rearview mirror, she confirmed she looked professional enough. Walking to the bank of elevators, she stabbed a button.

***

The lobby of the Sincore headquarters building was what Rachel expected for a high-tech company – made of glass and chrome, the ultra-modern, high-ceilinged open atrium soared to the tenth floor.

After flashing her credentials, she was led to the offices of four different employees, all top level managers. She interviewed each at length, spending several hours at the company. Although the high-level executives were helpful, solicitous even, she hadn't been able to generate any new leads. Unfortunately the executive vice-president of the firm, the man now at the helm since Zach Stevens' murder, was not at the office that day. She'd have to return the next day.

Exiting the building, Rachel drove the motorcycle a short distance to the hotel where she was staying, the Sheraton at Fisherman's Wharf. It was dinner time, and after showering and changing clothes, she walked the four blocks to Pier 39. A popular destination for tourists and locals, the festive Pier area overlooked the Bay and contained a multitude of restaurants and shops. Colorful street musicians played jovial music, while throngs of people perused the stores along the pier. The aroma of appetizing food smells mingled with the sea-air scent. The area was a cacophony of sound – the festive music, the multitude of conversations, and in the background, the loud calls of the sea lions that congregated along the pier.

Picking a restaurant at random, Rachel had a leisurely seafood dinner. The Dungeness crabs and sourdough bread were scrumptious, as was the chardonnay. But throughout the meal she had the nagging feeling someone was watching her.

***

The following morning Rachel was shown to the penthouse level office of the company's Executive Vice President. The glass-walled office had a breathtaking view of San Francisco Bay. It was a sunny day and the water sparkled from the reflection.

"Agent West," the man said, coming around his desk, "I'm Peter Carrington. I'm in charge now that ... Zach is gone. My people told me about your visit yesterday and said you'd be in to see me."

"Good to meet you, Mr. Carrington." The two shook hands and she sat across from his wide, cherry wood desk.

"Would you like some coffee, Agent West?"

"Sure," she replied, taking a moment to study the man as he went to a credenza and began pouring two cups. Carrington was a tall, slender man in his mid-fifties, with a patrician nose and neatly trimmed, salt-and-pepper hair. He wore what looked to be a very expensive charcoal gray suit with a red paisley necktie. He looked every inch the part of a corporate chief executive.

A moment later he handed her the coffee and sat down behind his desk. "I hope my staff provided you with all the information you needed."

"They were extremely cooperative," she replied with a smile.

He tented his hands in front of him. "Good. This has been a tragic loss for our company ... we ... I ... are still in shock over what happened. Is the FBI any closer to finding out who murdered Zach?"

"It's an ongoing investigation. I've been assigned to follow up."

"I see." He spread his hands flat on the desk. "I want to do everything I can to help you catch whoever did this. Tell me what you need."

Rachel breathed a sigh of relief. Dealing with Sincore employees was a welcome change from the surliness of Mrs. Stevens. "Your staff filled me in on your company and what it does, but I'd like to hear it in your own words. It'll help me get a better perspective."

"Of course," he said. "Sincore Technologies manufactures networking systems that, in layman's terms, connect computers to the Internet. We're a diversified company, with many divisions, but computer network connectivity is our main product. Commonly known as routers, our equipment transmits over seventy percent of the Internet's worldwide traffic." He paused a moment. "I'm sorry if I'm being too technical, Agent West."

"I have a degree in computer science – I'm following you fine."

"Good. Sincore routers, I believe, are the most advanced in the world."

She took a sip of the hot coffee. "I'm sure you're right. I've read several reports that indicate the same thing. Now, tell me more about the business side of things."

"Unlike many of our competitors, Sincore is a privately held company. Zach owned a large number of shares, as do I. The other shareholders are also employees of the firm."

"As I understand it, the company was founded by a small group of engineers."

"That's right. Zach and I, along with several others, started the company in his garage."

"You've come a long way."

"Yes, we have," Carrington replied, fidgeting with his necktie. "But now, without Zach, things ... won't be the same." By the sound of his voice and his subdued manner, it was clear the man really would miss Stevens.

Rachel leaned forward in the chair. "Tell me about the pending sale of the company."

"Of course. It was all Zach's idea. He came to me about it several months ago. He thought it would make all of us, the majority stockholders, incredibly rich." The man paused, drank some coffee. "Actually I was against the idea. I thought we would lose too much control."

"But you finally agreed?"

"Yes. Zach could be very persuasive. And since he was much smarter than I was, although I hate to admit it, I agreed."

"Who was the buyer?" she asked, trying to see if he would lie. She already knew Zhao Deng was the front man for Prism.

He shook his head slowly. "I don't know. Zach conducted all the negotiations himself."

"I see. Did he mention someone in particular?"

"No. I asked, but he never told me. Said it would be best if he handled the whole thing."

"Did he ever mention a group called 'Prism'? Were they the ones planning to buy Sincore?"

"He never mentioned that to me."

"So, now that he's gone, what happens to the pending sale?"

Carrington waved a hand in the air. "Who knows? As far as I'm concerned, the deal is dead."

"You've heard nothing from the other party since the murder?"

"That's right."

Rachel leaned back in the chair and absorbed this information. "Tell me about Mr. Stevens's demeanor, before his death. His wife said he was distraught."

"That's the strange part about it. As I told you before, Zach was very bullish about the sale of the company. But something changed in the last couple of weeks. He seemed worried about it for some reason. And he was secretive about the reason, wouldn't tell me why. I almost got the feeling he wanted to pull out of the deal, but couldn't figure a way out."

"Okay. I asked your staff yesterday about Mr. Stevens's travel itinerary – where he went and who he met with in the last couple of years."

The man arched his eyebrows. "Yes?"

"They had no record of him traveling to Helsinki nor to Shanghai in all that time."

"Let me think." He paused a moment, as if in deep thought. "I agree with that. I don't remember him ever going to either place. Is that important to the investigation?"

"Yes. But it's better if you keep this information to yourself."

"Of course. What else would you like to know?"

"Can you think of any enemies Mr. Stevens had? In your company, or in the industry?"

"None. In fact everybody –"

"Loved him," she interjected, finishing the man's sentence.

"That's right."

She nodded, then took another sip of the coffee, which was now lukewarm.

Rachel continued questioning the man for another hour, going over the same ground again, trying to gather additional information.

***

Rachel was in her hotel room later that day, when her cell phone buzzed. Pulling it out of her jacket, she held the cell to her ear. She immediately recognized her boss's voice.

"How's it going?" Alex Miller asked.

"Frustrating," Rachel snapped. "I've spent two days questioning people and I don't have much to show for it. I don't know any more than I did before."

"I'm sure that's not exactly true," Miller said in a calm voice.

She took a deep breath. "Yeah, you're right about that. I know that Stevens' widow, who is a real bitch, by the way, is not guilty of murder."

He chuckled, obviously finding her crack about the woman humorous.

"I also believe," she continued, "that the Sincore staff is not complicit."

"So your working theory is that the sale of the company was the reason for his death?"

"Yeah." She took the next ten minutes to fill him in on the details of her Q & A with the company's employees. At the end of this she said, "Carrington told me he thought that Stevens was getting cold feet about the sale, but didn't know a way out of it."

"Interesting. Maybe this 'Prism', whoever they are, realized this and took him out?"

"That's my thought, Alex."

"Okay. I've got something to brighten your day."

"Don't tell me I got another crappy commendation from the Agency."

He laughed again. "No. Nothing like that. We may have gotten a lead, on our end here at the Factory."

Her sour mood brightened. "Yeah?"

"Our tech guys just traced a phone call from Stevens's office on the evening he was murdered. It was the last one he made right before he left the Sincore building. Unlike the other calls to his office that day, this one was encrypted, and we weren't able to decipher it until now."

Rachel's enthusiasm surged. "What was in the conversation?"

"The voices were scrambled, so the conversation was unintelligible, but we know where it originated."

"Who made the call?"

"We don't know who, but we know where it originated. The reason we hadn't been able to trace the call before was that it bounced around several phony cut-out phone numbers from around the world."

"Sounds sophisticated, Alex."

"Yeah. It's clear they didn't want to be traced."

"What's the location?"

Then he told her.

Chapter 10

Marin County, California

Rachel West turned off the motorcycle. She leaned back on the seat and stared up at the two-story, cedar and stone contemporary home. The house was nestled on the rise of the heavily-wooded lot, set well back from the rural road that it fronted. There were no cars on the gravel driveway, nor was there any movement or sound coming from inside. Besides the chirping of the birds and the rustle of the leaves from the breeze, she heard nothing.

Rachel climbed off the bike and removed her helmet. She stretched her arms and legs, stiff from the hour ride up from San Francisco. Checking the street number again on the roadside mailbox to confirm it was the address Alex had given her, she strode on the driveway and up the wooden steps to the entrance. After removing her FBI ID from her pocket, she knocked on the door. There was no answer, and after a moment she rapped again.

Glancing into the home through one of the windows, she scanned the foyer and a living room beyond that. She saw overturned chairs and smashed glass on the floor.

Her heart racing, she pulled the Glock from her jacket and twisted the doorknob. The door was unlocked and she slipped inside and crouched, holding the pistol in front of her.

"FBI!" she shouted.

She heard nothing but the ticking of a clock.

Cautiously, she stepped into the living room, holding the handgun with both hands. There was no one in the room, but she saw evidence of a fight – broken dishes on a table, the overturned chairs, blood splatter and shards of glass on the floor. "This is the FBI!" she yelled again. "Anybody here?"

There was no answer. She advanced forward slowly, following the bloody tracks – boots by the looks of it – down the hallway and up a staircase.

Reaching the top of the landing, she saw more blood on the second floor corridor leading into an open doorway. The smell of gore increased as she approached.

Crouching by the door, she peered inside. It was bedroom. A man was sprawled on the bed, facing up, half covered by blood-soaked sheets.

She stepped inside, studied the inert body on the bed. She had seen enough death in her line of work to know the man was gone. Nevertheless, she leaned over and felt his neck for a pulse; there was none.

Turning away from the corpse, she quickly searched the large bedroom and adjoining bathroom, found no one else. She left the room and explored the rest of the house and found it unoccupied.

Returning to the bedroom, she studied the bloody scene. The dead man was in his mid-twenties, Caucasian, with a pock-marked face and tousled, jet-black hair. He was wearing a long-sleeve dress shirt and slacks, both now covered in dried, dark-red blood. The cause of death was likely the gunshot wound in his abdomen. The blood was congealed, and by the size of the wound, it appeared to Rachel that a large caliber handgun had been used. She examined the carpet and bed for ejected shell casings, found none. The killer had used a revolver or had cleaned up the brass, she realized. A pro.

She took a deep breath – the smell of cordite was gone, the only thing she smelled was the sickening copper scent of blood. She touched the corpse again – the body was stiff and cold. The man had been dead at least four hours, she knew, the typical time for rigor mortis to set in, and less than forty-eight hours, the time for rigor to dissipate.

Rachel glanced at her watch – she had been in the house eight minutes. Realizing the last thing she needed was for cops to show up and find her with a dead body, she hastily searched the corpse. Finding a wallet, she pocketed it, then inspected the rest of the room and house. She was looking for a computer, a laptop, or a tablet, but she found none. In a spare bedroom which had been turned into an office, she found a desk and a computer printer, but no PC. Cables had been disconnected – the killer had taken the computer.

She glanced at her watch again – fifteen minutes. Time to get the hell out.

Removing a handkerchief from her pocket, she retraced her steps through the house, wiping down everything she had touched, wanting to leave no trace of her visit.

Four minutes later she was gone.

Chapter 11

St. Petersburg, Russia

Ivan Illich Petrov stared out his office window and weighed his options for the upcoming phone call. It would be one of the most difficult calls he would make this year. The man on the other end, the American, was not a forgiving business partner. Petrov was acutely aware of the recent setbacks.

But if the group was successful, the reward would be great. It would make Petrov, a soldier-turned-businessman, incredibly wealthy. Although the Russian had the trappings of success – a large *dacha*, an expensive automobile, and an even more expensive mistress, he had acquired most of that with borrowed money. Now he was deeply in debt – the only reason he put up with the American and his acerbic personality.

It was a gray, overcast day in St. Petersburg, and he watched the commercial boat traffic as it made its way along the Neva, the wide river his building overlooked. A red tugboat was guiding an oil tanker. They were followed by a commercial fishing vessel, its smokestack spewing a trail of black smoke. Across the river he could make out the Winter Palace and next to it the Hermitage Museum with its distinctive white, green, and gold facade.

Realizing he could no longer postpone it, he picked up the receiver and tapped the keypad next to the phone to encrypt and scramble the call.

The phone rang for a long time before the person on the other end picked up.

"Yes?" the American said.

"It's Petrov, sir."

"You have good news for me, I hope."

"Good and bad, I'm afraid."

There was no response for a long moment. "You disappoint me, Ivan," The American growled. "I trusted you with this operation and now you keep bringing me bad news ...."

Petrov's stomach began to churn. "I'm sorry, sir. But it's not all bad."

"Give me the good first. I've sunk a lot of money into this. I could use some good news."

"The purchase of the European tech companies is going as planned. I've secured three of them, and a fourth is pending."

"At least you haven't fucked *that* up," the American spat out, venom in his voice.

Petrov swallowed hard, keeping his anger in check. "Yes, sir."

"What's the bad news?"

"The Sincore deal appears to be dead."

"We needed that one. Without Sincore, completing our operation is going to be difficult."

"I understand, sir. I've already started to work on alternatives."

"See that you do!" the American shouted.

"Yes, sir. On a related topic, I've covered our tracks. The authorities in the U.S. are still investigating Stevens' death, but I've erased the middleman. I don't believe we'll have a problem."

"I hope not, Ivan. My patience with you is wearing thin. We've already had two lapses ... first Zhao Deng and then Zach Stevens. I won't tolerate any more mistakes. By the way, did you take care of the Finland location?"

"Yes, sir. I burned down the house ... there's no trace of it now."

"Good. From now on, we'll have to talk by phone only. It's too dangerous for us to meet in person."

"Of course."

"What about the Chinese situation, Ivan? Has that been contained?"

"Yes. The bodyguard who eliminated Zhao was on our payroll, and we've erased him as well."

"See? When you put your mind to it," the American snarled, his voice full of sarcasm, "you *can* do something right."

Petrov didn't reply, only took a deep breath to calm his anger.

"What else do you have for me, Ivan?"

"I believe that's all for now."

There was click from the other end and Petrov realized the bastard had hung up without saying goodbye. *Screw him*, the Russian thought.

Chapter 12

Helsinki, Finland

Rachel West steered the Saab sedan to the curb and parked the car. Climbing out, she looked up at the nondescript ten-story apartment building. It was located on Kaivokatu Street, not far from the city's train station.

Most of the building's lights were off, she noted. The only lighting to the not-quite-dark nighttime scene was provided by one streetlamp and a flickering fluorescent bulb over the entrance. It was summer in Finland and darkness at night only lasted a few hours, and even then it wasn't pitch black like Rachel was used to in the States. The land of the Midnight Sun, as this part of the world was known, was living up to its name.

Rachel went into the unmanned lobby and, skipping the elevator, walked up the stairs to the second floor, then located the right apartment.

She checked the time on her watch: 3:23 a.m. Perfect, she thought. Shubert should be sound asleep. She stabbed the apartment's buzzer several times and waited.

After a moment she heard shuffling of feet from the other side of the closed door and a muffled, "*Joo?*"

"Mr. Shubert," she snapped, "it's Rachel West from Interpol. Open up."

Locks clicked and the door opened partway. The Belle Epoque concierge, dressed in sleepwear and a robe, stood there yawning. His hair was tousled. "Can't this wait until morning, Agent West?"

"Sorry, it can't," she said, pushing the door fully open and barging into the man's apartment. She shut the door behind her.

"What's this about?" he demanded, pointing a stern finger at her. "This is no time to come see me. I was asleep. You'll have to come back tomorrow. And make an appointment first!"

Frustrated from her lack of progress on the case and irritated at the man's surly attitude, she dispensed with pretense. Instead of answering him, she grabbed his outstretched hand with both of hers and twisted his wrist sharply. Still gripping his wrist, she sidestepped and yanked his arm behind his back. It felt good to put her CIA training to use.

"Ow!" he yelped. "Let go of me!"

"I don't have time for bullshit, Shubert. Either you tell me what I want to know or I'll break your arm."

"Please," he pleaded, "let go."

"You'll talk?"

Rachel pulled his arm up sharply again, not because she needed to but because she didn't like the man.

"Stop!" he yelled. "Yes, I'll talk."

She released his arm and he backed away from her, his eyes wide. "What do you want to know, West?"

"Information."

"I told you everything before, when you came to the hotel."

"We'll see about that. Anybody else here?"

He shook his head. "I live alone."

"Easy to see why." She pointed to the sofa in the living room. "Go sit down and shut up. I need to look around."

Shubert did as he was told and she quickly searched the small apartment, confirmed no one else was there.

Coming back to the living room, she stood over the seated man and put her hands on her hips.

"You don't act like a police officer," Shubert grumbled, as he massaged his arm. "All the ones I know are polite."

She gave him a hard stare. "You ready to talk or do you want to really piss me off?"

He raised his palms in front of him. "Okay, okay. What do you want to know? I told you before about the prostitute, Erica."

"I've already talked to her."

"What then?"

"When Zhao Deng stayed at your hotel, he would go to meetings."

"I don't know anything about that."

"Erica told me these meetings were at an estate in the countryside, about an hour's drive from Helsinki."

A flash of recognition crossed his face and his brow furrowed. "I don't know about that," he repeated.

"I think you do, Shubert."

"I'm sorry, I don't."

She took a step closer to him. "This estate is owned by a Russian. I need his name and I need an address."

His lips pressed into a thin line and she noticed beads of perspiration on his forehead. But he said nothing.

"We can do this the easy way," she spat out, "or the hard way. Which is it?"

"I'm calling the police," he stated, his bluster of earlier returning, "and my attorney. If you want to question me further, we'll have to do it at your office."

Grabbing the lapel of his robe with one hand, she cocked her other hand into a fist and punched him, hard, on the nose.

Shubert howled, his head snapped back and blood trickled from his nostrils.

Her knuckles ached from the jarring blow and she shook her hand to alleviate it.

The concierge shrank away from her on the sofa. In obvious pain, he gingerly touched his bent nose. "You broke it," he whimpered.

"You wanted the hard way, Shubert. I gave it to you. Now tell me about the Russian."

"His name is Arsi Lendel," he blurted.

"Doesn't sound Russian."

"He's from Finland, but he works in Russia. The house in the countryside, outside of Helsinki, is registered in his name."

"Who owns it?"

"I don't know. His Russian boss, I assume."

"Who's that?"

"I don't know. I only dealt with Lendel."

"What's the address of this estate?"

Shubert told her and gave her directions. She considered the information. Was the concierge lying? It wasn't likely, she thought. The man was in evident pain. In her experience, people with broken noses didn't want to aggravate the ache. "Okay. I'll go check it out. But if you're lying, I'll come back, you hear?"

She clenched a fist and held it in front of his face. "In the meantime, don't make any phone calls to your lawyer, or the police, or anyone else. Understand? This is between you and me."

He nodded furiously.

"Good. I'm glad we understand each other, Shubert."

***

Rachel drove the Saab out of the city and past the suburbs, then headed northeast, following the concierge's directions. Traffic was light on the two lane road and she reached the small city of Kouvola in half an hour. Driving through, she continued into the rural and beautiful Finnish countryside. Besides a few farmhouses, the heavily wooded area contained little signs of life.

She reached Lake Saimaa soon after and wound around the narrow road that bordered the sprawling lake. The early morning light cast a pink and gray glow on the dark blue, almost black water.

Ten minutes later she spotted a high stone wall which surrounded a wooded property. She drove past the wall and soon after found an open gate. Driving in, she followed a winding gravel road for another three miles. Apart from the trees and an occasional clearing, there was nothing else on the property except a very long airplane runway, paved in asphalt. By its length and width, the runway appeared to be able to accommodate a large jet.

Finally, after a bend in the road, she saw the large house. Or what was left of it.

Rising from a crumbled foundation was a burnt-out structure – blackened brick walls, a collapsed roof, and the remnants of three stone fireplace chimneys.

Behind the main house were two other smaller structures – perhaps a garage and a barn. But they also had been torched. Beyond the burnt-out buildings she could see Lake Saimaa at the end of the property. The area was deserted; no cars or people.

Parking the Saab in front of the main house, she got out.

The acrid stench of smoke hung in the air. Although the fire was extinguished, the smell was still overpowering. Her eyes began to water and she coughed. Pulling out a handkerchief, she covered her nose and mouth.

Then she strode forward for a closer look.

The estate had been completely burned down, and from the look of it, a strong incendiary device or accelerant was used. This was no accidental fire.

Whoever did it wanted no evidence left behind.

With a sinking feeling she realized Prism was once again covering its tracks.

Chapter 13

Langley, Virginia

Alex Miller was in his office when his phone rang. Putting aside the budget report he was reading, he picked up the receiver.

"It's Rachel," he heard the woman say.

"Where are you?" he asked. "I tried calling you earlier but there was no answer."

"I'm in the middle of nowhere Finland. I guess these satellite phones aren't always what they're cracked up to be." There was a pause, then, "I kind of miss the old landline days, Alex."

He chuckled. "I know what you mean."

"I'm driving back to Helsinki now. Just left the house Prism held their meetings."

His pulse quickened. "Tell me you got some good leads."

"The place was torched. Nothing left."

Miller's surge of excitement faded. "Damn."

"That's what I said, Alex, except I used stronger language."

He chuckled again, in spite of his disappointment. The woman's sense of humor was one of the reasons he was so fond of her.

"Tell me some good news, Rachel. I've been working on the department's budget, day and night. Damn HQ keeps cutting it and I need something to take my mind off that."

"You're in luck. I did get one good lead from Shubert, the concierge. He told me the estate was registered to a Finnish man named Arsi Lendel. Apparently this Lendel works for a Russian who owns the estate. You remember Erica Anheim, Zhao's prostitute?"

"Yes, I remember," he replied.

"Well, she told me the same thing – that a Russian man owned the place where Prism met."

"Okay. Any idea where you can find this Arsi Lendel?"

"No. But I'm on my way back to Shubert's place now. If he knows, I'll get it out of him."

"You are persuasive," he said, knowing the operative's interrogation track record. "In the meantime, I'll start searching the databases for Lendel."

"Good."

"One last thing before you go, Rachel. Be careful. This group, Prism, may be businessmen, but they're also killers. Watch your back."

"Careful is my middle name," she said with a laugh. Then the call clicked off.

As he replaced the receiver, he glanced out of his office window. It was nighttime, and all he could see was the mostly empty parking lot, illuminated by harsh floodlights. The weather report had said tomorrow would be a sunny day, a welcome change from the area's typical overcast sky.

Miller's thoughts turned from the details of the call to the caller. In his mind he visualized Rachel's sculpted good looks, her long blonde hair, and her vibrant personality.

A widower in his sixties, Miller lived a solitary, almost boring life. Besides his work, he had little else. He lived vicariously through the actions of his agents, operatives like Rachel. But she was special, he mused. Although he knew a beautiful woman in her thirties would never be interested in a dinosaur like himself, sometimes the fantasy made him feel alive.

Pushing those thoughts aside as unprofessional, he looked away from the window and went back to working on the budget.

Chapter 14

Helsinki, Finland

After grabbing breakfast at an outdoor cafe on Market Square, Rachel West drove the short distance to Shubert's apartment. The man wasn't home so she headed next to the Belle Epoque, figuring he was already at work.

She strode into the hotel's marbled lobby and looked around. Curiously, the concierge's station was staffed by a young brunette.

Rachel approached her. "I need to see Mr. Shubert."

"I'm sorry," the young woman replied, "he's not in today."

"Where is he?"

A worried look crossed the brunette's face. "We don't know. He's always very punctual. Never misses a day. But today ..." She held up her palms.

"I see." Rachel flashed her badge. "I'm with Interpol. Can you check your records and tell me his address and phone number?"

The hotel worker did so, confirming the apartment she had just visited was Shubert's only address. Thanking the woman, the agent left the hotel, located her car and climbed in.

Pulling out her cell phone, she punched in the concierge's number. Ominously, she reached an operator who informed her that the number had been disconnected.

Her leads were drying up fast, she realized.

Glancing at her watch, she calculated the time in Langley – it was the middle of the night back home. Taking a chance Alex Miller was still working, she dialed his number.

Miller picked up on the second ring.

"Don't you ever sleep, Alex?"

"No."

She smiled, knowing it was probably true. Her boss was a workaholic. "Alex, it looks like Shubert is missing."

"Damn. You think it's Prism?"

"I'd put money on it."

"Okay, Rachel. I've got something for you. I was able to track down Arsi Lendel. Like you said, he's a Finn. Has a place in Helsinki. But it appears his main source of income is from Russia. Regular deposits from a Russian bank are wired into his bank account."

"Give me the details."

He told her Lendel's address and she wrote it down. "Any info on the Russian bank account, Alex?"

"It's a numbered account. I traced it back to a dummy corporation in St. Petersburg, Russia. It was a dead-end after that."

"Okay. I'll start looking for Lendel right away. And Alex?"

"Yes?"

"Get some sleep."

He chuckled as he hung up.

***

Lendel's upscale apartment building was near the Uspenski Cathedral, the red-brick onion dome structure that is one of the city's landmarks. His building overlooked the Pohjoissatama Marina, an exclusive part of town.

After showing her badge to the attendant at the building's lobby, she took the elevator to the seventh floor and found the apartment.

Once again pulling her badge, she knocked on the door. There was no answer so she knocked again.

Figuring the man wasn't home, she scanned the corridor. Confirming the hallway was empty, she took out a miniature lock-pick set and bending over, fiddled with the lock. A moment later it clicked open and she went inside, quickly closing the door behind her.

"Mr. Lendel?" she called out. "I'm with Interpol."

Getting no answer, she stepped into the large, lavishly appointed living room. The far wall was floor-to-ceiling glass, with a spectacular view of the marina.

"Mr. Lendel?" she said again, as she moved past the living room, through a dining room, and lastly into a bedroom. The apartment was unoccupied. And from the musty smell, it appeared no one had been there in some time.

In the bedroom was an office nook, complete with a laptop and a printer.

She turned on the computer, but the files were password protected. She spent the next minute guessing at several different password combinations, with no success. Knowing the tech guys back at Langley would have better luck, she began disconnecting the cable wires.

But before she was done, she heard the apartment's front door open and close.

Stopping what she was doing, she removed her badge from her jacket and stepped back into the living room.

A huge, barrel-chested man stood by the doorway. His blond hair was cut into a crew cut and his suit and shirt were wrinkled and stained. Even from across the room, the smell of onions and cigarettes was overpowering.

Rachel held up the badge. "Interpol. Are you Lendel?"

The huge man sneered. "No. And I saw you on the security camera. You used a lock-pick to get in here. You're no police."

"Look, I'll call Interpol – I can have backup here in a couple of minutes."

Crossing his beefy arms across his massive chest, he sneered again. "Go ahead."

She swallowed hard. This thug, whoever he was, was smarter than he looked. It appeared she couldn't talk herself out of this – she'd have to fight. But she was no match for the giant of a man. She guessed he was 6'8" and over 350 pounds, all of it muscle. Rachel was strong for a woman, and well trained. But she knew training only got you so far. As he stood there, towering over her, she could tell he was itching for a fight.

"Do you work for Lendel?" she asked, stalling for time as she got ready to strike.

"Maybe I do and maybe I don't. The question is, who the hell are you and what do *you* want?"

"I'm investigating a case. I just need to talk to him."

"He's not here."

"I can see that. Do you know where he is?"

"I'm tired of your questions."

The man advanced, crossing the space between them quickly, his arms outstretched. He was surprisingly fast for a big man. It was obvious he was attempting to bear-hug her and throw her to the floor.

Sidestepping first, she then kicked him in the kidneys.

She heard him grunt as she circled behind him.

He whirled around, his eyes full of hate. "You'll regret that, *nartuu*!"

She tried a front kick next, aiming for his groin, but he swatted it away. Her leg burned from the ache of his powerful blow.

Running out of options, she lowered her head and ran into him, head-butting his solar plexus.

He groaned, but instead of staggering back as she'd hoped, he seized her with both arms, easily lifted her off the floor and threw her crashing to the ground.

Ignoring the jarring pain, she kicked up at him, once again trying for his groin.

Swatting her kick away, he laughed, then leaned over and punched her viciously in the stomach.

Rachel gasped for breath, the intense pain nearly blinding her. She rolled on the floor, trying desperately to get away from the brute. But he lunged at her, grabbing her with both hands and lifting her off the ground. Then he flung her across the room like a rag doll, where she crashed against the wall.

Slumping to the floor, she instantly lost consciousness.

Chapter 15

St. Petersburg, Russia

Arsi Lendel was in Ivan Petrov's office when his cell phone rang. Lendel took out the cell and held it to his ear.

"It's Terso," Lendel heard the man say. "I just caught a woman going through your apartment."

"Who is she?"

"She has an Interpol ID, but I don't think it's real. She broke into your place."

"Is her name Rachel West?"

"How do you know, Arsi?"

"I've run into her before. Is she alive?"

Terso laughed. "I roughed her up, but yes, she's alive. She's unconscious."

"I want her alive. Where are you now?"

"Still at your place."

"Tie her up. Take her to the safe house. I'll leave for Helsinki immediately. Don't hurt her anymore. I have to interrogate her."

"Too bad. She's a pretty thing. I could really enjoy playing with her."

"Later, after I'm done with her, she's all yours."

Lendel heard the man laugh crudely, and he disconnected the call. He turned toward Petrov, who was sitting across from him behind his desk.

The Russian man leaned forward in his seat. "Well?"

"That was Terso, sir. He's caught West, the agent I thought I had killed. But he doesn't think she's with Interpol."

Petrov nodded, then smiled. "That's good. We don't need any police agency nosing around our business. Find out what she knows."

"Yes, sir."

The Russian's face turned into a scowl. "And afterwards, make sure you finish the job this time. Eliminate her!"

Chapter 16

Glacier County, Montana

In the den of his massive home, the American was brooding.

He stared out through the transparent wall, made of military-grade, bullet-proof glass. Although he could clearly see out, from the outside, the wall's bronze, mirror-like opaqueness allowed no one to see inside.

Not that there were any strangers out there for tens of miles. The American owned a vast track of property, over 10,000 acres. It was very secluded, and all of it ringed by a ten-foot-high, razor-topped, electrified fence. He was a very private man. And extremely wealthy, affording him the ability to hire an army of well trained security guards, some of whom he could see now, patrolling the property in Humvees.

He stood there gazing out the window, his frame of mind tormented.

It was a clear day outside, the sun shining brightly. From his vantage point he could see a vast stretch of his property – the low foothills, leading to the mountains beyond.

He took a deep breath of the purified air to calm his nerves. A specially-constructed filtration system ensured he only breathed the cleanest air. A germaphobe, the American was constantly washing his already clean hands. A special cleaning crew came to the house several times a week to sterilize it and all of its contents.

But he wasn't thinking about any of that right now.

His only thoughts were on Prism. An operation that should already be complete.

A surge of disgust filled him as he recalled the recent setbacks.

Then he took another gulp of air to steady his nerves.

I will succeed! he screamed silently in his mind. *In spite of the incompetence of the others. I will succeed!*

Turning away from the sweeping vista, he left the room.

Chapter 17

Helsinki, Finland

Every part of Rachel West's body ached. A sharp pain emanated from her back, through her torso, and down her legs. Her head throbbed, the ache feeling like a vise around her forehead. The fight with the huge man had left her badly bruised, but luckily, she'd suffered no broken bones.

Rachel had regained consciousness a minute ago and found herself in a windowless, concrete room. A basement, she guessed. The place had a dank, moldy smell. A dim light bulb hung from the ceiling, providing the only light.

Sitting with her back against the wall, she stared at the closed door on the far side of the room, the only way in or out.

Ignoring the pain, she stood and approached the door. She tried the knob, and as she expected, it was locked. She ran her hands across the door and the frame around it. Both were constructed of heavy metal. Without tools or explosives, she wouldn't be able to break it down. And she had neither. In fact, as she'd realized moments earlier, she didn't have much of anything. She was still dressed in the blouse and slacks she was wearing earlier, but the giant had taken away her jacket, wallet, belt, and even her shoes.

As she stood there, her bare feet on the cold concrete floor, she gazed around the basement, looking for anything she could use as a weapon. But the room was empty – no furniture or fixtures of any kind.

Her thoughts churned, knowing the man could return at any moment. The fact he hadn't already killed her probably meant he was waiting for someone. His accomplice or boss, Arsi Lendel, she figured.

Just then she heard locks clicking and she moved away from the door. She went into a fighting stance, one leg forward, the other back, both arms up.

The metal door creaked open and the huge man stood there, pointing a Sig Sauer semiautomatic. Even from this distance he reeked of onions and cigarettes.

"Against the wall," he ordered.

She stepped back away from him but kept her stance.

As she watched, the giant, still training the handgun on her, pulled three large buckets into the room.

"What's that for?" she asked.

He laughed crudely. "For you. One bucket with water, another of food, and the last one for your shit and piss. You're going to be here awhile."

"Are you going to kill me?" she said, trying to draw him out.

He laughed again. "Of course. But not now. Arsi has to question you first."

"He's coming here?"

"Yes."

"When?"

"Later."

She continued asking him questions, stalling for time, as she quickly assessed the situation. Could she rush him, overpower him, and escape? She'd tried that before, with no success. And this time he had a gun. Would guile work? If he let his guard down she might be able to get at the handgun.

It was worth a try, because she knew that when Lendel arrived, her chances of surviving were even less.

Dropping her fighting stance, she faced him and flashed a smile. "Sounds like Lendel won't be here for quite awhile. We could have some fun, you and me, before he gets here."

A confused look crossed his face. "What do you mean?"

Still smiling, she began to slowly unbutton her blouse.

"You're trying to trick me!" he bellowed, still aiming the pistol at her. But his eyes were tightly focused on her chest. She could tell her actions were having the desired effect.

When she finished unbuttoning her blouse, she seductively removed the garment. Dressed in only her bra and slacks, she said, "You like?"

"I'm not stupid," he replied, "I know what you're trying to do." But his voice was raspy now and his eyes had a hungry look.

She pulled down one of her bra straps. "My name's Rachel ... what's yours?"

"Terso," he whispered.

She pulled down the other bra strap. "You want to fuck me, Terso?"

The huge man lowered the gun to his side, his eyes still locked on her.

She laughed seductively. "I know you do. I bet you're already hard as a rock."

His face was a mixture of emotions – lust and confusion.

After playing with the front snap of her bra, she unfastened it, then very slowly removed the garment. "I know a lot of ways to please a man ..."

His black eyes were burning with anticipation and he strode toward her until he stood close, towering over her. His stench was overwhelming.

Ignoring the disgust she felt for the man, she pasted on another phony smile. Sometimes she hated her job. Now was one of those times.

Using both hands, she began to slowly massage her bare breasts. "You ready to fuck me, Terso?"

"Yes," he grunted, breathing heavily. "Yes!"

She reached out with one hand and touched his pants crotch. "Oh yeah. You're more than ready." She rubbed him as he moaned with pleasure.

"Take off your clothes, Terso. I'm tired of playing games. I want your cock inside me."

The man quickly stuffed the pistol in his hip holster and eagerly took off his shirt. She had him primed now, she knew. Once he was undressed and distracted, she'd grab the handgun and blow his head off.

But as he was about to unbuckle his belt, she heard a phone ring.

With a groan he stopped what he was doing, backed away from her, and removed a cell phone from his pants pocket.

"Terso," he snapped, holding the phone to his ear. His facial expression went cold as he listened.

"Yes, sir," he said.

The man listened some more, and after a final "yes, sir", hung up.

Grabbing his shirt off the floor, he began to put it back on.

"Don't you want to fuck, Terso?"

"No time. That was Arsi. I've got to do something for him before he gets here."

She licked her lips suggestively. "You sure?"

"Don't worry," he said, his voice hard now. "After Arsi's done with you, he promised me – you're all mine." He leered. "I'll fuck you so hard I'll split you in two. Then I'll kill you and burn your body. Nobody will ever find you." He laughed. "How does that sound, *nartuu*?"

He turned and left the basement, slamming the door shut behind him.

Then she heard the locks click into place.

Chapter 18

Langley, Virginia

Alex Miller glanced at his watch and began drumming his fingers on his desk.

Rachel West should have called him hours ago – it wasn't like her to miss her daily call-in. He was about to pick up his phone when there was a knock on his office door.

"Come in," Miller said.

The door opened and a tall, rugged looking man entered. He had short brown hair, coal-black eyes, and a chiseled face. He was wearing a gray suit, a buttoned-down white shirt, and a solid gray tie. The man approached the desk and stood at attention.

"Have a seat, Turner."

"Yes, sir."

The man sat on one of the visitor's chairs and Miller studied him a moment. Matt Turner had been a Factory agent for over four years, and was one of Miller's best operatives. Taciturn by nature, he'd been adept at whatever operation he'd been assigned – be it a simple investigation or a complex, multi-person assassination. He went about his business quietly and efficiently, and he reminded Miller, by his looks and temperament, of the Marlboro man in the ads from years ago.

"You wanted to see me, sir?"

"Yes." Miller steepled his hands on the desk. "I've been working on a case, and I want to bring you in."

"Yes, sir."

"A couple of things you should know, before I read you in. If you're okay with the parameters, then I'll give you the details."

Turner's brow furrowed, but he said nothing.

"You've been with the Factory for a long time," Miller continued, "so you know we don't deal with the simple problems that most government agencies deal with. We tackle the ... let's say ... more intractable problems our country faces ... and we use unconventional methods sometimes."

Turner nodded, stayed silent.

Miller leaned forward in his chair. "In this particular operation we face an external threat, and also, I believe, an internal one. I have reason to believe that certain elements at Central Intelligence have been compromised." He lowered his voice for emphasis. "I think we have a mole at the CIA."

Turner's eyes went wide, but he said nothing.

"And because of that, Turner, I'm running this operation totally in-house. Factory personnel only."

"You've cut HQ out of the loop?"

"That's right. Are you okay with that?"

Turner's eyes narrowed, but then he nodded. "Yes, Director."

"Good. A second thing. This operation will likely require you to work within the United States."

"But the Agency charter expressly forbids us to. That's the FBI's role."

Miller shrugged. "Rules are made to be broken. And this operation is a matter of national security. Are you all right with this?"

Turner gave him a thin smile. "Yes, sir. I'm a good soldier. If you're giving me the green light to work in the U.S., I'm okay with it."

"Excellent." The director paused a moment. "One last thing. I have three people already working on this case – two tech guys, and one field agent."

"Who's the field agent?"

"Rachel West."

Turner rubbed his jaw. "West likes to work alone."

"I know that. But we don't always get what want in life, do we? I know Rachel prefers the lone wolf thing, but this case is too big for one person, no matter how good they are."

"Yes, sir."

Miller gave the agent a hard look. "So you agree to the parameters of the operation?"

"Yes, Director."

Reaching into one of his desk drawers, Miller removed a thick file. The folder had no markings on the cover. He placed the file on his desk and slid it in front of the agent. "This is for your eyes only. Read it, memorize it, and return it to me later today. Make no copies of it. Is that crystal clear, Turner?"

"Yes, sir. What's the operation called?"

"Since HQ is not involved, I'm not giving it an official name." Miller paused a moment. "In fact, our conversation today never took place."

Chapter 19

St. Petersburg, Russia

Ivan Petrov was roaming the labyrinth of gold-leaf covered rooms of the Hermitage Museum, something he did at times to relieve tension.

Just then his cell phone rang. Turning away from Leonardo da Vinci's *The Madonna Litta* painting, he answered his encrypted sat phone.

"Petrov," he said into the cell, and recognized the voice on the other end immediately. He listened in rapt attention for several minutes, then hung up.

A wide grin spread on his face.

Quickly marching out of the room he was in, he strode through the crowded, marble-floor hallways, down the ornate main staircase of the Winter Palace and exited the museum building complex. He reached the park-like side courtyard moments later, and was now well away from the swarm of tourists that invaded the legendary museum on a daily basis.

Once again pulling out his cell, he quickly punched in a number. After ringing for a long time, the American picked up.

"It's Petrov, sir."

"Ivan. You have good news for me?"

Petrov's grin returned. "As a matter of fact, I do."

"It's about time, damn it."

"Sir, I just heard from my contact in Stockholm. The European deals are all complete. We now have all the necessary tech companies in that area."

"Very good, Ivan."

"Thank you, sir. And since we already had the Asian contingent in our pocket, we're almost there."

After a pause, the American said, "What's happening on the U.S. side?"

"We've made a lot of progress on that as well. I expect to finalize those deals soon."

"See that you do," the American demanded, his voice dripping with venom.

"Yes, sir."

"And Ivan, now that the European part of the plan is in place, I want to test it as we discussed previously."

"I'll let our tech group know. When should I implement the test?"

"Now."

Chapter 20

Helsinki, Finland

Rachel West, once again dressed in her blouse and slacks, paced the basement like a caged tiger as she confronted her grim situation. It had been hours since Terso had left –
she knew Lendel could arrive at any moment.

Rachel still felt like hell, her body throbbing from the beating she'd taken from the big man. She was cold too, and suddenly realized it wasn't just from walking on the chilly concrete floor on bare feet. It was because she hadn't eaten in a day.

Not hungry but knowing she had to eat to maximize her strength, she squatted by one of the buckets Terso had left. With one hand she scooped up the green paste and held it to her nose. The food, a combination of beans and vegetables she guessed, smelled rancid. But it was all she had. Stuffing some into her mouth, she ignored the gag reflex and swallowed. She continued eating the slop for another few minutes, then scooped some water from the second bucket and washed it down. Her mouth tasted awful from the foul-smelling food, but at least she was full. After wiping her lips with the back of her hand, she stood.

Just then she heard muffled footsteps from the other side of the closed door and a loud clicking noise.

The door opened and Terso came in, still brandishing the Sig Sauer. He was followed by a short, wiry man.

She backed away from them, once again going into a fighting stance.

The short man laughed. "You think you can overpower two armed men?" He took out a small revolver, and aiming it her way, said, "Terso, tie her up so I can get started."

The big man, sticking the Sig Sauer in his holster, pulled out a rope from a pocket and walked up to her. "Turn around, bitch, or I'll beat you some more."

Rachel, not seeing an opening for escape, grudgingly dropped her arms and turned around. She felt her hands being tied behind her back.

The big man laughed. Then he kicked her savagely on her side, toppling her to the floor. Grabbing her roughly, he hauled her up into a sitting position and pushed her so her back was against the wall.

Gulping in deep breaths as she recovered from the painful blow, she stared up at the two men.

"Now we can start," the short man said, putting his weapon in his pocket. He walked up and stood in front of her. Terso leaned against a nearby wall and lit up a cigarette.

The short man crossed his arms and stared down at her. "Do you know who I am, West?"

"An asshole?"

He seemed surprised at her response. "Feisty, aren't you? Believe me, after we're through with you, you won't be feisty anymore. I'm Arsi Lendel."

"Should I be impressed?"

He ignored the remark. "We've met before."

"I don't think so, Lendel. I'd remember an asshole like you."

"I was driving the BMW, the one that ran you off the road."

"Our paths *have* crossed. I want payback for that."

Lendel's head reared back and he bellowed out a long laugh. Afterwards, he shook his head slowly. "Enjoy your humor now, West – soon you'll be begging for mercy."

She went quiet, trying to figure out an angle for her escape. Finally she said, "What is it you want?"

"I checked out your Interpol ID – it looks real enough, but I made a few calls – nobody at that agency has heard of you. Who are you, really? And who do you work for?"

It was clear her cover was blown – should she tell the truth?

Bypassing his question, she said, "I'll tell your boss. I'm not talking to a nobody like you."

"How do you know I even have a boss?"

"I can always tell an underling – and it's not just that you're a runt, which you are, but by the girlie way you walk."

Lendel's face turned red.

He glanced back at Terso, who had a smile on face. "Told you, Arsi. She's a *narttu*. A pretty one, but still a bitch."

The short man turned back to Rachel and kicked her. She jerked her head in time and the blow struck her shoulder instead.

She gasped from the pain, closed her eyes for a moment.

"Who are you?" Lendel bellowed. "Who do you work for?"

She stayed silent.

"If you talk I'll let you live."

"That's bullshit, Lendel. You're going to kill me no matter what."

Lendel kicked her again, this time in the side, and she twisted away from him, trying to crab away on the rough floor. But he kept at it, the blows landing. The pain was intense and a minute later she passed out.

When she came to, Lendel was still standing there in front of her, looking down at her.

"Once again," the man said, "who do you work for?"

She said nothing, her eyes burning with hate. She considered kicking Lendel in the balls, but Terso was nearby, his hand on the butt of the Sig Sauer. She'd be dead in a second.

"Should I keep beating you?" the short man uttered, between clenched teeth. It was clear he was still angry about her earlier remark questioning his manhood. "I'll break your ribs – maybe that'll puncture your lungs."

"Doesn't matter, I'm not talking."

"Arsi," Terso chimed in, "let me at her. I can make her talk."

Lendel turned toward the other man. "Go ahead. This *narttu* is stubborn." The short man walked away from her, pulled out his revolver and held it at his side.

Terso, a wicked grin on his face, squatted in front of her. His body odor was repulsive. "I'm going to enjoy this, West."

Leering, he grabbed her roughly with both hands and ripped off her blouse. Then he grasped her bra and tore it off. Staring at her now exposed breasts, he let out a long, guttural laugh. She struggled to get away from him, but he held her firmly in place with a vice-like grip. His eyes were transfixed on her bare chest.

"Arsi, give me a lit cigarette," Terso said.

Lendel took out a cigarette, lit it and handed it to the other man.

A cold shiver ran down her spine as soon as she saw what was happening. She knew instinctively what the brute was planning on doing. Terso was going to burn her breasts with the cigarette to get her to talk.

"Pity I have to do this," the huge man said with another leer, "since you have such sweet breasts." He laughed vulgarly. "Doesn't matter, though. There's other parts of your body I can play with later that'll be just as much fun."

"Get on with it, Terso," Lendel called out from behind him. "We don't have all day."

The giant grunted, an irritated look on his face. It was clear Terso didn't want to be rushed. He was having too much fun. Then he shrugged and held the tip of the lit cigarette an inch from her nipple. "Last chance, West. Want to talk now?"

"Yes!" she screamed, "I'll talk!"

Terso seemed surprised by the outburst, and in that split-second when he pulled the cigarette away from her, she lashed out with her leg, kicking the big man in the groin. She caught him at his most vulnerable spot and he groaned, dropped the cig and clutched his pants crotch.

Rolling away from him, she sprung off the floor.

Lendel, who was standing a few feet away, took a step back, his eyes wide. He brought the revolver up from his side, but Rachel didn't give him time to aim. Instead, she ran headlong towards him, her hands still tied behind her back.

The crown of her head caught him squarely on the chest and he toppled backwards, landing with a thud on the concrete floor. The revolver flew off and clattered to the ground.

From behind her she heard Terso still groaning, and as she turned, she saw him begin to get to his feet.

Spotting the revolver on the floor, she dropped to her knees, then quickly sat on the ground. Feeling blindly behind her with her bound hands, she managed to grab the gun.

Twisting her body as best she could, she turned toward Terso, aiming the gun his way. The giant was running towards her, an expression of utter hatred on his face.

She pulled the trigger in rapid succession, missing with the first shot, but hitting him in the torso with her second, third and fourth shots. But the big man kept coming, staggering forward until he was on top of her. Pulling the trigger again, she fired two more rounds point-blank into his gut and he collapsed on top of her. She kept pulling the trigger, but all she heard was the clack of dry fire – the gun was empty.

The giant's huge body, now inert, covered her completely as she lay on the floor. She gasped for breath from his crushing weight, but eventually managed to push off the corpse partway and slide out from beneath him. Her half-naked body was covered with his blood.

She scanned the basement for Lendel. He was now on his knees, in the process of getting up. *Where the hell is the other gun?* she thought, glancing desperately around the room.

Out of the corner of her eye she noticed Lendel on his feet, staggering toward the basement's open door.

She rushed toward him, turned her body sideways, and lashed out with a powerful martial-arts side kick. The blow struck him in the back, sending him crashing to the wall. He howled as his body slumped to the floor.

Every part of her body screamed with pain. Standing there, bent over and gasping for air, all she wanted was to rest. But she knew more of Lendel's accomplices could show up anytime.

She sprinted out of the basement, partially nude and soaked in blood, her hands still tied behind her back.

Chapter 21

Langley, Virginia

Alex Miller was in his office working at his laptop, when he heard a knock on the door. Looking up, he saw the door open and his assistant step in.

"Sir," the young man said, "we just got notification from HQ. The Internet is down across most of Europe. I just checked on CNN and they're also reporting the story. Thought you should know."

"Thanks, Carlos," Miller replied as the assistant reclosed the door behind him.

Logging into his email, the director read the Agency notice. Then he went online to the CNN site, curious as to their take.

After quickly reading the story, he checked the AP and Reuters news sites. From everything he read, it appeared the reports were accurate. Internet service throughout Europe had been down for over an hour, and was now just recovering. Although it was not unusual to have sporadic outages of the Internet at specific companies or even in whole countries, it was very rare for such a large-scale interruption to take place.

He closed the news sites and leaned back in his office chair. Was this some crazy hacker? It appeared way too massive for that.

An uneasy feeling settled over him. Could this be the work of Prism?

Chapter 22

Helsinki, Finland

When Arsi Lendel regained consciousness hours later, he sat up slowly and leaned his back against the basement wall. He had a massive headache, and gingerly touching the back of his head, realized he was bleeding.

Then it all came back to him – the fight, that *narttu* West, or whatever her name was, getting away. Laying in the middle of the room like a huge sack of potatoes was Terso's motionless body. Judging from the large pool of blood that now covered much of the floor, his accomplice was obviously dead.

"Damn," he growled. Not at seeing his friend's corpse, but at knowing West had escaped a second time. Petrov was going to be furious.

Chapter 23

Helsinki, Finland

Rachel lay on the narrow bed of the cheap motel, trying to get some sleep. But the noise from the other rooms on either side of hers was deafening. The paper-thin walls didn't keep out the loud music, or the groans of the hookers and johns who frequented the place.

Despite the commotion, she was glad to be here, nursing her pains. Lucky to have escaped. In the building where she'd been held, she'd found a knife to cut the bindings and some clothing, which she put on. Then, after making the long trek on foot to her hotel downtown, she checked out and found this place, a motel were no names where needed, only cash.

Her Interpol cover was blown. And it was too dangerous to use her real name on this assignment – she'd need a new identity.

She turned on her side, trying to find a comfortable spot on the lumpy mattress. But all she managed to do was release a cloud of noxious odors from the bed. She didn't want to even contemplate their source.

Even though her entire body was throbbing from the beating she'd endured, a glimmer of a smile creased her lips. The thought that she had killed that bastard Terso made her feel good. Really good. Sometimes, she mused, her job was satisfying.

Rachel finally fell asleep and when she awoke hours later, realized with alarm she hadn't checked in with Langley for days.

Getting off the squeaky bed, she stood and went to the room's scarred wooden dresser. There was a cracked mirror above the dresser and she looked at her reflection – she was now wearing her own clothes, but she had one black eye, and cuts and bruises covered her face. Her long hair, pulled back into a ponytail, was matted and unclean. She looked like hell.

Ignoring that, she opened a drawer and removed her spare sat phone. Sitting down on the bed, she stabbed in a number and held the cell to her ear.

"It's Rachel," she said, when Alex Miller picked up on the other end.

"Where the hell have you been?" Miller shouted. "You missed your call-in for two days!"

"Sorry, Alex." She rubbed her aching forehead. "It's been a tough week."

"Are you okay?" the man replied, calming down a bit. "I've been worried sick."

"Yeah, I'm alright. Some bumps and bruises, that's all."

"I'm sure it's more than that," he said sternly.

"I'm a big girl; I can take care of myself."

"One day, Rachel ... I'm going to get a call from the local authorities of some God forsaken place in the middle of nowhere, telling me they're scraping your body off the floor. I don't know if I can deal with that ..." He sounded genuinely concerned, maybe even more than that. *What the hell is that about?* she wondered. *I'm an operative, nothing more and nothing less.*

"I told you, Alex, I'm fine. I just need some rest and a long, hot shower. Now let me fill you in on what happened."

She spent the next ten minutes telling him the recent events. When she was done, she lay back on the bed, still holding the phone to her ear.

"Rachel, I've got some news for you. Today there was a widespread blackout of the Internet in Europe. It's back on now, but it looks suspicious; it was very well coordinated."

"You think Prism is behind it?"

"Could be." He paused, then said, "There's something else, and you may not like it."

She sat up on the bed. "What?"

"I've assigned another field agent to work with you."

Standing up abruptly, she clutched the cell tightly. "Bullshit! I always work alone!"

"I knew you'd say that," he responded, his voice calm. "It's for your own good. This is too big for one agent."

She began pacing the small room. "I won't stand for this shit! I don't want a partner, never have. You know that!"

"I'm sorry, it's done."

"You ... you can't ... I don't ... need a babysitter!" She was so angry she could barely get the words out. "Why didn't you check with me ... before you did this?"

"Because I knew what your reaction would be. Anyway, he's not a babysitter, he's a good agent."

She slumped on the bed, realizing she wouldn't be able to change Alex's mind. "Okay, who the hell is he?"

"Matt Turner."

"The Marlboro Man? You've got to be kidding."

"He's one of our best operatives."

"Not as good as me."

Miller chuckled. "That may be, but his case closing ratio is outstanding."

"Blah, blah, blah. He's a by-the-book, buttoned-down shirt, perfect hair kind of guy. I bet he spit-shines his shoes every morning."

Miller laughed again. "You'll make a good team."

"That remains to be seen." Then she hung up.

Chapter 24

St. Petersburg, Russia

"My American partner," Ivan Pretrov said into the phone, "has been checking into the background of this West woman." He paused, looked out his office window at the river below. A large cargo ship, being guided by a tug boat, was moving slowly past, blocking his view of the Hermitage Museum. "You were right in your assessment, Lendel. She's not with Interpol."

"You found out her real identity, Mr. Petrov?" Arsi Lendel replied, his voice somewhat distorted by the scrambled call.

The Russian turned away from the window, instead focused on the painting of Stalin, which hung on the opposite wall. The long-dead leader of the motherland was Petrov's idol. "Yes. The American has a source at Central Intelligence. It appears West is an agent there."

Arsi Lendel let out a low whistle. "No wonder she was so well trained."

"That's still no excuse." Petrov replied, his voice hard, "You let her escape. Twice." He paused to control his rage. "You've let me down, Lendel. Which means I've let the American down. Do you have any idea what that means?"

"I'm sorry, sir. It won't happen again."

"How can I be sure of that?"

"Sir, it was my employee, Terso, who let her get away. It really wasn't my fault."

Petrov didn't reply at first, instead focused on the painting. "Have you at least dealt with *that* issue?"

"Yes, sir. He's no longer an employee of mine. I put a bullet in his head."

"Well, at least you did something right."

"Yes, Mr. Petrov."

"Find West. Kill her. I don't care how. I don't care about collateral damage. Just find her and kill her. The last thing we need is the CIA involved."

"Yes, sir, I'll take care of it."

"One more thing, Lendel. This will be your last failure. Next time you won't be so lucky. And neither will the rest of your family in Finland. I know who they are and I know where they live."

Chapter 25

Helsinki, Finland

Rachel West picked him out of the crowd right away. The tall, rugged man was the only one wearing a business suit – the other passengers coming out of baggage claim were all dressed casually.

She waved and Matt Turner nodded and strode over.

"How was the flight, Turner?"

"Long."

As they left baggage claim and exited Vantaa Airport, they made small talk, part of their training to blend in with the crowds around them.

After they got in her rented Saab in the parking lot, she turned and faced him. "This is a bad idea, Turner. I've had a couple of days to let it sink in, but I'm still pissed. I told Miller I didn't want a babysitter."

The man frowned, but he said nothing.

"I always work alone," she added.

"Look, West, I know that. You have quite a rep at the Agency. But I had no choice."

"Yeah, yeah. You're a good soldier," she said with disdain, "and good soldiers always follow orders."

He frowned again and his cheeks flushed, but he stayed silent.

"You got a rep too, Matt. The big, quiet guy. A by-the-book Boy Scout. They may not tell you to your face, but people call you the Marlboro Man, because of your looks."

"I know. But I get the job done."

"Yeah, so I've been told," she said, grudgingly knowing he was right. She raised an accusing finger at him. "But remember this. This is my operation. You can tag along, but I'm the lead agent."

"Miller didn't tell me that."

"He didn't have to – you should have figured it out on your own. I was assigned to the case first, so I'm lead. Right?"

The handsome man thought about this for a moment, then nodded.

"Okay, Turner, I'm glad we got that out of the way." The roar of a plane taking off from a nearby runway filled the car's interior and she waited for that to subside. "You brought me my new ID?"

Turner reached into his suit, took out an envelope and handed it to her.

She scanned the forged contents, memorized her new name and cover. Grinning, she said, "I've never been a 'cultural attaché' at the U.S. Embassy before. That'll work. What are you?"

"Different name, same position." He pointed to her face. "How'd you get the black eye and bruises?"

"It's a long story and I won't bore you with it. Let's just say the other guys are worse off. Don't worry, a little makeup and I'll be good as new. I assume Miller gave you details of the operation."

"I read the file. Though I'm concerned we're doing this off the books."

She gave him a sidelong glance. "It's true what they say about you – you really are a Boy Scout, aren't you?"

He didn't reply.

"Miller thinks we may have a mole at the Agency," Rachel said, as she watched a plane on the horizon begin its descent. "That may or may not be true, but it's his call."

"Yes, it is. By the way, I've booked us rooms at the Sokos Vaakuna in downtown Helsinki," Turner said, as she glanced toward him again.

"Good. The place I'm staying in now is a dump. Did you bring the tools I requested?"

"Yes, West. The Glock 42 with the silencer and the carbon knife."

"Okay. This temporary partnership may just work out." She gave him a questioning look. "How'd you get that through airport security?"

He smiled. "The embassy ID helped."

Rachel started up the Saab and began driving out of the airport complex and toward the city.

Chapter 26

Helsinki, Finland

Matt Turner sipped a beer and studied Rachel West as she ravenously attacked her large platter of veal and noodles. The two were seated at an outdoor restaurant overlooking Toolonlahti Bay.

Although he had never worked with her before, their paths had crossed at meetings and briefings. She was stunning – probably one of the best-looking women he had ever seen. But as their earlier meeting at the airport proved, her reputation was well deserved. Described as a bitch-on-wheels if you crossed her, he now knew it was an apt description.

But Miller had given him his marching orders – Turner had a job to do, and by God, he planned to do it.

After taking another sip of beer, he said, "I guess you're hungry." He kept his voice low as not to be overheard, although there were only a few other customers at the restaurant and they were seated far away.

Rachel put down her fork and knife and looked up at him. "All I've had to eat was Lendel's slop and the crap they had at the fleabag motel."

The waiter brought them fresh drinks and Turner waited for the man to move away. "By the way you're walking and the bruises on your face, looks to me like you're in pain. Maybe you should see a doctor."

Her eyes flashed in anger. "And what, leave you to run this case? Forget it. This is my operation, remember?"

"Whatever you say. Just trying to be helpful."

"Listen. I don't need a babysitter, or a daddy. It's tough being a female agent in a male culture. I've worked my ass off, put in the hours, did whatever I had to do to get to this point. I'm not giving that up. Understood?"

"Keep your voice down," he said quietly, holding his palms up. "I apologize if I offended you. I didn't mean to."

Her expression softened. "Look," she replied, this time more calmly, "I run into a lot of characters in this line of work – men at the Agency and in the field – they take one look at me and usually want sex." She paused, took a sip of her wine. "Since we just started working together, I want to set the record straight. I've never had sex with anyone at Central Intelligence. I never, ever, mix business with pleasure. Secondly, although I've used my looks to entice criminals, I don't put out." She leaned forward in her chair. "And if for some reason I get close to crossing that line," her eyes flashed with a ferocity he found a little frightening, "I always make them pay for it afterwards." She picked up her steak knife and held it up. "If you get my drift."

"I do," he replied, then took a long swallow of his drink.

Rachel put the knife down and leaned back in the chair. She smiled, a soft, almost shy smile. "I'm sorry to come on so strong. I can tell you're a decent guy. Better than most I've come across. I ... I had some rough times when I was a teen, things I'm still trying to sort through." She paused. "And my job hasn't helped."

The woman went quiet a moment as if in deep thought, then extended her hand toward him and smiled. "Let's start over, okay?"

He shook it. She had a firm, strong handshake, but her skin was warm, soft, and sensual. He held her hand for a bit too long and she snatched it away.

Pushing aside her empty plate, she said, "You read the file, right?" The friendliness and femininity that had seeped out for a brief moment was gone. Her tone was all business.

"Yes, I did."

"Okay, let me fill you in on some of the details that aren't in there." A soft breeze blew and she tucked her long blonde hair behind her ears. It was dusk, but the still strong sunlight cast an orange glow that accentuated her sculpted features. "I've had good leads on Prism, but as soon as I get close, they've shut me down. I was held hostage by Arsi Lendel and his goon. The goon is dead, but Lendel is still out there." She motioned with her hand. "Somewhere. He's not the ringleader, but I think through him we can find the Russian who appears to be the key to this operation."

Turner nodded. "Where does Lendel live?"

"He has an apartment here in town. He wasn't there when I went the first time. We need to go back again."

"How did you get captured?"

A look of disgust crossed her face. "The goon, Terso, got the drop on me."

"He's dead?"

"Yeah," she replied with a smug smile. "I made him pay in the end. Now we just have to find Lendel – I want payback with him too."

Turner glanced at his watch. "You want to head over there tonight?"

"No, we'll get an early start in the morning. You're probably jet-lagged and I need you fresh. And I'm still nursing some pain."

He arched a brow. "If you want, I could check it out tonight on my own."

The woman gave him a hard look. "Forget it. We do this my way, or you go home now."

Chapter 27

Helsinki, Finland

The drive from the Sokos Vaakuna Hotel to Lendel's apartment building took ten minutes, and since it was five a.m., Rachel West had no trouble finding a place to park close to the high-rise.

"This is it," Rachel said as she turned off the Saab.

Matt Turner, sitting in the passenger seat, nodded and stayed quiet. He, like her, had dressed in dark, casual clothing. Beneath that clothing they wore ultra-light Kevlar suits he'd brought from Langley.

Rachel glanced out the car's windows – all was quiet in the marina area, which the building overlooked. Rows of pleasure boats, power and sail, rocked gently in their moorings. Few people were out. The early morning light, a combination of pink and gray, reflected off the deep blue water.

"Remember," she said, "I'll take the lead."

The man frowned, then shrugged. "Fine."

She checked the load on her Glock and tucked the weapon back in her jacket. Climbing out of the car, they made their way into the upscale building, took the elevator to the seventh floor and stepped out.

"Wait here," she whispered, and, hugging the left side of the corridor, crept toward the apartment. As she got close, she glanced up toward the ceiling, scanning for what she'd missed the last time, the special security camera Lendel had installed.

She didn't see it at first because of its tiny size, but then she spotted it, a small black dot where the wall met the ceiling.

Pulling out a compact can of spray paint, she reached up on her tip toes and sprayed the camera lens. Then she motioned for Turner to join her.

Taking out her lock-pick set, she fiddled with the apartment door lock. It clicked a moment later. Putting away the lock-pick, she pulled her Glock, turned the knob and stepped inside. She went into a crouch as Turner, drawing his own gun, followed her in and closed the door behind him.

The lavishly appointed living room was dim and quiet. In fact, there were no lights on anywhere in the place. All she heard was a slight hum coming from the kitchen, probably the refrigerator. As before, the air in the apartment smelled stale as if no one had been there for some time.

Rachel waited a moment to let her eyes adjust to the dim light.

Facing Turner, who was crouching next to her, she murmured, "Looks like no one's here, but I'll go check the other rooms to make sure. You stay here. I don't want to be caught by surprise again."

Turner glared, obviously not happy with taking orders from her.

Standing, Rachel slowly made her way forward, holding the gun in front of her. She searched the kitchen, dining room, bathroom, and lastly the large bedroom. The whole apartment was vacant. She noted that the bed cover was undisturbed, the corners neatly tucked in.

Flicking on a bedside lamp, she scanned the room and noticed the laptop computer in the adjacent office nook.

"All clear," she called out to Turner. "But there's a computer here in the bedroom. We need to check it out."

The other operative joined her in the bedroom and they walked over to the office nook.

After lifting the lid on the laptop, she turned on the machine. The screen came to life, displaying a small white box in the center of a solid blue background. She knew the computer could be a treasure trove of information, but they'd need a password to access it.

She tried several combinations, simple things like 'Lendel' and 'Arsi', spelled normally and backwards, without success.

"This is as far as I got last time," she said, "before I was interrupted."

"Let me try," Turner replied. Stepping forward, he input a series of letters and numbers into the white box with no success. But on his third attempt, the screen's color abruptly changed from blue to red.

Just then a phone rang in the room and both agents froze.

She spotted a landline phone on the bedside table, but it was quiet. She glanced around, trying to pinpoint the ring, which seemed to be coming from the bedroom closet.

Stepping over to the closet's open door, she looked inside. She had searched the space earlier, had found nothing suspicious, just clothing and shoes.

Then she spotted a gray backpack on the floor, tucked on one side of the closet. The ringing sound was coming from inside the backpack.

With a sinking feeling she instinctively knew what it was.

Suddenly everything happened in a flash.

From behind her she heard Turner shout, "Rachel! It's a bomb!", as he rushed toward her and shoved her out of the way.

Tumbling to the floor, she looked up as the man slammed the closet door shut. She heard an earsplitting roar, felt the concussion of the blast, and saw the door burst into shards of wood.

Turner's body flew backwards in the air, striking the opposite wall before collapsing to the floor.

She felt intense pain, then everything went black.

Chapter 28

Glacier County, Montana

"I saw the results of the test," the American said into the phone. "The Internet in Europe was down for hours. You did well, Ivan."

"Thank you," Ivan Petrov replied, his voice sounding slightly distorted from the scrambled call.

The American was sitting behind the mahogany desk in the den of his massive home. As he talked on the phone, he gazed out the glass wall at the nighttime scene. A full moon cast a bluish pall over the wooded foothills and the mountain range beyond.

It was a desolate scene, just the way he liked. Except for the occasional moving headlights of the Humvees patrolling the extensive property, there was no other sign of life.

He took in a deep gulp of the purified air and slowly breathed it out. "My faith in you has been restored, Ivan. After your many fuckups, it's reassuring to see you can still deliver."

"Yes, sir."

"Where are we on the U.S. side of the operation?"

"Good news on that front as well," Petrov eagerly said. "The final deals have been completed. We now control the necessary tech companies there."

A surge of excitement filled the American. "Excellent. You're to be commended."

"Thank you, sir."

"So – we can now proceed with the next phase of the operation?"

"That's correct, sir."

"Very good. Keep me informed as things proceed." The American turned off the call and replaced the receiver. He leaned back in the leather chair, his usually tortured thoughts for once quieted. *My plan is finally coming together*, he thought. A smile spread on his lips. *I should celebrate.*

He picked up the phone receiver once again and spoke briefly.

Then he reached into a desk drawer, removed the surgical mask that was there and slipped it on, covering his nose and mouth. He also took out a pair of sterilized rubber gloves and put them on. These were precautions he always took before meeting anyone, no matter who they were.

A minute later the door to the den opened and a middle-aged, bespectacled man wearing a white lab coat stepped in. He was carrying a thick manila folder.

"You wanted to see me, sir?" the man said as he approached the desk.

"Yes, Doctor. I want to spend time with Lorraine tonight," the American replied, referring to his wife. "But first I need to make sure she's clean." Although his wife had always been faithful to him, his paranoid nature clouded everything.

"Of course, sir."

"You tested her recently?"

"Yes. Today in fact."

"Any diseases or infections?"

The doctor shook his head forcefully. "Of course not," he said with a sigh. He was used to his boss's aversion to germs and his other abnormal proclivities. He was also extremely well paid for his services, and accepted the odd behavior as just another part of the job.

"Let me see the results."

The man reached in his folder, took out a sheet of paper and placed it on the desk.

The American picked it up, read it thoroughly, then slid the report back across the desk.

"Very good, Doctor. You may leave. Go find Lorraine and send her in to see me."

"Yes, sir."

As soon as the physician left the room, the American leaned back in the chair, his gaze on the vista outside. His thoughts turned to the pleasant aspect of the upcoming sex with his wife, a fairly rare event now that he had turned seventy. The woman was forty and beautiful and was always eager to please him. He had made her extremely wealthy.

The frequency of the sex had less to do with his age, and more to do with other factors. His business dealings always took priority. But a more crucial reason was his irrational fear that she would contaminate him. Even though he realized how ridiculous this thought was, it was something he could never quite shake.

As he waited for his wife to arrive, he didn't remove the surgical mask and gloves. He would keep them on during the whole time he spent with Lorraine. In fact, when he disrobed, he would put on a condom. After the sex, and after she had returned to her own bedroom, he would take a blistering hot shower to remove any potential germs.

Standing, he walked around his desk and went into the adjacent bedroom to wait.

Chapter 29

Langley, Virginia

"Looks like you're getting your wish after all," Alex Miller said, his voice stern.

"What do you mean?" Rachel West asked.

She had just come into her boss's nondescript office and sat down on one of the hard plastic chairs that fronted his worn metal desk.

The director drummed his fingers on the desk. "I just talked with our medical team. Matt Turner is going to be out of commission for some time."

"I'm sorry to hear that, Alex."

He arched a brow. "You sure about that?"

"Of course. I'm not a heartless bitch. Yeah, I'm glad he won't be working the case, but hell, Turner saved my life. If he hadn't pushed me out of the way, it'd be me who would have been badly hurt."

Miller shook a stern finger at her. "You're lucky to be alive – both of you. I'm glad I insisted Matt take the Kevlar with him on the trip."

She smiled. "Me too."

His expression softened a bit. "Okay. But, damn it, you've got to be more careful in the future, Rachel."

Continuing to smile, she gave a mock salute. "You got it, chief."

He grunted, but she could tell the man had calmed down.

"I have half a mind to assign another agent to work with you while Matt recovers," he said, still drumming his fingers on the desk.

Her heart sank when she heard this.

"However," Miller continued, "I don't have anybody nearly as good." He glared a moment longer, but she could tell the anger was for show. "Anyway, you'd probably get him killed."

She chuckled.

"Don't get too excited, Rachel. As soon as Matt's cleared by the doc, I'm putting him back on Prism."

"He wasn't that bad to work with."

"That's high praise coming from you."

She laughed again. "Yeah, I guess it is."

"I read the report you turned in this morning, Rachel. You thought the explosion at Lendel's apartment was a trap?"

"I'm sure of it. Lendel knew I'd be coming after him and set it up in advance."

Miller stopped drumming and leaned forward in the chair. "So. Where are we?"

"Every time I get close, this group figures out a way to shut me down." She paused a moment. "I think the Russian, whoever he is, is a key player. If I can find Lendel, I'll get him to talk."

"I agree. I'm working my sources, trying to find an electronic trail to both of these guys, but so far we've come up empty."

"Alex, I need to get back to Finland."

He held up a palm and shook his head. "Not so fast. You're not in any shape to do the lone wolf thing just yet. The doc filled me in your condition. Your injuries were significant, not to mention a slight concussion from the bomb blast. Take a few days, a week would be better. Rest up."

"No way!" she shot back, her expression grim.

He glared again, but this time she could tell he was serious. "It's not up for discussion."

Rachel studied her boss for a long moment. He was one of the best men she'd ever met, and she considered herself lucky to have him as a supervisor. But once he made up his mind, it was tough to get him to change it.

"Look, Alex ..."

"You can't always get your way," he said flatly.

Finally, she shrugged. "Okay, fine, I'll take some time off. But as soon as I'm ready, I'll be knocking on your door." She smiled. "And then I'm not taking no for an answer."

Miller smiled and after a moment, laughed. "Go on, get out of my office. I've got work to do."

She pointed a finger at him. "I got you to smile. Imagine that." Standing, she turned and left the office.

***

Rachel took a cab home from the Factory. She hadn't been back to her apartment since she'd flown in from Finland three days ago. She'd spent that time at work, recuperating at the in-house clinic, writing reports, being debriefed, and checking in on Matt Turner. The wounded man was comatose and couldn't communicate, but she had sat by his bedside, watching him sleep. She owed him big-time. Deep down she felt responsible for his condition – the bomb had been meant for her.

The cab reached her apartment building on the north side of Langley fifteen minutes later. She paid the fare, got her bag from the trunk, and went into the lobby of the fifteen story building. Taking the elevator to her floor, she walked down the hall to her place and let herself in.

The apartment smelled musty and after doing a security check of all the rooms, she opened the windows. It was noontime in July and the breeze that blew in was hot and humid. Nevertheless it smelled fresh. She'd put the air-conditioner on later.

The apartment was nothing fancy. Simple, modern furniture, a couple of throw rugs on the hardwood floors. Inexpensive prints hung on the walls. Rachel, never concerned about what others thought unless it was part of a job assignment, liked simple things – casual clothes and a relaxed living environment. She had no pets, or plants.

After unpacking her bags, she went into the bathroom and placed her Glock by the sink. She was still jumpy from the trip, and although she was home, she still felt the need to keep the weapon close by.

Stripping her clothes, she inspected her body in the mirror over the double sink. Gingerly, she ran her hands over the bruises and welts that covered parts of her torso, legs and arms. As she touched several badly bruised areas, she realized Miller had been right. *I do need some time off.*

Leaning forward, she looked carefully at her face. Luckily the black eye was gone, as were most of the cuts on her face.

Turning away from the mirror, she entered the shower and spent the next twenty minutes scrubbing herself clean.

Then, after placing the Glock on her bedside table, she lay down on the bed. She was asleep in minutes and slept for the next ten hours.

Chapter 30

Langley, Virginia

As she lay on the plush bed in her boyfriend's upscale apartment, Rachel West stared at the ceiling. The light in the room was dim and there was a lingering scent of wine and sex.

She closed her eyes a minute, remembering the last hour. As usual, their lovemaking had been great. Brad had been extra-gentle, making sure he didn't hurt the bruised areas of her body.

Rachel rolled on her side and watched the handsome, dark-haired man as he slept peacefully next to her. She reached out, lightly caressed his broad shoulder. It felt good to be back with him, if only for a few days.

His eyes blinked open and he sat up on the bed. "You okay, Rachel?"

"I'm fine."

Brad lay back down, turned to face her. "I was worried, earlier, that I might have hurt you."

She touched his face. "You're sweet."

His face clouded with concern. "What the hell happened on this last trip?"

"You know I can't talk about it."

"We've known each other two years – you can't keep shutting me out."

"It's my job, Brad. It's classified."

"Then quit your damn job. I hardly see you."

"We've had this conversation before."

"Damn right," he shot back, anger in his voice. "How long do you expect me to wait for you? I want us to be a normal couple – get married, have kids."

A feeling of sadness filled her. "We've had that conversation too. I told you I wasn't ready for that."

"Will you *ever* be ready?" he whispered.

"You know I love you."

"What does that mean, Rachel? Does it mean fucking a couple of times a month when you're in town? You're good in the sack, but I want more."

Her face flushed and she took a couple of deep breaths to control her anger. "You mean lot more to me than sex."

He lay flat on his back and stared up at the ceiling. "Maybe. But all I know is you're always traveling, always getting hurt on the job. And you never tell me what's going on in your life."

She placed a hand on his shoulder. "It's never been easy for me to share. You know that."

He faced her. "I know you had a tough childhood," he said. "And I've always tried to understand. But ... I want us to have a normal life. Is that too much to ask?"

"No, it isn't. It's just, the timing isn't right."

Brad's eyes were sad. "I think you should go home tonight."

"I'd really like to stay," she murmured.

"It's probably better if you go."

"You're sure?"

He nodded, his expression as dejected as she'd ever seen.

Her eyes brimmed with tears but she said nothing more. Rising from the bed, she dressed quickly and left the apartment.

***

Rachel had parked her Kawasaki 1000 cc motorcycle in the underground lot of the apartment building. She made her way to the bike, put on her helmet and turned on the machine. The powerful engine throbbed to life. Putting on the headlights, she navigated out of parking lot and up to street level. It was past nine in the evening and there was little traffic out.

She cruised aimlessly, reflecting on what Brad had said. *Could we ever be a normal couple?* she wondered. Part of her wanted that, wanted to settle down and live a regular life with the man she loved. *But can I give up my job?* She loved the adrenaline rush of being a field agent at the Agency. *Can I give that up?*

Rachel twisted the throttle and the motorcycle's engine roared, the sound drowning out her thoughts. The Kawasaki surged forward and when she merged onto the highway, she debated what to do next. She was too wired to go home and sleep, and her martial-arts dojo, the place she typically went to find solace, was already closed for the day.

Taking the off-ramp, she downshifted and headed to the 24-hour gym near her apartment. Parking the bike in front of the gym, she input her access code and entered.

There were only a few people at the place, regulars she recognized. Going to the locker room in the back, she changed into shorts and a loose T-shirt and donned boxing gloves. Then she spent the next two hours pounding the heavy punching bag. She ignored the soreness of her ribs, focused instead on delivering solid jabs, uppercuts, front-kicks, and side-kicks.

Drenched in sweat and exhausted, she showered, changed clothes, and left the gym, still agonizing over her troubled personal life.

Chapter 31

St. Petersburg, Russia

With his thoughts focused on his upcoming meeting, Ivan Petrov drove the Mercedes sedan along Nevsky Prospekt, the city's main boulevard.

Turning right, he went through the upscale commercial areas and then, after a few miles, into the gritty warehouse district. He located the shabby, two-story building minutes later and parked the sedan at the rear, well away from street traffic.

Climbing out, Petrov scanned the deserted alley and let himself into the warehouse. He used the building, one of several he owned in the area, when he wanted to meet in private with associates.

The elevator was broken so he took the stairs to the second floor. At the top of the landing, he glanced out the filthy window to the scene below, once again confirming there was no one around. The second floor was a large open space with a high ceiling, and was empty except for stacks of wooden pallets arrayed by the walls. The place reeked of machine oil. Faint daylight streamed in from narrow windows, the glass in most cracked or simply missing.

In one corner of the space was a partitioned area with a door. He headed in that direction, stepped inside the room and closed the door behind him.

Nicholas Yeltsin was already in the small, windowless room, waiting for him. Seeing Petrov, the other man beamed, approached, and the two shook hands. Yeltsin was a thin, balding man with a hooked nose. He wore a business suit and a tie. The man had worked for Petrov for many years.

"How was the flight from Stockholm, Nicholas?"

The man shrugged. "Same as always. Aeroflot never improves. But, what's the use in complaining?"

Petrov nodded in agreement. "You are right, my friend. Aeroflot will never change."

"On the phone you said you had something important for me?" Yeltsin asked.

"That I do. But first let me congratulate you on finalizing the tech company deals. You've been the perfect intermediary. We couldn't have done it without you. You did an excellent job, my friend."

"Good enough for a bonus, Ivan?"

Petrov returned the smile. "Absolutely. You've certainly earned it." Reaching into his jacket pocket, he removed a sound-suppressed Makarov PB. Aiming the pistol quickly, Petrov fired off three rounds.

Yeltsin, an incredulous look on his face, clutched his chest and crumpled to the grimy concrete floor.

Petrov bent over the fallen man and put a fourth bullet behind his ear.

Chapter 32

Glacier County, Montana

The American spent five minutes washing his hands with anti-bacterial soap, a ritual he followed religiously once an hour. Satisfied they were finally clean enough, the man dried his now red hands, left the bathroom and went into his underground study.

Known to his associates and even his wife as 'John Smith', the American had assumed this identity many years ago. Due to his ever-growing penchant for anonymity and secrecy, he had shed his previous identity once he made his wealth in the stock market. He had picked his new name because it was the most generic he could devise – 'John Smith' was the most common name in the United States. He preferred to be called 'sir', but everyone has to have a name, even someone as secretive as he was.

Sitting behind the large desk, he began to study the five computer monitors lined up in front of him. He was a highly unattractive man, some would say repulsive, bordering on deformed. His hands and head were excessively large for his torso, and his back was hunched. His brow was heavily pronounced, his eyes were small and too close together, and he had a weak chin. But he had so much money it didn't matter. Men and women alike, including his wife, overlooked his appearance, knowing he was willing to lavish them with more money and assets than they would ever need for several lifetimes.

His looks belied the great intelligence and business savvy he possessed. An intelligence that had served him well, and afforded him the secrecy and behind-the-scenes power he craved.

He continued studying the monitors in front of him, occasionally writing notes for himself, based on what he saw. Each computer monitor displayed a dizzying array of multi-color charts and graphs, depicting movement in the various stock exchanges around the world – the NYSE and NASDAQ from New York, the DAX in Germany, the JPX in Japan, and the SSE in China. Mounted on the wall of the underground study were ten flatscreen TV's, five across and two high. He glanced at them now.

Each TV screen was broadcasting a different news feed from across the globe – CNN, Fox News, Univision, Skynews, Telemundo, the BBC. All were muted for sound. Each feed showed a different scene. An oil refinery fire in Texas, a ten-car pile up on the Ventura Highway in Los Angeles, rioting in Greece, a famine in the Congo, a brewing war in the Middle East, a flood in Bangladesh. Everyday things that happened constantly, and affected billions of people around the world with a repetitive regularity. The names and places changed, but there was always a new problem and a new crisis.

A slow smile spread across John Smith's deformed face. What if you could shape these events, even for a short time? *That is true power*, he mused.

His smile grew into a dark, sardonic, almost maniacal grin. *Information is power! He who controls the Internet, controls the world.*

Chapter 33

Helsinki, Finland

Rachel West approached one of the available charter vessels at the dock area by Market Square. After negotiating a rate with the boat captain, she climbed into the powerboat and settled onto one of the seats at the stern.

It was a cool, windy day and as the boat sliced through the choppy bay, saltwater sprayed up, dampening Rachel. It was refreshing, a welcome change from the heat and humidity of Langley.

They headed south along the coast, toward the city of Turku, and then east to the island of Ekenas, which was located a few miles offshore. If Miller's information was correct, Arsi Lendel's family had a home on the island. Since Lendel had blown up his own apartment in Helsinki, she figured the man might be there. With no other leads, it was as good a place as any to start her search.

Thirty minutes later they were there and the boat pulled into a slip at Ekenas's waterfront marina. Paying the fare, she climbed off and strode into the picturesque village. Restaurants and quaint shops clustered close together around a town square. Stopping at a cafe, she got directions to Lendel's home, which was only two miles from the town. She had studied a map of the island the day before and had learned that there was only one paved road, a two-lane street that circled the place.

Wanting to scout the area anonymously, she decided to skip a taxi and began walking along the main road. The island was sparsely populated, and after passing several neighborhoods, the countryside turned rural, with only a few homes, all spaced far apart from each other.

Soon after she spotted Lendel's place in the distance – a white, two-story, wood and stone house. It was set well back from the road and protected by a high stone wall.

Getting off the road, she trudged through a wooded thicket and climbed up a hillside. Taking out a small pair of binoculars, she scanned the scene below. The property consisted of the main house and a smaller structure, probably a garage. She guessed the wall that surrounded the place to be about seven feet high with spikes along the top. All was quiet. No one was about, nor did she see any dogs. The only car she spotted was a Volvo sedan in the driveway.

Should I wait for nightfall to make my move? she wondered. She was itchy to find Lendel and exact revenge. *The hell with it, I'm going now.*

Putting away the binos in her jacket, she made her way slowly through the vegetation, being as quiet as possible. When she reached the wall she crouched by the base and looked up. The spikes on the top ledge were made of cut metal, their sharp edges glinting in the sunlight. The wall was about seven feet high. She knew she'd have to get a running start, jump, and grab the top ledge, being careful to avoid the spikes.

After tying her long hair into a ponytail, she strode away from the wall and eventually turned back. Then she sprinted full force, and when she reached it, leapt up, her arms outstretched. She was able to get a handhold on the top edge, but struck the wall with her still-sore ribs, making her wince from the pain.

After waiting a moment to catch her breath, she carefully spaced her hands further apart and began to pull herself up to the top. When she was high enough, she thrust one of her legs up, so that her shoe caught the edge.

Knowing she couldn't stay there any longer without attracting attention, she hauled herself all the way to the top, but not before feeling one of the spikes cut into her leg. Ignoring the trickle of blood, she dropped to other side of the wall, crashing down on a flower garden.

Then she heard it and froze. The growling of what was probably a very large dog.

Glancing up, she spotted it immediately – a Doberman, its snarling jaws open. The animal, which was only a short distance away, began barking, its muscles tense and ready to pounce.

Quickly pulling the Glock from her jacket, she fired, but the dog was already in a gallop and the shots missed.

The Doberman launched into the air and she fired again, and this time the rounds hit the mark. Just as the dog's huge, gaping jaws were about to reach her, the animal staggered and plunged into the bed of flowers.

"Drop the gun!" she heard someone shout in Finnish.

She turned and saw him ten feet away – a big, rugged man in his twenties, aiming a Sig Sauer automatic with both hands. Even if she got off a shot, he wouldn't miss at this distance.

"Don't shoot," she replied in English.

"I said drop it!" he said in the same language.

"Okay, okay." Rachel let the Glock fall into the garden, then slowly raised her hands.

"Come out of there," he ordered, "and no sudden moves."

She flashed a wide smile. "This is all a big misunderstanding. I'm a tourist, and my car broke down."

He shook his head. "You look a lot like West, the CIA agent Arsi told me about. He said you were dead, that you had been blown up in the explosion."

Rachel smiled again and stepped out of the garden. She was only seven feet from him now. "Do I look dead to you? Like I said, this is a misunderstanding. My name is Susan Richards. I'm a Canadian tourist – my car broke down back there, and I was trying to find help. I'm sorry about your dog – it attacked me and I had to defend myself."

"Let me see your ID."

"Sure, no problem," she replied, moving a few feet closer. "It's right in my pocket."

"Take it out slowly. And remember, no sudden moves or I shoot."

She carefully removed the ID and handed it to him.

In that split-second when he took it, she whirled around in a martial-arts spin kick, her foot striking the pistol. As the gun flew off, she kicked him again, this time with a powerful front kick to his groin.

The man howled in pain and buckled to his knees. With the heel of her hand she struck him hard on the chin, snapping his head back. He toppled over, groaning and clutching his crotch.

Rachel was exhausted, her ribs were sore, and she had a cut on her leg. But she was also exhilarated, the adrenaline rush blocking out the pain. It felt good to put the big man down. Really good.

Then she felt a blinding pain on the back of her head, and everything went black.

***

Rachel came to sometime later, the pain in the back of her head a dull throb.

She was tied to a chair, the rope bindings tight around her chest, arms and legs. In front of her stood Arsi Lendel, his arms crossed, a wicked smile on his lips.

"We meet again," Lendel spat out. "And this time there is no escape, West. You outmaneuvered Pirjo. Luckily I was around. But as you can see, you're going nowhere except to an early grave."

She quickly scanned the room and guessed it was the large garage she'd spotted from the hillside. In one corner was a black BMW sedan – probably the car that had rammed her off the road a couple of weeks back. Leaning against the sedan was the large Finnish man she'd kicked in the groin. He was holding an MP-5K sub-machinegun and his eyes were a blaze of hate.

Her situation was grim, she knew. She'd have to come up with something, and fast.

Making a split decision, Rachel turned back to Lendel. "Thank you, Arsi."

His brows arched. "Thank you for what?"

She smiled. "For falling into my trap."

A perplexed look crossed Lendel's face. "What are you talking about, West?"

"Do you think I'd come here, with no backup?"

Lendel's frown deepened. He turned to the other man. "Go outside, Pirjo. Check the grounds. See if anyone else is around."

Pirjo nodded, and with the MP-5K at the ready, left the garage.

Lendel pulled out a revolver and held it at his side. "I'm sure you're lying, West. You're a fucking *nartuu*, a crazy American bitch, and now you're going to die." He raised the pistol and aimed it at her face.

Her heart skipped a beat as she stared down the muzzle of the gun. There was no back up coming, and it was obvious her lie hadn't worked.

Her adrenaline pumping, she forced herself to stay calm. Shrugging, she said, "Go ahead, kill me. I don't give a shit. Once my backup CIA team gets here, you'll be dead too." She shrugged again. "Go ahead. Pull the trigger. But if I were you, I'd keep me alive. A live hostage is worth a lot more than a corpse. Without me to bargain with, you're a dead man."

Lendel hesitated a moment, then took a step back from her and lowered the gun. He glanced at his watch, as if deciding what to do.

Pirjo came back into the garage, his face flushed. "Nothing out there, boss," he said, panting.

"We'll load her in the car," Lendel said, "and take her to the boat. It may not be safe here anymore." He turned back to Rachel. "I'm not taking any chances with this *nartuu*."

Then he moved closer to her and, after raising the revolver above her head, swung down hard, striking the back of her neck.

She saw a bright flash of stars and lost consciousness.

***

When she awoke sometime later, she realized she had been jammed into a small, cramped space. It was pitch black, and stuffy, and from the jostling, she guessed she was in the trunk of the BMW, traveling at high speed. No doubt Lendel and his goon were taking her to their boat. After that, she figured they'd kill her and dump her body in the Baltic Sea.

Her hands and feet were still bound, and now a piece of duct tape covered her mouth. She struggled against the rope bindings, but it was no use.

Rachel's head was throbbing, the massive headache a result of the multiple blows she'd received. But she knew she was lucky to be alive. She also realized her predicament was, to some degree, her own fault. She should never have rushed into the situation so quickly. It was a character flaw that had gotten her into trouble before. Her boss, Alex Miller, was always telling her that. And although she would never admit it to him, he was right.

Pushing those thoughts aside, she focused on now. *How in hell am I going to get out of this?* she wondered. It was a small island, and the car would reach their destination at any moment. She needed to come up with a plan.

But before she could come up with something, she felt the car slow down.

Chapter 34

Glacier County, Montana

The American was standing in front of the bathroom sink, and as he put on his latex gloves, he studied his appearance in the mirror. No doubt the woman he was about to meet for the first time would find his behavior odd. And she would find his looks strange, even repulsive.

From his own perspective, meeting someone outside his close circle of associates was something he avoided. But it could not be helped. A decision of this magnitude required a one-on-one meeting. Too much of his own money was at stake.

After one last look at the three-piece suit he was wearing, he adjusted his tie. Lastly, he slipped on his white surgical mask, covering his mouth and nose. Turning away from the mirror, he left the bathroom and went into his massive study.

The woman was already there, sitting in front of his large, mahogany desk. Seeing him, she stood, and as he approached, her eyes grew wide. She stepped back a moment, a look of disgust crossing her face. It was a reaction he received often and he was used to it.

She recovered quickly, the repulsed look replaced by a charming smile. The woman was wily, he realized, no doubt the reason she was such a good politician.

"Mr. Smith," she said, "thank you for taking time out of your busy schedule to meet me."

He didn't offer to shake hands. "On the contrary, Governor Blakely. It's I who is honored to make your acquaintance. Please have a seat."

The American sat behind his desk and she took a seat in one of the visitors' chairs. He had seen many photos of her in newspapers, and seen her on TV news, and in real life she looked no different: a middle-aged woman with short, curly black hair; a stocky, some might say pudgy, figure; and plain facial features – a pug nose and thin lips. But it had never been her looks that had gotten her to a position of power, he knew – it was her high intelligence and cunning political skill. The rumor was that she had never married because she had never met a man who could match her intellect.

"As we're both busy people," he said, "I'd like to get down to business, if that's okay with you."

Blakely flashed the charming smile again. "Of course."

"I've followed your career for many years, Governor. I've seen your influence grow, first as a congresswoman, then a senator, and now as a governor of Massachusetts. You've accomplished many things."

"Thank you, Mr. Smith."

"But it's your political leanings that have always fascinated me, Governor Blakely. I've studied your background in detail. I've watched hours and hours of your TV news interviews, and read transcripts of your speeches. Although you've always campaigned as a moderate, I've suspected that, deep down, you were a socialist. It's something I picked up from off-hand comments you've made, and when you've spoken to smaller, more liberal groups."

She cocked her head. "That's very perceptive, Mr. Smith. From your tone I take it you share these beliefs?"

"I do. Very much so. Although I've spent my whole professional career as a capitalist, making obscene amounts of money, deep down I always believed socialism was the answer. In fact, I would go further than that, and classify myself a communist. You could say it was something I was born into."

Blakely nodded. "I see. In that case, I'll lay my cards on the table. It's true, I am a socialist. I've had to disguise my real beliefs in order to get elected. It's not something I'm especially proud of, but as a politician ... well, I think you know how it works."

"Perfectly understandable, Governor. I *do* know how politics works. The most important thing is to get elected. And once you have the power, you can make a difference."

She smiled that disarming smile again and he realized the woman was a master of manipulation.

"But the country has changed," he continued. "Years ago the U.S. was more conservative, but now America is changing and becoming a more liberal place. You see it everyday with the growth of the welfare state. Many people want handouts. Less people want to work – they're relying more and more on government assistance programs. Slowly, but surely, the U.S. is moving toward a socialist state."

"That's true, Mr. Smith."

"Yes," he said, "we've come a long way." He paused, leaned forward in his seat. "But we still have a long way to go. Unfortunately, for many Americans, capitalism is still considered the norm, but as we both know, that's a bankrupt system." He lowered his voice for emphasis. "True socialism is the answer. The only answer. Redistribution of wealth shouldn't be the exception – it should be the norm in our country. But to make that happen, we have to make some changes, some serious changes. Even if it means eliminating the Constitution. That old, tired piece of paper is holding us back."

Blakely nodded her head. "I agree. I totally agree. Of course, there are still plenty of Americans that don't share our socialist philosophy."

He shrugged. "They'll always be those that cling to their guns and religion. But, with a new administration, with new thinking, we can squash those that resist the new way." He chuckled. "Even if we have to do it by force. Would you agree?"

"Of course – but it's not something I can talk about before the election."

"That's true, Ms Blakely. First you have to get elected. And that's where I can help. I have extensive financial resources and I'm willing to spend that capital to back the right candidate. But before I commit to that, I have to make sure my thinking and that of the candidate align. You think our views are compatible?"

She nodded and smiled that charming smile again. "From what I'm hearing, our views align perfectly. One of the people I admire most is Karl Marx. He said it best when he declared in 1845 that, *'Communism for us is an ideal to which reality will have to adjust itself. We call communism the real movement which abolishes the present state of things.'*"

"Marx is one of my favorites also, Governor. So, you're in agreement that to accomplish our goals, we may, and probably will, have to suspend the Constitution? And as part of the process, we'll confiscate all the guns in the country, except for law enforcement. Once we do that, no one can stop us from implementing our socialist agenda."

"Yes, those are the necessary steps," the woman replied.

He leaned back in the chair and studied her closely. Although he had just met her, he liked her. Liked her very much. *I can work with her. No doubt about it.*

"Well," he said, "in that case, my decision is made. You are the right candidate."

She beamed. "Thank you, Mr. Smith."

"How soon before you begin the campaign?"

"Actually, I've already started preparing for it. Although I'm still governor and I have those duties to attend to, I've hired consultants for the campaign."

"Excellent," he said. "The sooner we get started the better. I assume you'd welcome an initial donation to your campaign? I'd like to be one of the first."

"That would be lovely, Mr. Smith. How much would you like to contribute?"

He mentioned a very large sum, and her jaw dropped. She recovered quickly, and flashed that smile again. "That's very generous of you."

"That's just for starters. As we get closer to the election, I'll be contributing more. Much more."

He stood to signal the meeting was over. "My assistant will make out the check for you, Governor Blakely. By the way, I think your new title, after you're elected, has a nice ring to it. Don't you think, Madame President?"

Chapter 35

Ekenas Island, Finland

Rachel West felt the car slow down and come to a stop. She was still in the dark, cramped trunk of the BMW, her hands and feet bound, duct tape covering her mouth.

She figured they had reached the island's marina. It was probably the best opportunity for her to escape from Lendel and his goon. If she could get someone's attention, hopefully they'd call the cops.

The car's doors creaked open, then slammed shut, and a moment later the lid to the trunk opened. The two men peered down at her, grabbed her roughly by the legs and shoulders, and jerked her out. Then they began to carry her down a wooden dock. As she glanced around the nighttime scene, her heart sank. They weren't at the busy marina, but rather at a remote part of the island. Lendel probably anchored his vessel away from the town in order to insure privacy for his criminal activities.

Now what? she thought. She struggled against the rope bindings, but they were secure.

They reached a large powerboat a moment later, and as they came alongside the boat, the men swung her aboard like a sack of potatoes. She landed on the wooden deck with a *thud* and she groaned from the sharp pain in her ribs.

Silently, the two men untied the mooring lines, and within minutes the boat engine came to life. As she stared up at the nighttime stars, she felt the boat move away from the dock. She took in a deep breath, smelling the salt water and the smoke of the diesel engine.

Lendel must have gunned the motor because the powerful engine howled, the boat went up on plane, and she felt the large vessel cut through the choppy waters of the Baltic.

After that they left her alone for a long time. Lying there, she tried to figure out their position. The boat was moving away from land, and by her estimate, they were many miles out. She had yet to see or hear any other boats. In fact, all she heard was the sound of waves slapping the sides of the boat.

Eventually the engine powered down and the boat slowed to a crawl and began to drift. She heard the cranking of the anchor as it was lowered. A moment later, Pirjo, towering over her, grabbed her by the shoulders and slammed her into a sitting position against the bulkhead.

Pirjo moved off to one side and Lendel appeared in her line of vision, a smirk on his face.

"So, West," Lendel said, "how does it feel to be utterly helpless?" He crouched in front of her and, with a quick motion, tore the tape off her mouth.

She winced, and took in a few deep breaths.

Lendel waved a hand in the air. "Look around, West. We're ten miles from shore. Far away from your CIA backup team." He smiled. "If there ever was one. But no matter; it's only you, me, Pirjo, and ...." He jerked a thumb, pointing out to the dark blue, foreboding water. "And lots, and lots of sharks. You probably don't know this, but there are over 30 species of sharks in Nordic seas."

She glanced out at the Baltic, realizing he was right – it was a well-known fact that the seas around Finland were shark infested. A shiver of fear ran down her spine – she'd always had a fear of drowning at sea, and worse yet, of being eaten by sharks. No doubt from watching too many Hollywood movies.

"I called my boss," the man continued, "before we left the house. He was thrilled I had captured you. He told me to kill you, as you would expect, but he told me to find out all you know first. So, here's the deal, you bitch. You tell me everything, and I mean *everything* you know about us, and I'll go easy on you."

With a glint in his eyes, he added, "Talk, and I'll simply put a bullet in the back of your head. It'll be quick and almost painless. But say nothing, and I'll start by cutting off your fingers and tossing them in the water, one by one, to chum for sharks." He laughed, a dark menacing laugh. "Then I'll start on your toes. How does that sound, *nartuu*?"

She stared at him, her eyes burning with hate. "I knew you were just a middleman, Lendel. Who's your boss, the mystery Russian?"

He laughed again, but there was no humor in it. "You are persistent, I'll grant you that." He turned to Pirjo, who was standing a few feet away. "Can you believe this bitch?"

Lendel faced her again, and with a grin, took out a large switchblade from his pocket. He flicked it open, the long blade gleaming in the moonlight. "Okay, West, what's it going to be?"

What the hell do I do now? she thought, her mind racing, trying to come up with a way, any way, out of this mess.

"What do you want to know?" she said, stalling for time.

"Everything. Who do you work for?"

"Central Intelligence, but you already know that, Lendel."

"At least you're not lying. Good girl." He closed the switchblade and placed it next to him on the deck of the boat. "How did you find out about Prism?"

She moved her bound feet slightly, and as she continued talking, began tucking them underneath her. "From Zhao Deng, the Chinese businessman."

He nodded, obviously satisfied with her answer. "How did you find out about me?"

"From the concierge at the hotel in Helsinki."

"Okay, that makes sense. What else do you know about Prism?"

"I know you're part of it, and that you work for a Russian."

Lendel nodded again. "What else?"

She tucked her legs a bit more. "I know you're an asshole, Lendel."

A startled look crossed his face and in that split-second, she kicked out with her bound legs, knocking him backwards. The man hit the railing of the boat, and as he fumbled to get his balance, she struck again, kicking him a second time, and this time his body went over the railing. She heard a loud splash.

Still sitting on the deck by the railing, she whirled around, only to see Pirjo running towards her, aiming the MP-5K sub-machinegun her way.

"You better get your boss out of the water," she said, "before the sharks get to him."

The man halted, clearly unsure what to do next.

Since her feet and hands were still bound, Pirjo probably figured she couldn't escape. Lendel was thrashing around in the heavy seas, screaming for help.

Slinging the sub-machinegun over his shoulder, he ran toward one of the life vests clipped to the bulkhead. Grabbing it, he ran back to the railing and flung it overboard.

Scooting toward Pirjo on her backside, she came up behind him, lifted her legs and kicked out. She struck him in the ass, and she kicked him again, this time harder, and he tumbled into the dark seas.

Wasting no time, she slid over to where the switchblade lay on the deck. Her hands were still bound behind her back, so she fumbled awkwardly until she felt the knife beneath her. Flicking the blade open with her fingers, she grabbed the handle as best she could and began cutting the rope. A moment later her hands were free and she quickly cut the binding on her legs.

Springing to her feet, she rushed to the entryway of the cabin below deck and sprinted down the stairs. Frantically searching cabinets and closets for several minutes, she finally found what she was looking for – a weapon. After checking the load on the semi-automatic pistol, she took off the safety and ran back up the stairs.

Reaching the deck, she heard screaming and thrashing coming from the side of the boat. Crouching behind the railing, she peered toward the water, aiming the weapon with both hands.

The bright moonlight illuminated the seas clearly, and what she saw turned her stomach. Not more that ten feet from the boat were dozens of shark fins moving fast on the now crimson water, churning up the waves. She saw a human arm shoot up out of the sea for one second, heard a strangled scream, then the arm was gone. All that remained of the two men was their blood, mixing with the dark blue sea.

Chapter 36

St. Petersburg, Russia

Ivan Illych Petrov parked his Mercedes by the side of the Church of the Spilled Blood and climbed out of the sedan. The historic church, built in 1883 and one of the city's landmarks, was closed to tourists today and Petrov knew the place would be quiet. The church was his favorite spot when he needed time to be alone and think.

Before going inside, he glanced up at the beautiful onion dome spires, its multi-color mosaic tile work and gold leaf design reflecting the day's sunlight. The sunshine was a rare sight in Russia, he knew. He welcomed the change from the usual gray dreariness.

Going in, he stepped past the vestibule and walked into the cavernous, almost vacant church. Kneeling at the third row of pews, he observed as an altar boy extinguished the candles that lit up the ornate altar. A mass must have just concluded, he realized. All the better, since he disliked the religious pageantry, preferring the simple, quiet time with the Lord.

Kneeling in the hushed silence, he inhaled the aromatic scent of candle wax and incense. The altar boy, finished with his duties, genuflected in front of the gold-plated and bejeweled crucifix above the altar. Then he exited, leaving Petrov alone in the church.

The vaulted ceiling of the church depicted various scenes of Christ and the saints, as did the massive stained-glass windows, which admitted the room's only light, now that the overhead lights had been turned off. As he stared at the crucifix, he prayed silently. Prayed for forgiveness for his many sins, but more urgently, prayed for the success of his current project.

During his service as a high-ranking military officer, he could never practice his religion openly, especially during the Soviet years. Later, after *perestroika*, when the country once again became Russia, Catholicism and the other faiths were tolerated, though not totally accepted. The country was still ruled by the Communist Party after all.

Finishing his prayers, the man crossed himself, got off his knees and sat on the hard wooden bench. His thoughts turned dark, as he mulled Prism's operation. He'd suffered a blow with the loss of a key player, Arsi Lendel. Lendel had been one of his main go-to-guys. Now that he was dead, the colonel no longer had an intermediary – he'd have to get more personally involved in the execution phases of the plan. That was unavoidable now.

And another thing bothered him – it appeared Lendel had been killed by the American agent, West. Once again the elusive woman had survived.

His anger boiled at the thought, causing his blood pressure to spike. Gulping in a lungful of the aromatic air, he forced himself to stay calm. Whatever he did, he knew it was imperative his American partner not learn of West's escape. Petrov realized he was already on a short leash with John Smith – one more fuck up and he would be cut out of the financial bonanza the operation would bring.

And they were close now. Very close to success. A few more tests and Prism would be ready. He could almost taste it. The colonel wouldn't just be affluent, but set for life, with riches far beyond his dreams. He'd be able to retire to someplace warm, ditch his homely *babushka* wife, and live openly with Nikita. As he thought about his mistress, a smile crossed his lips. The woman was a joy, a blessing really. His smile widened as he comprehended the irony of it – he was in the Church of the Spilled Blood, one of Russia's holiest sites, and he was thinking about sex with his mistress. *Life is like that. Full of irony.*

Feeling a pang of guilt at his impure thoughts, he vowed then and there that if Prism was successful, he would donate ten per cent of his new wealth to the church. And maybe, just maybe, after his death God would overlook his many sins and grant him a spot in heaven.

Silently saying another prayer, he crossed himself, stood, and left the church.

The fleeting sunlight outside had already evaporated, replaced by a gray, overcast sky.

As soon as he got in the Mercedes, he pulled out his cell phone and punched in his home number. His wife picked up and he informed her he would not be home for dinner. She was used to his absences and the reason for them, and after uttering a few choice profanities, she hung up.

Then he made a second call, this one to Nikita, telling her he'd be over soon. His mood lifted at the prospect of seeing her again.

Starting up the car, he headed east on Nevskiy Prospekt avenue and soon after reached her upscale condo building. Parking the car, he made his way to her apartment, which overlooked the Fontanka River. He'd bought her the place a year ago, something he'd never regretted.

Nikita met him at the door, carrying a tumbler of vodka which she handed him. He was delighted to see what she was wearing – a see-through negligee, high heels, a wide smile, and nothing else. She gave off a heavy, musk-like scent from the expensive perfume that he'd also purchased for her. Even though they'd made love countless times, seeing her aroused him every time they met.

"Ivan Illych," she said, going up on her tiptoes and giving him a quick kiss on the lips, "I wasn't sure you'd be over tonight. I thought the old hag wouldn't let you out of the house."

Petrov chuckled. "Nothing could keep me from seeing you."

He reached out to hug her, but she slipped away with a sly grin.

"Not yet, Ivan, you know how I like to play this game."

"But Nikita, all I've thought about today is you."

She gave him a phony pout. "All you think about is work."

"That's not true," he protested weakly, knowing she was mostly right. Taking a sip of the vodka, he relished the strong, refreshing taste. Over the rim of the glass he studied the beautiful woman as she sat leisurely on the sofa in the living room. She leaned back, giving him a clear view of her full, curvaceous figure. Nikita was twenty-five, with short, straight black hair parted in the middle. She had luminous green eyes – beautiful to him, although his friends said her eyes were cold, almost cruel. But he just laughed at his friends. Nikita had full, red lips and a small scar on her cheek, the result of a childhood cut that hadn't healed properly. But that was the only imperfection on her soft, alabaster skin, and now he never even noticed it. He had fallen for her instantly.

Petrov approached the sofa and was going to sit next to her, but she pointed to the armchair across from her.

With a sigh, he sat in the armchair and took another sip of his drink. He was used to her games, had accepted them long ago. In the end, she was always worth the wait.

"So, my dear Ivan Illych, how was work today?"

He shrugged. "It was work."

"Are you ever going to tell me about that secret project of yours?"

"You know I can't do that, Nikita."

Her eyes narrowed. "Did you earn lots of roubles today?"

"Of course. I make money every day. I even made a deposit to the trust fund I've set up for you."

She smiled. "That's what I like to hear." She shifted her legs, uncrossing them briefly, giving him a clear view of her inner beauty. She re-crossed them quickly.

His adrenaline kicked in. "You're killing me, Nikita." He took a long pull of the vodka.

"Soon, Ivan Illych. You'll be rewarded very soon. But you have to be patient. You know that."

He leaned back in the chair and drained his drink.

Seeing this, she got off the sofa, took his glass and going to a sideboard, refilled it. Handing it back to him, she went back to the couch.

Nikita absent-mindedly rubbed the scar on her cheek. "How soon before the project is finished?"

He took a large swallow. "We're almost there."

"Good." Her green eyes flashed with intensity. "Then you'll dump the old hag?"

"Yes. I told you I would."

"I'm not getting any younger, Ivan."

"You're hardly old."

She sneered. "Women age much faster than men."

"You'll always be beautiful to me."

"Don't placate me, Ivan. I don't want to be a Russian whore my whole life. I want to get married. *And soon.*"

"You'll get your wish. You know it's not easy to get rid of my wife. Her father has connections with the *gruppenova*," he said, referring to the Russian mob. "I have to pay her off – a lot. As soon as my operation is complete, I'll have plenty of money."

Her green eyes stayed cold another moment, but eventually a sly grin spread across her face. She patted the sofa cushion next to her. "Why don't you come here."

Setting his drink down, he crossed over and, inhaling her strong musk scent, sat next to her on the sofa.

Nikita loosened his tie and unbuttoned the top buttons of his shirt. After nibbling his earlobe, she kissed his neck while rubbing his bare chest with her hand.

Not able to contain his excitement, he pinned her against the sofa, kissed her on the lips forcefully and thrust his tongue down her throat.

She pushed him away and once he was off her, she slapped him hard across the face.

Rubbing the sting on his cheek, he stared at her.

"You're rushing it, Ivan. You know I like to be in control."

"I couldn't help myself."

Her eyes shone with intensity. "Are you going to behave?"

Physically he was much bigger and stronger, but he'd learned a while back that she had a strange, almost hypnotic power over him. Petrov had many mistresses in his lifetime, but only Nikita had this effect on him. He sighed and said, "Yes."

"Good," she replied sweetly. "Now sit back on the sofa and relax. Would you like another drink, my Ivan Illych?"

The two vodkas had already made him lightheaded. "No. You know what I want."

"In that case, let's get started." Nikita stood up and faced him. Slowly, she pulled down the shoulder straps of her negligee and let it fall to the floor.

His eyes narrowed as he watched her, the anticipation building. She took off her heels and walked forward so that she stood over him. He was breathing heavy and he reached out and caressed one of her luscious breasts. Her soft, white skin felt wonderful.

She gave him a stern look. "You said you were going to behave."

Petrov stopped what he was doing. "I'm sorry, Nikita ... it's just ...."

"I said lean back on the sofa. Or you go home now."

Leaning back, he watched as she finished unbuttoning his shirt and began rubbing his bare chest.

Noticing the bulge in his pants, she caressed it lightly and he gasped as he almost released.

Pulling her hand quickly away, she gave him a self-satisfied smile. "It appears you're ready."

As he sat there, panting, and looking up at the beautiful woman, he fought the urge to grab her, throw her on the floor and fuck her brains out. He'd done that on previous occasions and her response was always the same – she would lay there, limp as a dishrag, unmoving, mute, her eyes burning with hate.

So he sat there quietly, waiting for Nikita to make the next move.

Leaning over, she kissed him on the lips. It was along, passionate kiss, and when she pulled back eventually, she said, "See what happens when you behave?"

He nodded, once again breathing in her sensual scent.

Nikita knelt in front of him. With a sly smile, she reached over and unbuckled his belt. Then she undid his pants and reaching in with both hands, began to stroke him. He was on fire, ready to explode at any moment.

As she increased her tempo, he groaned with pleasure. He grit his teeth to prolong the moment and stave off the inevitable.

He watched in horror a minute later as she pulled her hands away and sat back on her haunches. His heart sank, knowing the woman was playing another one of her games.

"Please Nikita," he said with a grunt, "you can't stop now!"

She crossed her arms in front of her, a stern look on her face. "Do you love me, Ivan?"

"Of course I do!"

"You're going to marry me?"

"Yes! I said I would."

"Prove you love me."

"How?"

"I want a new car."

"I gave you one last year."

"A piece-of-shit Russian Lada. I want a Jag, or a BMW."

He didn't hesitate in answering. "Yes, whatever you want."

Her eyes lit up. "Really?"

"Yes! Now *please* finish this!"

"Of course, my dear Ivan."

"And no more games!"

She smiled sweetly. "No more games, I promise."

Kneeling in front of him once again, she used both hands to stroke his cock and fondle his balls. His heart pounded from the excitement.

Still caressing him with her hands, she parted her lips and leaned in. She began licking the tip of his cock with her skillful tongue. He groaned from the pleasure.

She kept at it, gradually increasing her tempo, her hands and tongue moving faster and faster until he was ready to burst. Knowing he wouldn't be able to hold off much longer, he whispered, "*Please* Nikita, do it now ..."

Nikita complied, opening her mouth wider, and began taking him in. An expert in giving pleasure, she did this slowly, taking him in a bit at a time, until eventually his whole cock was fully in her mouth.

He exploded in one long, delicious rush.

When she pulled away moments later, she got to her feet.

"See how better it is when you behave, Ivan Illych?" she said, grinning. "All you have to do is let me be in control – then you get everything you want. Now, let's go to the bedroom. I'm not done with you yet. Our fun is just beginning."

Petrov knew he had a long, satisfying night ahead of him.

***

As Petrov fought the heavy traffic during the city's morning rush hour, he reminisced about the previous incredible evening. Nikita had kept him up all night, giving him one satisfying sexual jolt after another. Totally satiated and exhausted by six a.m., he'd finally told her he'd had enough. He'd be sore for a week, but it was worth it. The woman was that good in bed.

Pushing aside the pleasant thoughts, he focused on the heavy St. Petersburg traffic.

Seeing a break ahead, he changed lanes, sped up the Mercedes, and soon he was in the city's upscale shopping areas. Going past those, he eventually arrived at the gritty warehouse district. Here the vehicles were trucks, delivery vans, and semis. Their diesel engines coughed a bluish smoke that tinged the air with an acrid smell, penetrating the air-conditioned interior of the sedan.

Locating the right warehouse minutes later, he parked the car at the rear of the building and climbed out. Unlike the other warehouses he owned in the area, this one was not run down. He'd outfitted the two-story structure with the latest technology and security.

After scanning an ID card and inputting a code on a wall-mounted device by the rear entrance, he stepped into the building. Walking down a corridor, he stopped at an unmarked, closed metal door, which was flanked by a barrel-chested man carrying an assault rifle. Nodding to the man, Petrov once again scanned his card and went inside, closing the door behind him.

Petrov saw his associate right away, hunched at a computer console, furiously tapping away on the keyboard. Arrayed along one wall of the windowless room was a long row of bulky computer hard drives, emitting a muted hum.

His associate, Andrei Lechenko, was a typical cyber geek. Lechenko wore black frame glasses with extra thick lenses that gave his eyes an owlish appearance. His black hair was greasy and unkempt. The man was tall and lanky, almost emaciated, because he often forgot to eat. He lived and breathed for his computer work and thought of little else.

Lechenko was wearing what Petrov remembered seeing him in a week earlier – a wrinkled, plaid flannel shirt and baggy, stained khakis. And from the long stubble on his face, it appeared he hadn't shaved in days.

"Andrei," Petrov said, approaching the man. "How is it going?"

Lechenko abruptly stopped working and glanced up from his keyboard. By his startled look it was clear he hadn't realized Petrov had come into the room.

"Mr. Petrov. Everything is almost ready. Just a few more minutes and I'm done."

"That's what I wanted to hear." Petrov pulled up a chair and sat with good view of Lechenko's computer screen.

"You were able to break through the firewalls, Andrei?"

The computer geek pushed his glasses up the bridge of his nose. "Now that we have access to the tech companies' router technology, it's a breeze."

"Excellent. What's next?"

"I've been testing my programs for the last two days. They all worked perfectly. I'm just waiting for one last sequence to kick in."

"My American partner will be very pleased," Petrov said, leaning back in the chair and letting out a long breath.

Lechenko smiled. "When this is over, I want to visit the U.S. I've never been there and I'm dying to see Silicon Valley." He gestured toward his computer and the hard drives by the wall. "I want to see the places where all this technology originated."

"Maybe, Andrei, you'll get your chance. You'll certainly have enough money to afford it."

Lechenko nodded. "I've been practicing my English. It's very good now."

Petrov smiled. "I'm sure it is, my friend."

The computer on the desk emitted a long beep and Lechenko glanced at the screen. "It's ready." He tapped on the keyboard again and a new image appeared, this one displaying an official looking logo. Below the symbol was a paragraph of warnings. Below that were three blank boxes for a username and two separate passwords. The writing on the screen was all in English. Petrov, from his long association with his American partner, had no trouble reading it.

"All I have to do now," Lechenko said, "is this last step." Leaning in, he began inputting a series of numbers and letters into the blank boxes.

Petrov held his breath as he stared intently at the computer.

A moment later the image on the screen changed again. It now displayed a very long list of city names. Next to each city was their web link.

We're in! Petrov realized.

Prism now had access to the electric grid of the U.S. state of Texas.

Chapter 37

Langley, Virginia

"Calm down," Alex Miller said. "From what you've told me, you're lucky to be alive."

Rachel West's hands formed into fists. "Easy for you to say, Alex. Every time I get close to a good lead on Prism, it vanishes."

They were sitting in Miller's office at the Factory; she was briefing him on her trip to Helsinki.

She placed her hands flat on his desk and took a deep breath to calm down. "All I needed was half an hour with Lendel – I would've gotten him to talk. Now he and his goon are history. All I can hope for is that the sharks got indigestion."

Miller chuckled. "It's good *you* weren't the shark bait. Don't forget, you were tied up, guns pointed at you. I know you think you're superwoman or something. But let's face it, you're an agent, one of my best, but ... you were damn close to getting killed again."

She shrugged, and after a moment a smile crossed her lips. "Guess you're right."

He pointed a stern finger at her. "You know I'm right. I have half a mind to assign you another partner."

"What?" she said, raising her voice, her anger returning. "You can't do that!"

Miller stared at her, his face showing no emotion. He was quiet for a minute, then said. "I can. And I should. But we both know what happened last time I did that."

A feeling of regret filled her. "How is Turner?"

"Still in rehab at the medical facility. He's getting better, but we haven't cleared him for duty yet."

"Glad to hear he's improving."

"Me too, Rachel." He paused, leaned forward in his chair. "There's another reason I'm not assigning you a new partner."

"Because I *am* superwoman?" she said with a sly smile.

He rolled his eyes. "No. As you know, I've had a feeling there's a leak at Central Intelligence. And certain things have come up recently confirming my suspicion there's a mole at Headquarters. So we're going to continue keeping this investigation in-house. Factory personnel only. My budget is limited and I can't spare another agent right now."

"Not a problem, Alex."

"I figured you wouldn't be upset," he replied sarcastically.

Rachel considered what her boss had just shared. "Any idea who the mole might be at the glass palace?"

"Not yet, but I'm working on it. It's someone fairly high up, because they seem to have unlimited access to a lot of information."

She nodded and went quiet as she studied the man sitting behind the desk. Her boss appeared tired and seemed to have aged since she'd seen him last, which was only the previous week. She guessed the situation with the CIA leak was a factor.

"I do have some good news on the investigation," she said.

"What?"

Rachel reached in her pocket and removed a flash drive. She slid the device across the desk and he picked it up.

"I located a laptop computer on Lendel's boat," she said. "The files on it were encrypted as you'd expect, but I downloaded them to this drive. Hopefully the tech guys can decipher them."

"Good work, Rachel. We may get a lead yet."

"I hope so – we need it."

Miller pointed to his office door. "Okay. Now get out of here. Go home. Get some well-deserved rest."

"You'll call me as soon as you get anything?"

Laughing, he said, "Go, will you!"

Rachel left his office and made her way to the building's underground parking lot. Finding her Kawasaki, she put on her leather jacket and helmet. Then she climbed on and turned on the ignition. The powerful motorcycle roared to life, the big engine emitting a low-throated growl.

She left the building and reached her apartment a short while later.

After showering, she made herself dinner, which consisted of scrambled eggs, ham, and somewhat stale bread. Then she went to the bedroom and slept for the next twelve hours straight.

When she awoke, she continued to lie in bed for a time, feeling rested for the first time in a week. With her fingers she traced her bare abdomen and ribs, which were still sore but getting better.

Lying there, nude, staring up at the ceiling, she thought about her boyfriend Brad. *Maybe I'll call him*, she mused. Their last night together had ended badly. Very badly. But she still had strong feelings for him. *He's a good man.* A good lover, but he was more than the great sex. He was someone she wanted to share her life with for a long time, maybe forever.

The hell with it, she told herself. *I'm calling him.*

Reaching over to the bedside table, she picked up her cell phone and began punching in the number.

Just then an incoming call interrupted her and she answered it. "This is West."

"It's Alex. That flash drive you gave me. The tech guys were able to break the encryption."

"That's great!" she replied.

"Get back to the office, Rachel. Now."

Chapter 38

Glacier County, Montana

The American could hardly contain his excitement.

He was in his underground study, closely studying the five computer monitors on his wide desk. The various stock exchanges from around the world were displayed on the screens. They showed normal activity for a weekday in late summer – low volatility on below average trading volume. The multi-color charts depicted the buying and selling of shares on the indexes; the typical ups and downs, with nothing out of the ordinary happening. John Smith had made his living trading stocks for many years, and from his experience knew everything was calm right now in the markets.

Smith glanced up at the ten flatscreen TVs mounted on the wall. As usual, each TV was tuned to a different news feed from across the world, all muted for sound. He paid particular attention to two TVs, one showing CNN Headline News, the other tuned to the local CBS affiliate in Houston, Texas. He was sure that once the event took place, they would be among the first to report it.

He looked at his Rolex as he ticked off the minutes. He had been coordinating closely with Ivan Petrov all day, wanting to make sure the timing was as close to perfect as possible. Petrov, from his warehouse in St. Petersburg, had activated Prism's pre-arranged plan five minutes ago.

Ten minutes ago Smith had executed his own program trades, purchasing very large quantities of oil company stocks. He'd bought sizable blocks of Exxon/Mobil, Shell, and Amoco shares. Now he was just waiting for the news to break. Although the American was an expert trader, he knew the stock market was like placing a bet on an unpredictable outcome, with odds not much better than the games of chance at Las Vegas casinos. Even using sophisticated mathematical models like quantitative analysis and computer generated regression logarithms, your odds were still not much better than 60/40. In fact most day traders, who didn't use sophisticated programs like Smith did, lost more money than they made on a typical day on Wall Street.

That's why Smith was so eager for the news to break.

Never before in his trading life had he been able to predict what was going to happen with such certainty. Of course, in the back of his mind, he knew Petrov and his computer expert Lechenko could fail. All the previous tests had worked perfectly. But those had just been tests, technical exercises with no money involved.

This time it was different – very different.

This time the American had invested a fortune buying the oil company stocks. True, the stocks would still have value if things didn't go as planned. But what if the stock market tanked suddenly for some unexplained reason? He'd lose big time.

Pushing the negative thoughts aside, he resumed watching the TV monitors, while occasionally glancing at his watch.

Still nothing.

He swallowed hard, fighting the urge to call Petrov and find out what the hell had happened.

Looking at his Rolex once again, he realized they were still 30 seconds from the event.

Beads of perspiration formed on his forehead, and he felt hot, although he kept the temperature of the room at a cool 68 degrees.

As the seconds ticked off, he pulled out a handkerchief and wiped his brow, his eyes still glued to the TVs.

Then in a split-second, he knew it had happened. The screen showing the Houston TV station went dark.

As he waited for CNN or Fox News to pick up the breaking story, he switched one of the other TVs to a Dallas station. As he had expected, that broadcast was not affected.

The Dallas TV station was showing one of those mindless talk programs he so detested. He watched as the talking heads, two blonde, well-dressed women, discussed the latest fad diet. A '*Breaking News*' tag line began to scroll at the bottom of the screen, reporting that a major power outage had just occurred in the south Texas area.

With a smile, he turned back to the other TV screens. The one from the Houston station was still dark, but CNN was beginning to report the story.

He turned up the volume and watched the anchorwoman.

"*We have breaking news,*" the attractive brunette said, "*coming to us from the Houston area. Much of south Texas has suffered a severe electrical outage. The power blackout is extensive, and includes Houston, Galveston, and many other cities. This area is well known for its petroleum refining. A large portion of the U.S.'s oil refining operations, so important to the Texas economy, is located there. Local authorities have told us they are actively working to resolve the issue ....*"

The American leaned back in his chair, a self-satisfied smile on his lips. The plan's working, he knew. Texas oil refining plants accounted for approximately half of the U.S.'s capacity. And although the refiners had backup generators, a long shutdown of the electrical grid in the area would still cripple production and cause havoc in the world's oil markets.

According to Smith's specific instructions, the computer program Petrov had put in place would take days, and possibly weeks, for the affected power companies to override. That was plenty of time for his newly purchased oil company stocks to react. Since oil refining production would be curtailed, oil supplies would be at a premium in the U.S. and worldwide. The stocks would soar in price.

Smith turned his attention to the stock trading screens on his desk.

The market was already beginning to react. Several of his oil stocks were surging. One of them, Shell Oil, had jumped in value by twenty percent.

His smile widened.

Chapter 39

St. Petersburg, Russia

The Aeroflot commercial jet touched down at Pulkovo Airport and began taxing to the gate.

Rachel West looked out the plane's window, watched as other planes landed and took off. Although she was fluent in Russian and had operated in the country several times before, she was apprehensive about this trip.

In her previous assignments here she'd had backup close-by, provided by CIA personnel at the U.S. Embassies. But since this was a Factory-only operation those resources weren't available. Not having back-up wasn't a major problem in a European country like Finland. But here in Russia things were very different, including the political system, which made her current operation daunting. Although Russia was ostensibly a democracy, she knew that was window dressing – the government, controlled by old-style Communist *apparatchiks*, ruled with an iron fist. She'd have to be extra careful and keep a low a profile.

Still, Rachel couldn't blame her boss for his decision to keep the mission in-house. The leak at Central Intelligence was real and had already impeded her investigation of Prism.

Luckily, she realized, St. Petersburg was unlike Moscow. St. Petersburg had a growing tourism trade, making Westerners more accepted.

The jet reached the gate and the passengers began deplaning. It had been a connecting flight, stopping in London before making its final destination here. Many of the passengers were British tourists, she surmised, and some businessmen, including the overweight, middle-aged man in the seat next to her. He was wearing a charcoal gray pin-stripe suit and a silk tie. It was clear he had been coming on to her, and she in turn had been polite while making it obvious she wasn't available.

After removing her backpack from the overhead bin, she turned to the man, who was in the process of getting up. "Hope you have a good business trip," she said.

The man smiled, reached into his suit, removed a business card and handed it to her. "I'm staying at the Gushka Inn," he replied in his clipped British accent. "It overlooks the Moyka River. It has a nice bar. I'll buy you that drink I promised you."

"I'm going to be pretty busy." Then she returned the smile, not wanting to shut him down completely. It might come in handy to know a Westerner during her trip. "But then again, I might get thirsty."

"Excellent! I'll buy you dinner, too. Cheerio, then."

Turning, she followed the other passengers out of the plane.

After collecting her other bags from the luggage area, she cleared customs and made her way to the money exchange on the main concourse. The value of the Russian currency was low, and she traded dollars for a thick wad of roubles.

Her cover this trip was as a tourist so she had dressed appropriately, wearing casual clothes, a simple blouse and jeans. She wore her long hair in a ponytail, covered by a ball cap with no inscription. Glancing at other women as she strode through the terminal, she realized she would not stand out. Here in Russia, unlike in China, there were plenty of tall blondes with blue eyes.

Making her way out of the airport, Rachel found a taxi stand. Bypassing a newer model Saab, she got in an old, dented sedan with faded yellow paint.

The cab driver, a balding man in his sixties, turned and faced her. "*Dobryy den. Gde?*" *Good morning. Where to?*

"I'm a tourist," she replied, continuing in Russian. "I'm looking for a cheap hotel."

He nodded, mentioned a name.

"Do they take cash?"

"*Da.*"

She agreed and the driver took off.

It was an overcast day, and she observed the other traffic as the cab made its way into the center of the city. The driver was quiet, not curious about her trip or supplying her with useless chit-chat, something she appreciated.

When he stopped in front of a run-down, four-story building, she gave him the fare and added a large tip. "I may need more transportation during my stay," she said.

"Here's my name and phone number," the man replied, giving her a wrinkled slip of paper.

Rachel checked into the hotel and found her cramped, but at least clean room on the third floor. It had scarred, wood furniture, and the only window overlooked a grimy alley. But it had easy access to the fire escape, something that would come in handy if she had to make a quick exit. A cheap print of Russian leader Vladimir Putin hung on one of the walls, the only decoration in the room.

After taking a shower, she changed clothes and began pacing the room, trying to plan her next move. The Factory tech guys had extracted key, although limited information from the flash drive. Arsi Lendel had been receiving regular payments from a St. Petersburg bank, and now she had the account number. Unfortunately, that's all she had. Rachel was sure that Lendel's partner in Prism, the mysterious Russian, lived here. Her dilemma was finding him while keeping a low profile.

In one of her previous missions to the area she had used the services of a local informant, a sketchy character she didn't completely trust. Gorky Pushkin was a poet who supplemented his meager writing income by selling information to foreigners. She needed information, along with a few other things, and Pushkin was her best bet right now.

Rachel stopped pacing, pulled out her cell phone and punched in a number.

After ringing a long time, the call went through and the man answered.

"*Kak vee pozhivaete, Gorky*?" she said. *How are you, Gorky?*

"*Zdravstvuyte. Kto zto?*" Pushkin replied. *Hello. Who is this?*

"It's Rachel."

"Ha. Of course. Now I recognize your voice. It's been awhile."

"Yes, it has, Gorky. How's the writing going?"

"I write, but I make no money at it."

She chuckled. "Life's like that sometimes. Listen, we need to meet."

"*Da*. You want to come to my apartment?"

Rachel remembered his grimy, warren-like place that made her current hotel room seen luxurious in comparison. "*Nyet*. How about someplace public."

After a brief pause, he said, "How about the park close to St. Isaac's – by the statue?"

She knew the area well and it was not a far walk from her hotel. "Perfect. When?"

"You have roubles?"

"Of course, Gorky."

"Then I'll meet you there in an hour."

She hung up and immediately headed out of the room, wanting to get there early and scout the area to make sure the man wasn't setting her up.

Fifteen minutes later Rachel walked by the imposing facade of St. Isaacs Cathedral, its tall golden dome providing a welcome contrast to the cloudy grayness of the afternoon. Crossing Admiralteyskiy Prospekt after a break in traffic, she entered the park through the south entrance.

Striding through the wooded areas, she reached the clearing a moment later and sat on one the benches by the statue of the Bronze Horseman. Designed by sculptor Etienne Falconet, the magnificent bronze sculpture depicted Peter the Great, the city's founder, on horseback. It was one of St. Petersburg's most notable landmarks.

From this vantage point she had a clear view of the park – if Gorky was being followed or if he had alerted the *politsiya*, she'd have a chance to slip away. But the only people she spotted were tourists or workers from the nearby buildings.

The man walked into the park half an hour later, and seeing her, approached with a wide smile on his face.

"*Dobryy den*," he said, extending his hand.

She shook hands. "*Zdravstvuyte*."

He sat next to her on the bench, which faced the statue and the Neva River beyond. "You picked a good time of the year to visit our city, Rachel. If I remember correctly, the river was partly frozen last time you were here."

She gave him a sidelong glance. Gorky was a small, wiry man, with straight, slicked-back hair. His heavily pocked-marked face attested to bad acne in childhood. "You have a good memory, my Russian friend."

He rubbed his hands together. "Are you in need of information again?"

"*Da*. That and a few other things."

"Then you came to the right man." He gave her a crooked grin. "I may not be the most polished writer in Russia, but I have other talents that keep a roof over my head. What do you need?"

"First, Gorky, I need information. I have the name of a local bank and an account number. I need to find out the person who owns the account." She handed him a slip of paper.

He read the note and nodded. "I can do that. But it will be expensive."

"How much?"

The man mentioned a large sum of roubles.

"Don't be ridiculous," she said, knowing he was testing her. "I'll give you half that."

He laughed. "Such a game we play. All right. I'll do it for half."

"Good. I want a few other things. I need a car – something that can't be traced back to me. And a lock-pick set, a collapsible metal baton, and a switchblade."

"No problem, Rachel."

She nodded. "Something else. Russian security is very good at the airport, so I couldn't bring it with me. I need a pistol."

Gorky frowned. "Can't you get that from the Agency people here in town?"

"Not this time. This operation is off-books."

His face clouded with concern. "A car is one thing, but a gun ... things in the country are better after the Soviet Union broke up, but still, the *politsiya* are everywhere."

"I'll pay."

"How much, Rachel?"

She mentioned a large sum.

The man looked nervous, and he glanced around the park for a long moment before turning back to her. "*Da.* I'll do it. But it'll take a day or so."

"No problem."

"And like last time, Rachel, I'll need half the money up front."

Nodding, she reached in her pocket and counted out the bills. Holding up the money, she said, "But don't skip town. Remember, I'm a resourceful woman. I'll find you and break both your arms."

"I would never do that. You're a good customer. Don't worry, I'll get you everything you need."

She handed him the money and he put it away quickly. "How do I get a hold of you, Rachel?"

"It'll be easier if I call you," she replied, still not trusting the man completely.

"*Da.*"

They both stood and after a brief good-bye, they headed in different directions.

***

Rachel found a sidewalk cafe that fronted the Neva River, and after being seated, glanced at the menu. She ordered borsch and *kulebiaka*, a local favorite consisting of fish, eggs, and rice. She had never found Russian food to be especially good, but these items were usually edible.

Leaning back and sipping black tea, she watched the commercial boat traffic wind their way on the Neva. Her uneasiness about dealing with Gorky hadn't dissipated, but she knew her options were limited.

Just then her cell phone vibrated in her pocket and she pulled it out and held it to her ear. It was an encrypted call, and after listening to several odd clicks, she heard Alex Miller's voice, sounding tinny and faraway.

"It's your uncle," he said, employing the typical code word that indicated her boss didn't fully trust the phone's scrambling technology in a country like Russia. "Visited any good tourist spots yet?"

"Not yet, just got here," she replied. "I'll visit the Hermitage tomorrow and Tsarskoe Selo the day after."

"Glad to hear it. Listen, I wanted you know about something. Your cousin in Texas was in a car accident – you may want to give him a call."

Rachel realized Miller was telling her something bad had happened in that state and that she should check into it. "Thanks for letting me know, Uncle. Soon as I finish eating, I'll call him."

"One last thing. Be careful on your trip – I know you want to have fun and see all the sights, but ... I'm an old man, and all your other relatives are even older. If you get in trouble, you're on your own."

"I'm aware of that, Uncle. I have a local contact, he's helping me out."

"Is that the guy you met on your last trip there?"

"Yeah, that's him."

"In that case, be doubly careful."

"Roger that, Uncle." She hung up just as the waiter brought her meal. The soup was lukewarm and the *kulebiaka* bland, but she ate it anyway, in a hurry to find out what Miller was trying to tell her.

Thirty minutes later Rachel was back in her cramped hotel room, sitting on the bed, her notebook computer open in front of her. Using the hotel's Wi-Fi connection, she went to Pravda's news website. Although not the most objective, the Russian newspaper's online site was the most widely referenced news source in the country, and her use of it would arouse the least suspicion. Going to the international news section of the site, she scrolled to the U.S. headlines. She saw the story right away and read it thoroughly.

According to Pravda, a widespread power blackout had occurred in southern Texas. The blackout was in its third day already, and was causing massive problems. Texas authorities blamed the problem on a computer malfunction, which had shut down the electrical grid of several power companies. State and Federal authorities were aggressively working on restoring electricity to the area, the report said, but no timetable was given for the recovery.

Her gut twisted as she re-read the article – in the back of her mind, she suspected Prism was behind the event.

***

A day later Rachel knocked on Gorky Pushkin's apartment door and waited. Although she didn't want to meet the man here, it was the most private place she could think of.

A moment later the door opened and he let her in. Gorky was wearing sleepwear and a ratty robe, not surprising as it was the middle of the night.

"We could have waited until morning, Rachel," he said with a yawn, closing the door behind her.

"It's too important to wait. Anyway, I figured you could use the money."

His face lit up. "You have the balance?"

"Of course."

"Have a seat; I'll get some vodka while we conclude our business."

She scanned the tiny, unkempt living room – like the last time she had been here, the only furniture was a soiled, lumpy sofa and an ancient wooden cabinet. Litter and stacks of books covered most of the grimy concrete floor.

"I'll take that drink, Gorky – but I prefer to stand."

He shrugged, went to the cabinet, pulled out a bottle and poured the clear liquid into glasses. Handing her one of the containers, he downed his drink in one gulp.

She eyed the somewhat soiled glass suspiciously before taking a sip. The cheap liquor burned her throat, but she drank it anyway.

"If you don't mind, Rachel, I'd like to see the money first, then I'll give you what you came for."

"Bullshit. I already gave you half up front – I need to see the merchandise first." She pointed to her pocket. "I've got all your roubles right here. Don't you trust me, my Russian friend?"

He held his palms up in front of him. "Of course I trust you. We'll do it your way. I'll go get it." Turning, the man went into one of the other rooms and came back holding a cardboard box. He placed the box on the sofa, opened it, and removed a set of keys, which he handed her.

"These are the keys to the car. It's parked on the street in front of this building."

"What kind of car is it?"

"A Lada."

Rachel grimaced, knowing the reputation for that brand of Russian cars. "A piece of crap. That's the best you could do?"

He shrugged. "You needed something fast. Don't worry. It's dented and the bodywork's a little rusted, but it runs well."

"It better, Gorky."

He smiled. "You'll like the next thing a lot more." Reaching into the box once again, he removed a chrome-plated pistol and handed it to her.

It was a Makarov 9 mm semi-automatic. Although it was not new, it was in very good condition, Rachel realized. She ejected the clip, then checked the slide action, which worked perfectly. Makarovs, she knew, were one of the most widely used handguns in Eastern Europe, and in fact had been standard issue for the Russian military and the KGB for many years. Because of their simplicity and good stopping power, they were even available in the U.S.

"You did well, Gorky." She checked for the serial number on the gun and was pleased to see it had been filed off. "What about ammo?"

"Two extra clips, and 50 rounds of ammunition. It's all in the box, along with the lock-pick set, and the other things you needed."

"Excellent, my Russian friend. What about the information?"

"What about my money?"

She pulled a large wad of roubles from her pocket and held it up. "It's all here."

His face lit up in a wide grin. "*Da.*" He reached in the box and took out an envelope. "The information you were looking for is all here."

She took the envelope and handed him the wad of bills. Opening it, she quickly read the contents that were inside. "You're sure about this, Gorky?"

He nodded. "*Da.*"

Rachael gave him a hard look. "If it's wrong, I'll be back. And I won't be my usual charming self."

"For a pretty lady you worry too much." He counted the money she'd given him, and with a satisfied smile, put it in his robe's pocket. "Would you like more vodka? I have plenty."

Shaking her head, she said, "No, thanks. I've got to get going."

***

Rachel found the Lada just where Gorky had said, parked on the street in front of the building. Even in the dim light given off by the streetlamp, she could tell the boxy sedan was a piece of crap. With dented bumpers, rusted side panels, and balding tires, the car looked like a reject from a used-car lot. It was painted gray, but the color was faded and scratched. The sedan certainly didn't look like classy Aston Martins spies drove in the movies, she mused.

She unlocked it and climbed in. Starting it up, she was surprised to find the engine sounded powerful.

Pulling away from the curb, she drove off in the almost deserted street. She floored the gas pedal and the Lada jumped in response, accelerating strongly. The car may look like crap, she realized, but at least it had some guts.

It was three a.m. when she reached her hotel a short while later. Removing the box Gorky had given her from the trunk, she made her way up to her room.

After loading the Makarov's clips with ammo, she inserted one of them into the handgun. Then she packed the gun and all the other items from the box into her backpack.

Instantly she felt better.

Gorky had found out that the bank account that made the payments to Arsi Lendel was owned by a trust fund titled *N. Ivanova Trust Fund.* The fund had a local address.

Opening her notebook computer, Rachel logged on to the Internet search engine Yandex, Russia's version of Google. Inputting the information into Yandex, she was surprised to find that the trust fund was set up for a woman named Nikita Ivanova, who lived here in St. Petersburg.

Rachel had been sure that Lendel's boss, the mysterious Russian, was a man. *So who the hell is this Nikita Ivanova?* she wondered. Was Gorky's information wrong? Rachel gritted her teeth, silently cursing the shifty poet. Taking a couple of deep breaths to calm down, she continued her online search. Once again using Yandex, she did a search for the woman and what she found was interesting. Ivanova was a college dropout who appeared to make her living from modeling lingerie. Rachel found several photos of the young woman online. She was a stunning dark-haired, green-eyed beauty in her mid-twenties.

Maybe this Ivanova was married to Lendel's boss? It was a possibility, although the online information didn't say the woman was married.

At least now Rachel had a name, a face, and an address. A good starting point. Glancing at her watch, she saw it was past four in the morning. She badly needed to get some sleep before starting her search for the woman.

Yawning, she turned off the computer and set it on the floor. Then she stretched out on the narrow bed and still clothed, fell into a deep sleep.

***

Rachel had no problem finding the woman's apartment building, an upscale structure that overlooked the Fontanka River. It was mid-morning, and she hoped Ivanova would be home.

Rachel smoothed down the conservative black dress she was wearing, and then knocked on the apartment door. When there was no answer, she pressed the buzzer several times until she heard the shuffling of feet from the other side.

The door opened a crack, and the dark-haired beauty peered from behind it. "*Da?*"

"*Zdravstvuyte,*" Rachel said, "*Vee pozhivaete Nikita Ivanova?*"

"Yes, I'm Nikita," the woman replied in Russian. "What do you want?"

"I work for Vogue Magazine," Rachel continued in Russian, using the cover story she had devised earlier. "We're scouting for models in the city and we saw photos of you online. We're looking to find new faces for our future issues."

Ivanova's eyes grew wide and she opened the door fully. "Of course. Please come in."

Rachel stepped inside and quickly scanned the room, which was furnished in contemporary, expensive-looking furniture. The large apartment had a beautiful view of the river below. Ivanova was dressed in a silk blouse and skirt that, like the furniture, appeared expensive.

"My name is Sally Winters," Rachel continued. "I'm from New York City – as you probably know our magazine is based there."

Ivanova nodded, looking a bit star-struck. "You said you've seen my pictures online?"

"Yes. You're quite a beauty."

"That's a big compliment, coming from an attractive woman like you," Ivanova replied. The woman rubbed her cheek, and Rachel noticed a faint scar there. "Most of my modeling work has been in lingerie, as you can tell from the photos. But I always wanted to do more serious work."

Rachel smiled. "You may get your chance now."

"Please sit down, Miss Winters," gesturing to the brocade sofa. "I was having some tea. Would you like some?"

"Of course. Do you live here by yourself?"

"I do. Well, just me and my cat."

Rachel watched as the woman left the room, then inspected the large living room carefully, looking for clues. Next to the sofa was a baby-grand piano and resting on the piano's closed lid were an assortment of framed photos. She walked over, studied the pictures closely. All of them showed Ivanova with a much older man. *Her father maybe?*

Ivanova came back a moment later with two cups, and after handing one of them to Rachel, they both sat on opposing sofas.

"You said you're looking for new models, Miss Winters?"

"That's right. We've interviewed several candidates already, and we'll be talking with more over the next week."

"I see. I have a portfolio book of my work I can show you."

"That won't be necessary. I'm not interested in semi-nude photos. We have a photographer who would take tasteful, fully-dressed, test shots once we've selected the final candidates. Right now we're still in the preliminary stages, getting a feel for who would be the perfect face to represent our magazine. We're very particular, as you can imagine."

"I understand," Ivanova said, rubbing her scar once more.

"We're doing background checks on our candidates to make sure there are no surprises – illegal activity, that sort of thing. In fact we've done some checking on you, and I had a couple of questions."

"Yes?"

"There's a trust account in your name at a local bank, with a significant amount of money in it. Tell me about that."

Ivanova laughed nervously. "Ha – that. My boyfriend, fiancée actually, set that up for me. But I don't have access to it yet – not until we're married." She pointed to the framed photos on the piano. "That's him in the pictures – he's such a dear."

Rachel nodded, her interest peaked. This could be the mysterious Russian she was looking for. "I see. When are you getting married?"

"Soon." She made a face. "As soon as he gets a divorce from his wife."

"Tell me about him."

"He's a businessman now, but he used to be an officer in the Russian army – a colonel. His name is Ivan Illych Petrov, and he's the sweetest man I've ever met."

Rachel smiled. "I'm sure he is. What kind of business is he in?"

Ivanova waved a hand in the air. "I don't have a head for business; he makes money, that's all I know. He bought me this place."

"That's very generous of him. He lives here in St. Petersburg?"

"No, he lives outside the city, south of here." She mentioned an address. "He has a large home, an estate actually – but of course I've never been there."

Rachel nodded. "Well, you've been very helpful, Miss Ivanova."

"Please, call me Nikita."

"Okay, Nikita."

"Is there anything else you wanted to know about me?"

"Not at the moment. I think I have all the information I need for now."

"I'd be glad to pose for those test shots, Miss Winters."

Rachel took a sip of the tea. "Yes, that would be the next step. As soon as I've talked to the remaining candidates, I'll be sure to get in touch with you."

Ivanova seemed crestfallen at not nailing the photo gig right away. "What else can I do to make your selection easier? I know I'm the right woman for you."

Rachel smiled, trying to figure out how she could use the woman's eagerness to her advantage. "Well, you certainly have the right look. But I am concerned about one thing."

"What's that?"

"As you know, our magazine has a worldwide distribution – once we select a model and we feature her, her status soars. We've had several of our girls become international supermodels overnight."

"Yes, Miss Winters, I'm aware of that."

"So I want to be sure the person I select has a clean background." Rachel frowned. "But I'm concerned that in your case, dating a married man – that could lead to a drawn-out, messy divorce."

"It's not like that at all. Ivan loves me. He'd do anything for me. He's promised me that once he completes his current project, he'll divorce the *babushka* and marry me."

"Still. I need to be sure. I'd like to meet him."

"He's a very private man, Miss Winters. He doesn't like to meet strangers."

Rachel stood up abruptly. "Then I'm sorry, Nikita. And it's too bad. I think you'd make a perfect cover girl."

"I'd be on the cover of your magazine?"

"Yes. I can guarantee it."

"In that case, I'll talk him into it. I'll arrange a meeting."

Rachel smiled. "Excellent." She handed Ivanova a card. "Write down your phone number, and I'll call you in a day or so. We can set up a time and place for the three of us to meet."

The young woman jotted on the card and returned it to Rachel.

"It's been a pleasure talking with you, Nikita. I'm certain you're going to have a bright future with us."

***

Back at her hotel room later, Rachel logged on to her computer and began doing a search for Ivan Petrov. As Ivanova had said, the man had been in the Russian military for many years, and had retired as a colonel. After that his online trail went cold. Whatever business he was involved in was secretive, and Rachel suspected, highly illegal. She was sure now that Petrov was Lendel's boss.

All she had to do now was wait for Ivanova to set up the meet.

Chapter 40

St. Petersburg, Russia

"I don't like it, Nikita," Ivan Petrov said, peering over the rim of his tumbler of vodka.

They were in Nikita's apartment, and the young woman was sitting on the opposite sofa, a pout on her pretty face.

"This is important to me, Ivan Illych. Anyway, I'm not asking for much – all you have to do it meet Miss Winters and show her we're a normal couple. Is that too much to ask?"

"I know, I know. But you don't even need this photo spread. After we get married, you'll have all the money you'll ever want."

Her green eyes burned with intensity. "It's not just the money. I could be a famous model. Don't you want that for me?"

Actually, he hated the idea. All he really desired was to have Nikita all to himself. The last thing he wanted was to have her become well-known, jetting off to photo shoots around the world. "Of course I want the best for you. Didn't I give you this condo? And don't forget about the Jaguar I'm buying you."

Nikita pouted again and leaned forward, giving him a good look at the ample cleavage of her low-cut dress. "I appreciate all that. You know I do. But can't you do this one little thing for me?"

Petrov sighed and didn't answer, as he tried to figure out a way to finesse the situation.

Obviously sensing his reluctance, she patted the seat cushion next to her. "Why don't you come and sit over here, Ivan Illych. Let me show you how grateful I can be...."

Chapter 41

St. Petersburg, Russia

Rachel West put on the same conservative black dress and studied her appearance in her hotel room's mirror. After combing her long hair, she slipped on her high heels and went to the room's scarred wooden cabinet. Taking the Makarov pistol from one of the drawers, she put the weapon in her purse and slung it over her shoulder.

Glancing at her watch, she knew it was time.

***

An hour later Rachel was at Ivanova's apartment, knocking on the door. She was tense, not knowing what to expect. She had been in similar situations before, and knew that things could go bad fast. Touching her purse, she felt the outline of the Makarov inside, giving her a feeling of reassurance.

Nikita opened the door a moment later, a wide smile on her face. As before, the young woman was wearing a silk blouse and a short skirt. "Please come in, Miss Winters."

A tall, older gentleman dressed in a gray suit was standing in the living room; Rachel recognized him as the man in the photos. A stern, suspicious look was on his face.

"Miss Winters," Nikita said, "I'd like you to meet Colonel Ivan Illych Petrov."

"Pleasure to meet you, Colonel," Rachel said, offering her hand.

Petrov shook it, but didn't say a word.

"Please, have a seat, Miss Winters," Nikita said. "Ivan is having vodka. Would you like some?"

"I'd prefer tea," Rachel replied, as she perched on one of the sofas, and watched as the man sat down across from her and took a long pull from his drink.

While Nikita left the room, Rachel quickly assessed the situation. It appeared the man had come alone, without bodyguards, something that would have greatly complicated matters. But she noted the bulge in his suit jacket, indicating he was probably armed.

"I understand you were in the Russian military for many years," Rachel said, trying to put the man at ease.

"*Da*," he replied curtly. By his cold manner, it was clear he was uncomfortable being here.

Nikita came back into the room, and after handing Rachel a cup, sat next to Petrov. She looked adoringly at the man, then expectantly at Rachel. "I'm glad you've had a chance to meet each other. You'll be setting up the photo shoot soon?"

Rachel smiled. "Of course, Nikita. Colonel Petrov, tell me a little bit about the kind of business you're in. Nikita says you're very successful."

Still glaring, he said, "I don't see how that's any of your concern."

Nikita patted Petrov in the shoulder. "Don't be rude, Ivan. She's just curious."

Petrov said nothing, his lips set into a rigid line.

It was clear to Rachel that she wasn't going to get anything out of him by being pleasant. She had hoped to postpone using force until she was sure he was the right man, but realized now she had no choice or time to waste.

Her adrenaline flowing, she reached into her purse. Quickly taking out the pistol, she aimed it at him. "Colonel, slowly take the gun out of your jacket and place it on the floor. And no sudden moves, or I shoot."

The scowl on his face abruptly changed to shock.

"What the hell is this?" he shouted, turning his gaze from Rachel to Nikita and then back to Rachel.

Rachel gripped the Makarov tightly. "Remove the gun from your jacket, Colonel. Do it now!"

Grimacing, the man reached into his suit jacket and removed a semi-automatic handgun. He rested the gun on the floor by his feet.

"Kick it away," Rachel ordered.

Petrov complied and she sighed with relief. She glanced at Nikita, saw the terror in her eyes.

"What is it you want?" the colonel asked. "Is this a robbery? I have cash on me."

"Shut up, Petrov!" Rachel tossed her purse to Nikita. "There's a rope in there. Take it out and tie his hands behind his back. And don't screw it up or you'll regret it, Nikita."

The woman removed the strand of rope from the purse and began tying the man up while he remained sitting on the sofa. When she was done, Rachel said, "Lie on the floor, Nikita, and hold your hands behind your back. Now!"

Keeping an eye on Petrov, she watched Nikita comply.

Standing, Rachel picked up Petrov's gun off the floor and stuck it in a pocket of her dress. Then she approached the man, and holding the muzzle of the Makarov to his temple, checked the rope bindings. Satisfied, she went over to Nikita, now laying face-down on the floor. Striking the pistol across the back of the woman's head, Rachel watched her body slump.

That done, she turned back to Petrov.

"Please don't hurt Nikita!" the colonel pleaded. "I'll give you all the money you want."

"This isn't about money, Petrov."

"What then?"

"I need information."

"What? What are you talking about? Nikita told me you were with some famous magazine – I knew I should have never agreed to meet with you, you crazy bitch!"

Rachel swung her pistol across the man's face, and he flinched back, blood seeping from his nostrils.

"This is how it's going to work, Petrov. I ask the questions, you answer them. It's that simple. If you don't cooperate, I'll really hurt your pretty little girlfriend. Is that what you want?" Rachel hoped it wouldn't come to that. In fact, she would start beating up Petrov first, before she'd hurt Nikita. She knew a tough customer like Petrov wouldn't break easily, but would probably do everything in his power to protect his girlfriend.

"Please, whoever you are, please don't hurt Nikita!"

"You'll talk, Colonel?"

"*Da!*"

"Good." Pulling a chair close to him, she sat and leveled the gun at his head. "You're part of Prism, aren't you?"

A shocked expression crossed his face. "What? I don't know what you're talking about!"

"Don't lie, Colonel. I know you're Lendel's boss, and you're part of the group that's secretly buying tech companies."

He flinched, almost as if she'd struck him. "I ... I ... no ... I don't know what you're talking about ...."

"I've been tracking your group for a month. I know all about Zhao Deng, and Arsi Lendel, and your house in Finland, and Sincore Technologies. You might as well come clean, and spare yourself the pain of having me beat it out of you."

Just then his face lit up in a flash of recognition. "You! You're that crazy bitch West! The CIA agent."

Rachel grinned. "Not the compliment I was looking for, but I've been called worse."

Turning serious, she once again smashed the pistol across his face and this time his nose gushed blood, staining his shirt and suit a bright red. "I don't have time to play games. Tell me what I want to know now, or Nikita gets hurt."

The man glanced at his girlfriend, who still lay unmoving on the floor. "What do you want to know, West?"

"Tell me about Prism. What are you planning to do with the tech companies you're buying? And who else besides you is in the group?"

"You broke my nose." He gasped, gulping in air through his mouth. "I'm having trouble breathing."

"Fuck you, Petrov. Answer my questions, or I start on her next."

He glanced nervously at Nikita again, then back at Rachel. "Okay. It's simple, really. I was buying the companies to resell them for a profit."

"Bullshit! There's more to it than that. Why was the Chinese billionaire involved? Who else is in on it?"

Petrov glanced around the room – she sensed he was stalling for time. Finally he said, "It's just me. I was trying to buy Sincore and the other companies to make a profit."

"I don't believe it. There's more to it than that. And I think Prism is bigger than you – much bigger. You've got other help. I don't think you're smart enough to plan and execute the events taking place in Texas right now. That takes a lot of technical expertise."

"*Nyet!* I'm telling the truth!"

"Bullshit!" Angry, she approached Nikita's prone body and raised the pistol above the woman's head. "Talk now, or by God, I'll crush her skull!"

"Don't do it!" Petrov pleaded. "Please don't do it. I'll tell you."

Rachel lowered the gun and walked back, standing in front of the man. "I'm listening."

Petrov's shoulders slumped. "I have a partner. An American."

"What's his name?"

She heard the apartment's front door creak open and she whirled around, saw a brawny man in the doorway, aiming a gun at her.

Dropping to one knee, she fired off two rounds at the man; at the same time she saw the muzzle flash from his weapon.

Something heavy struck her in the back and she toppled forward. Her head hit the parquet wood floor and she lost consciousness.

When she awoke sometime later, her forehead throbbed with pain.

As she scanned the now vacant living room, she scrambled to her feet. Locating the Makarov under one of the sofas, she quickly searched the apartment. Petrov was gone, as was Nikita. In a corner of the living room she found the burly man she had shot. He was dead.

Now she realized the colonel had been stalling for time – he must have set off some silent alarm, and waited for his bodyguard to show up.

Gingerly, she touched her forehead and felt the bruise there. Luckily that was the only injury she had sustained.

Rachel glanced at her watch. How long had she been out? And more importantly, where was Petrov now? As she mulled this over, she heard the wail of police sirens in the distance. No doubt the colonel, involved in criminal activities, didn't want to wait for the *politsiya* to explain a dead body. Thinking Rachel dead, he managed to free himself, grabbed Nikita and hurried away. In fact, he had probably anonymously called the police after making his escape.

Not wasting any more time, Rachel rushed out of the apartment and out of the building.

Chapter 42

St. Petersburg, Russia

Rachel West drove south on Ligovskiy Prospekt and an hour later was out of the city and into the outer suburbs. When she saw the signs for the small town of Strelna, she slowed the Lada and looked for the right cross street. Nikita had given her Petrov's home address, and Rachel figured the man was probably there.

Ten minutes later she drove by the walled estate, which was situated on a heavily wooded property. As she slowed near the imposing entrance, she noted the security cameras posted on either side of the closed gate.

Rachel wound her way along the lightly-trafficked rural road as she followed the wall for another half mile or so. When the wall turned inward, she knew she had reached the end of the property line. Pulling off the road, she found a sheltered area under a thicket of trees and parked the sedan. Scanning the deserted area, she turned off the car and climbed out.

After retrieving her backpack from the trunk, she trudged through the trees to get a closer look at the estate's wall. It was well over six feet high, rustic-looking, and built with natural stones. Not spotting any cameras, she approached it, and after strapping on her backpack, she began climbing, using the jutting stones for support.

Reaching the top of the wall, she peered over the edge. All she saw was vegetation – more woods with heavy underbrush. No guards were in sight. She maneuvered herself over the top and dropped to the other side. Quickly, she pulled the pistol from a pocket and advanced.

As she made her way through the vegetation, the clothes she was wearing, jeans and a black windbreaker, became stained from the thicket. Her long blonde hair was tucked under a black watch cap.

Trudging through the grove, she listened for human sounds but all she heard was the chirping of crickets, the rustling of leaves, and the call of birds. The piney scent of the woods filled her lungs. And although the temperature was in the mid-sixties Fahrenheit, typical for a Russian afternoon in August, she began to perspire from the exertion.

The woods thinned out, and after another hundred yards she saw the estate in the distance. Pulling a pair of binoculars from her backpack, she scanned the scene. The *dacha* was a three-story estate with a high portico supported by circular columns. A semicircular driveway, empty of cars, fronted the large home. She spotted two men patrolling the grounds, both armed with AK-47 assault rifles.

Rachel glanced at her watch. It was five p.m., and if the empty driveway was any indication, Petrov was not at home. After weighing her options, she decided to remain in the sheltered thicket, keep an eye on the house, and wait until nightfall to make her move.

Sitting behind an outcropping of rocks, she trained the binos on the house and waited.

Her thoughts wandered, at first to the Prism investigation, then to more personal matters – her ailing mother and lastly to the man in her life, Brad. It had been weeks since they'd seen each other and worse yet, their last time together had ended badly.

Pangs of regret filled her as she thought about all the things she'd done wrong in their relationship. True, not everything had been her fault, but her constant travel and the demands of her job were significant. It was the one constant that had always made her love life difficult. She couldn't blame Brad for his anger. *But can I really give up my job?* she wondered.

Pushing those thoughts aside, she focused on her surveillance.

Three hours later she was rewarded.

A large Mercedes sedan pulled into the driveway in front of the estate. Ivan Petrov, along with two other men who appeared to be bodyguards, climbed out of the car and went into the home.

So far she had seen four guards – it was clear Petrov had beefed up his security since she had seen him last. Getting in the house and overpowering them was not going to be easy, not easy at all.

***

The St. Petersburg area was living up its reputation of 'White Nights'. Although it was midnight, total darkness had not yet settled over the estate grounds. Figuring it was the best she was going to get, Rachel began approaching the large home, using the gardens and sculpted bushes for cover. As she scurried from one set of shrubs to another, she kept a close eye for the two guards who roamed the property.

Fifty yards from the house she spotted one of the guards, his AK-47 slung over his shoulder. He was no more than twenty feet in front of her. She watched as the man stopped patrolling and lit up a cigarette. Seeing an opening, she pulled her switchblade from a pocket, flicked it open, and crept towards him, keeping to his back.

Sprinting the last five feet, she grabbed him around the shoulders and slashed the blade across his throat. He struggled briefly before collapsing to the ground.

After scanning the grounds for the other guard, she wiped off the bloody knife.

Then Rachel advanced again, creeping forward. When she reached an elaborate garden, she stopped and crouched behind a tall shrub. Scanning the scene, she realized that beyond the garden the vegetation thinned out. The areas around the home itself didn't provide any cover – she'd have to race the last twenty feet or so and hope she wouldn't be spotted.

But she still didn't want to use her pistol, hoping to maintain the element of surprise as long as possible. Putting away the knife, she took the collapsible metal baton out of the backpack and expanded it. After one last look around, she dashed forward.

But just then the second guard came around a corner of the house and her heart started pounding. Obviously spotting her, he began to unsling his assault rifle.

She sprinted right for him, and as he leveled the weapon at her, she ducked and swung the baton across his knees.

The man groaned and fired off a wild shot. She slashed him again, this time striking his face. She heard the sound of cartilage breaking and he staggered back. Hitting him with the baton a third time, this time in the solar plexus, he finally went down to the ground.

Rachel wacked him on the head and his prone body sagged.

Wasting no time, she picked up the AK-47 and ran the last few feet to the side of the house and hugged the wall. The element of surprise was long gone, she knew – the shot had seen to that.

And as if on cue, the outdoor floodlights came on clearly illuminating the property. She only had seconds before the rest of the guards found her.

Training the assault rifle in front of her, she sprinted to the rear of the house, and once there, looked for a back door.

Spotting the double doors to her right, she dashed toward them. After crossing the flagstone patio, she slowed and fired off a burst of shots at the closed doors.

The ornate wood entrance shattered, splinters flying everywhere. She fired another burst from the powerful AK and the door almost disintegrated.

Rachel crept inside, crouching behind a heavy wooden table. She was in a dining area, and could see into the kitchen just beyond. Although it was dim in this room, lights were on in the kitchen and an adjacent corridor. Although her ears were ringing from the AKs deafening sound, she could still hear shouting from inside the home.

She gasped for breath, a flash of fear forming in her gut. *How many guards were left? No way to know.*

Just then a bulky man pointing a handgun stepped into the kitchen. She fired, but she must have missed because immediately there was return fire. Several shots whizzed over her head, thudding into a nearby wall.

Rachel pressed the trigger again, but nothing happened. With a sinking feeling she realized the rifle had jammed; she dropped the weapon and pulled the Makarov from her pocket.

Training the pistol in front of her with both hands, she remained where she was, hiding behind the table in the dim dining room.

Suddenly the lights flicked on in the room and the guard burst in, firing his weapon. She returned fire and the man went down. But at the same time she felt a burning pain in her shoulder and knew one of his rounds had nicked her. Ignoring the seeping blood, she advanced slowly, and after insuring the guard was dead, crept into the kitchen. It was deserted, but she still heard shouts from other parts of the house.

Figuring Petrov was hiding on one of the upper floors, she carefully made her way through a long corridor. Passing a vacant study and a lavish living room, she stopped at the bottom of an ornate staircase, and using the banister for cover, glanced up. No one was visible, but she heard several hushed voices, at least two men and a woman.

Spotting the light switches on the nearby wall, she went over and flicked them off, sending the hallway and the staircase into shadows. At least they'd have a tougher time spotting her, she thought. She gritted her teeth as pain from her shoulder wound coursed through her.

Rachel began climbing the wide staircase. When she reached the top steps, she crouched. The corridor led both ways, to multiple bedrooms she assumed. She strained to hear more voices, but everything was quiet now. And the hallway was brightly lit – she'd be a sitting duck as soon as she stepped into it.

She needed a distraction, something to throw them off. *But what?* She had no smoke grenades, or flash-bangs, items typically carried by SWAT or CIA teams. She'd have to improvise.

Sorting through a couple of ideas, she selected one, went downstairs and back to the kitchen. There she found what she was looking for – dish towels, matches, and three bottles of vodka. Uncapping the bottles, she stuffed the towels into the necks and went back to the staircase. She climbed up, stopping several rungs from the top landing.

Using the matches, she lit one of the improvised Molotov cocktails and rolled it into the corridor to the right, as hard as she could. She heard glass breaking. Lighting the second bottle, she tossed it left. It also shattered.

Instantly a man's voice spoke from the right corridor; she peeked in that direction. A barrel-chested man holding an assault rifle was in an open doorway, tamping down the flaming carpet with his feet.

Rachel fired off two rounds and the guard staggered back and collapsed. Wasting no time, she raced to the doorway and crouching to one side of it, lit the third Molotov cocktail and tossed it in the room.

Shots rang out from the bedroom, and she hugged the wall as the rounds pockmarked the other end of the corridor.

She heard a woman's shrill voice from the room, and then a male response telling her to shut up. Smoke was now trailing out of the room, and sensing an opening, she poked her head around the doorjamb. Spotting the bedroom's overhead light, she shot it out. As soon as the room went dark, she couched and then rolled herself inside, the flames burning her pants in the process.

Hiding behind a dresser, she extinguished the smoldering jeans as she listened.

Smoke was filling the room and the woman's voice had turned into screams. Taking a quick look over the dresser, she couldn't see much in the dimness, but realized no one was in the large bedroom. From the nearness of the shouts, she presumed Petrov and the woman were hiding in the adjoining bathroom. That door was closed, but Rachel knew they couldn't stay in there forever, especially with a hysterical woman inside.

Training the pistol over the dresser, she waited.

Just then the bathroom door flung open and a woman in sleepwear rushed out. It wasn't Nikita, but a much older, unattractive woman. Rachel heard Petrov's voice now, calling to her from the bathroom.

The woman, coughing, stumbled around the dim bedroom and headed to the room's open door. Rachel ignored her as she left the room. She stayed hiding behind the dresser, pointing the Makarov at the bathroom. She needed Petrov alive – she had to interrogate him.

But she sensed the colonel was making his stand in the bathroom and from the looks of it, that room wasn't on fire. And she knew she couldn't wait him out this time – parts of the bedroom were already aflame; in minutes she'd have to flee herself.

"Give yourself up, Colonel!" Rachel shouted. "Or I'll kill your wife."

"Go ahead!" Petrov replied. "Kill the bitch. You'll do me a favor!"

"Damn," Rachel muttered, trying to figure a way to get to Petrov.

Just then a column of flames rose from the carpet in front of the open bathroom door and trailed inside the room. She heard coughing, and a moment later Petrov, wearing a bathrobe and holding a pistol, rushed out. He stumbled along, heading for the bedroom door.

She fired a round at his upraised pistol, and the gun flew off as the man yelled and grabbed his bleeding hand with the other.

"Stop right there, Petrov! Or this time I aim for your head."

The man froze, his gaze peering through the smoke.

Standing, Rachel crossed the room and trained the gun on him. "On your knees, Colonel! And hold your hands behind your back!"

The man complied and she took off her belt and tied his hands together.

The blaze in the room had increased and the smoke intensified, the acrid smell filling her lungs. Coughing, she realized they had to get out of there.

She prodded him with the gun. "Get up and walk forward. One false move and you're dead."

Petrov did so, and with her following behind, they went into the corridor and down the stairs. There was less smoke in the entry foyer, but she knew the whole house would be in flames soon. *Where the hell is Petrov's wife?* she wondered. The front door was wide open, so it was a good bet the woman had run out that way. *Are there more guards outside?*

She prodded the colonel with the gun again. "We're going out the front. Move!"

The two went outside, the fresh air a welcome change. She scanned the scene, saw no other guards on the grounds.

The Mercedes sedan was gone from the driveway – the wife must have taken it. Rachel realized they had to get away from the property soon – the woman had probably called the *politsiya* by now.

Noticing the attached four-car garage to the left of the house, she pointed and said, "That way, Colonel." Luckily the fire had not spread to the garage.

"I'm bleeding," the man said, coughing.

"Shut up and keep walking!"

There was a side door leading to the garage. Finding the door locked, she fired off one round, cracking open the mechanism. Kicking in the door, she glanced inside and flicked on a light. Three vehicles were in the garage – a Range Rover, a low-slung Porsche roadster, and a cargo van.

"Where are the keys to the Range Rover, Petrov?"

The man nodded toward the wall. "In that cabinet, over there."

Going over, she pried open the locked cabinet and saw a row of keys hanging on hooks. She selected one and pocketed it. Then she opened the back seat door of the Rover and said, "Get in, Petrov."

"I'm going to bleed to death!"

Her own shoulder was still bleeding, the pain acute – she had no sympathy for the Russian. "Get in the fucking car!"

He climbed in and she strapped the seat belt around him. With his hands tied behind his back and being belted in, it would be difficult for him to get away now. Slamming the door shut, she went around the car and got in the front. Starting up the vehicle, she hit the door remote and one of the bay doors creaked open.

She put the Range Rover in reverse and exited the garage.

A minute later they were away from the property and on the rural two-lane road.

As the estate receded in the rear-view mirror, her thoughts churned. *What the hell do I do now?* She had to interrogate him. *But where?* Usually she would have had a back-up team and a safe-house to use. But this time she was all on her own, and she was in an unfamiliar area. To make matters worse, she was injured.

But the most important thing was to interrogate the colonel about Prism. Before police arrived, or before the man died.

Spotting a sheltered, wooded area to her right, she made a hasty decision. Pulling off the road, she bounced over rocks and shrubs until the vehicle was under the trees and well away from the road.

She turned off the Range Rover, got out, and gun in hand, climbed in the back seat.

Petrov stared at her, hatred in his eyes.

"Tell me about Prism, Colonel."

He shrugged. "I told you about it before."

"Not all of it. You're holding back."

"*Nyet.* I told you, West. It's my operation. My plan was to buy the tech companies and sell them later at a profit."

"Bullshit. There's other people involved. And it's not just buying the companies for a profit – this is a lot bigger than that. Now talk!"

"I've told you everything, West."

She whacked the pistol across his already bent nose, and he flinched, screaming out in pain. It was the second time she had broken his nose in the last few days. Blood spurted from his nostrils, but he said nothing.

"We can do this all day, Petrov."

She struck him again and he howled; but once he recovered, he stayed mute. He was a tough customer, she realized. Last time she questioned him Rachel had Nikita to bargain with – but now it was just him, and he wasn't budging.

Pulling the switchblade from her pocket, she flicked it open. The sharp blade glinted in the early morning light.

For the first time, his eyes showed fear. "What are you going to do with that, West?"

"You'll see," she replied with a grin. Reaching over, she sliced open the bathrobe, then began cutting off his pajama pants. He tried squirming away, but the seat-shoulder belt held him firm.

With his genitals exposed, the man didn't seem so confident. "What are you going to do, you crazy woman?"

"I think you know."

"No, please! Not that!"

Her voice dropped to a whisper. "Tell me what I want to know and you can keep your cock intact." She moved the knife so it was almost touching his genitals. "You want to talk now?"

"*Da! Da!*"

"Good." She pulled the blade away a few inches. "Your American partner. Who is he?"

"His name is John Smith."

She let out a cold laugh. "You expect me to believe that?"

"It's true! His name is John Smith."

She thrust the knife forward and the sharp blade touched his genitals, almost cutting the skin. He screamed and flinched away from her.

"It's true, West! That's his name!"

She realized he had to be telling the truth. "Where does he live?"

"I don't know."

"Don't bullshit me, Petrov!"

"It's true! We always met in Helsinki, or talked on the phone. He lives in the U.S., but I don't know where."

"What's Prism's plan? Why are you buying all the tech companies?"

Just then she heard police sirens in the distance and she knew she was running out of time.

"They'll find us very soon," Petrov said, his confidence returning.

"How do you figure that? We're not near your house."

"This vehicle has GPS tracking – I'm sure my wife told the police – they'll be here in a matter of minutes."

"Damn," she muttered. *What the hell do I do now?* She'd never be able to get away on foot, with Petrov in tow.

Knowing she only had one option, she climbed out of the car and began running over the rough terrain at full speed. She had to get back to her Lada and take off before the *politsiya* located her. After sprinting through the forest, she went across a clearing, then darted into more woods, the branches tearing at her clothes. She kept well away from the road, instead crossing the rural countryside using the dense vegetation as cover.

Ignoring the pain in her shoulder, she kept moving for half an hour more until she finally found the sheltered area where she'd hidden her car.

Exhausted, sweating, and gasping for breath, she got in and listened for the sound of sirens. But all she heard was the rustling of leaves.

Starting up the Lada, she sped away.

Chapter 43

Glacier County, Montana

John Smith was in his underground study, logging off his computer. He had just sold off his large positions of oil company stocks at a huge profit. The Texas power outage was still ongoing, but it didn't matter to him now. The American had made his money and that's all that mattered. He knew the utility company authorities would restore electricity to the area in a matter of days, a week at the most. Although the malware programs Prism had inserted were very sophisticated, he knew that with enough time any programming could be overridden.

Turning off the multiple TV screens mounted on the wall, he stood and was about to leave the room when one of the phones on his desk rang. It was the one he used exclusively to speak with Ivan Petrov. He sat back down and picked up the receiver.

"Yes?"

"It's Petrov, sir."

"I know who it is."

"I've run into some complications, sir."

Smith didn't like the sound of that. "What kind of complications?"

"The CIA agent, West, found out about me."

"How in hell did *that* happen? You told me she was dead."

"Yes, sir, that's what I thought too."

Smith had known for weeks West was still alive, and that Petrov had lied to him about it. That one lie made Smith realize he could never trust the Russian again. "You say she found you? Where, in St. Petersburg?"

"Yes, sir – she knew where I lived, came to my house, held my wife and I hostage."

Bile rushed up the American's throat. This was serious – extremely serious. "She found out about our plans?"

"No, I didn't tell her."

"Did you tell her about me, you idiot?"

"Of course not, sir."

He sensed the Russian was lying to him again, but decided not say it. "Tell me what happened. In detail! I want to know everything, Petrov."

"Yes, sir."

The Russian gave Smith a ten minute account of his two meetings with West, and as he listened he tried to figure a way to contain the situation.

When he was done recounting the events, Petrov said, "I need to get out of St. Petersburg – it's not safe for me here."

Smith was quiet a moment, then in a flash it came to him. "I agree, Ivan. You need to get out of there, along with your computer programmer, Lechenko, and all his equipment. I'll send my jet. It'll pick you up. You'll come here, to my home."

"Come to the U.S.?" The Russian sounded skeptical.

"Yes, Ivan. You'll be very safe here. My house is a fortress."

"I don't know, sir. I was thinking about Moscow or another city in Russia ... but the U.S. ... I just don't know ...."

Smith's voice turned hard. "It's your only choice, if you want your cut of the profits."

After a minute, Petrov answered. "Fine. I'll go. But I need to bring someone with me in addition to Lechenko."

"Your wife?"

"No, not her. My mistress, Nikita."

"That's fine, Ivan. Just make sure the programmer is with you. He's the key."

"Yes, sir. When can your plane be here?"

"My pilot will be airborne in an hour."

"Thank you, Mr. Smith."

"Don't worry, Ivan. Everything will be fine." The American hung up the phone, a wide smile lighting up his face.

Chapter 44

Langley, Virginia

Rachel West rubbed her temple, trying to push away the growing headache.

"Are you okay?" Alex Miller asked.

Rachel stopped what she was doing and leaned forward in the chair. "I'm fine – just jet-lagged from the flight from Russia."

The two people were sitting in Miller's office. Outside it was a bright, clear day. Sunlight streamed in from the room's only window.

"Okay, Rachel. But right after you brief me, you're going to the medical facility downstairs. I want your shoulder injury fully checked out."

"And deal with that bitchy nurse again? Forget it."

"I insist," he said, a sharp tone in his voice. "I need you at 100%. If you don't get medical care and some rest, I'm pulling you off this assignment."

She shrugged. "Whatever you say. Let me fill you in on the last couple of days in St. Petersburg. After I fled Petrov's estate, I went to his mistress's condo. I hoped to use her as leverage again. But Nikita wasn't there, and her clothes were gone from the apartment – Petrov must have hid her at some other location. After that I spent a couple of days trying to locate Petrov again, with no luck. I went back to his house, but it was in ruins. Someone had torched it. The home was totally charred, and it looked like a sophisticated accelerant was used. Petrov probably did it himself – my Molotov cocktails couldn't have done that much damage."

"Were you able to get a lead on where he went?"

"No, Alex – there was no trace of him – my gut tells me he left the city; he may not even be in Russia."

"That's bad news – he's one of the architects of Prism."

She nodded. "I agree. But I think the American he told me about is a bigger fish – according to Petrov, this John Smith is the key player. He's the one that came up with the plan and the money to set it up. Have you been able to come up with anything on Smith?"

"You know how many John Smiths there are in the U.S., Rachel?"

"How many?"

"45,803."

"Ouch."

"That's what I said too," he replied. "You're sure that was the man's real name?"

"Don't worry, Alex; that was his name. When I was interrogating Petrov, I had him with his pants down – literally."

Miller raised a hand. "Spare me the details."

Rachel chuckled. "Whatever you say. It's a shame the Russian cops were headed our way. I would have had him singing choir chants in another five minutes."

"As soon as you called me from Russia and told me about this John Smith, I got our tech guys involved. They're working around the clock trying to find him. It'll take some time, but I'm hopeful they can do it."

"How are things in Texas, Alex?"

"The electric grid is back up. The power in the affected areas has been restored, but it was down for almost two weeks – the economic impact is significant."

"At least that problem is over. Have there been any other issues like that?"

He shook his head. "No. But I think Prism will be striking again. And soon."

Rachel felt a knot in her stomach. She felt guilty for not learning more from the Russian. She needed to get back in the field, actively looking for Smith. But they didn't have much to go on. "I agree. I got the sense from Petrov that Prism was just beginning its operation."

Miller pointed to his closed office door. "Okay. Out of here. I want you downstairs in the medical facilities."

She was about to protest, but he gave her a hard stare.

"Now, Rachel."

***

Rachel spent the next two days recuperating at the Factory clinic, suffering the bad food and the bitchy attitude of the nurse from hell. But the doctor on staff was first rate, and at the end of that time her shoulder was healed enough that he released her for light duty. That meant she couldn't return to the field, but at least could work at her office cubicle, doing paperwork.

During the downtime she tried to reconnect with Brad, but he didn't return her phone calls, a clear sign things were even worse than she had suspected.

Rachel also got a chance to visit her mother at the nursing home, and was pleased that her frail condition had improved.

Also on a positive note, Rachel learned how Matt Turner was doing. Her fellow agent had recovered from the injuries he'd suffered in Finland, and was now back on full duty.

Chapter 45

Glacier County, Montana

The Boeing 767 is a wide-body commercial jet with a flying range of 6, 385 miles and a seating capacity of up to 375 people. Years ago John Smith had purchased one and had it modified to his specifications. The passenger seats had all been removed and replaced with luxurious living accommodations for himself and a small group of his close associates. Well-appointed living areas, lounges, and bedrooms had replaced the crowded spaces and narrow aisles of a regular commercial jet.

Ivan Illych Petrov was in the airplane now, as it made its final landing approach over Smith's vast property.

Petrov had been in the plane many times when Smith had visited Finland. In fact, the Prism meetings had always taken place inside the plane, as it sat parked on the runway of Petrov's home in Finland. The American, an agoraphobic, never wanted to be far away from familiar surroundings.

Petrov was in one of the jet's lounges now, looking out a window at the majestic view below. Beyond the long runway beneath them, the vast property of rolling countryside stretched for miles, eventually leading to a pine forest that culminated in mountain ranges.

The Russian had never been to Smith's home. In fact, he never knew where the man lived. Petrov was extremely apprehensive about this trip. Was it the fear of the unknown, or something more? He wasn't sure. He hadn't wanted to leave Russia, but realized he had no choice. But once the operation was complete and he'd collected his share of the profits, he planned on leaving Smith's home and moving someplace warm, like the Caribbean, where he and Nikita could enjoy all the money he'd made.

Nikita was sitting next him now, a worried look on her face. She'd been fidgety the whole long flight over, obviously nervous about their abrupt move overseas. But he knew that once they were in the Caymans, or Antigua, or Jamaica, living in luxurious comfort sipping drinks by a pool, she'd be happy.

As he turned his gaze from Nikita back to the view outside, his mind wandered over the last few hectic days. It had taken his programmer, Andrei Lechenko, days to pack up all of his computer equipment and get it ready for the move. The tech geek was in another part of the plane right now, no doubt working on some new programming code. Unlike Petrov and Nikita, who were reluctant to go to America, Lechenko was thrilled. The young man was looking forward to resettling in the U.S., under a new name of course, and being part of the 'American dream'. It was a naive idea, Petrov knew. Dreams were fulfilled with cold hard cash, and once he had his, he'd be done with the quirky programmer and with John Smith.

Petrov felt the airplane pitch as the runway loomed larger. He heard the groan of gears as the flaps lowered and knew they'd be on the ground soon.

His apprehension intensified, and turning to Nikita, noticed she also was more unsettled the closer they were to landing. Reaching over, he held one of her hands, smiling with a confidence that was all for show. Then he turned back to the window, the feeling of impending doom growing by the second.

***

"Welcome to my home," John Smith said to the three people in front of him. They were in the den of Smith's palatial home. He spoke in English because he knew his new guests were fluent in the language. He hadn't offered to shake their hands, but had simply stood when they had been escorted into the room by one of his aides.

Smith motioned to the chairs in front of his massive desk. "Please have a seat." As Petrov, Lechenko, and the young woman sat, he studied the trio. He had met the two men many times before in Finland, but was not acquainted with Petrov's mistress. Nikita was a striking young woman, beautiful and exotic. It was clear why the Russian had brought her along.

"How was the flight over?" the American asked.

"Long," replied Petrov. "But your plane is incredible – we felt like we were in an exclusive hotel."

Smith smiled. "It's more than adequate for my needs. Before we get down to business, Ivan, I wanted to assure Andrei and Nikita that my staff has been working nonstop since you decided to come here, getting suites ready for you. We've spared no expense." He turned to Nikita. "I know you're far from home and in a different environment here, but you'll have every luxury at your fingertips. My whole staff is committed to making your stay as comfortable as possible."

Nikita nodded, but by the look on her face, it was clear she was taken aback by Smith's deformed appearance. Over time, he knew, she'd get used to his looks. Everyone did.

Then the American turned to Lechenko. "For you, Andrei, we've converted a whole floor of space where you can set up all of your computer equipment. And if you need anything, anything at all, please come to me personally and I'll take care of it."

The programmer beamed. "Thank you, Mr. Smith. I'm looking forward to working here."

"Excellent, Andrei." The American pressed a button on his desk and looked over at Petrov. "My aide will be in shortly. He'll show Nikita and Andrei to their rooms, so we can have a chance to talk."

"Of course," Petrov replied.

A moment later the aide came in the room and escorted the two people out. When the door closed behind them, Smith turned to the Russian. "I know a lot has happened over the last week, but I need to make sure everything is still on schedule." The genial tone Smith had used welcoming the group was gone now.

"Yes, Mr. Smith. Lechenko has done all the prep work. We can pull the trigger once his equipment is set up here."

Smith gave him a hard look. "You're sure?"

"Yes, sir."

"Okay. I want to proceed as soon as possible." The American settled back in his executive chair. "From the looks of it, it appears Lechenko will be very happy here."

"That's correct. He's wanted to visit the U.S. for a long time; has an appetite for all things American."

Smith smiled inwardly. "That's good to know. How about you, Ivan? You don't seem yourself."

"It's a big change, one I didn't expect to make."

"Life is like that, throwing us curves. Don't worry, once Lechenko is settled and the operation continues on schedule, you'll get your money."

"Thank you, sir."

"Turning to a more pressing matter, Ivan, I'm still concerned about this CIA operative, Rachel West. I'm amazed she found you."

Petrov shook his head and his cheeks flushed, obviously embarrassed by the situation. "Yes, sir. I couldn't believe it either."

"Do you know where she is now?"

"No idea, Mr. Smith."

The American steepled his fingers on the desk. "She's no longer your concern. I have a source at Central Intelligence. I'll locate her and deal with her appropriately."

"Yes, sir,"

Smith stood up abruptly. "That will be all for now, Ivan."

Chapter 46

Langley, Virginia

Rachel West was in her cubicle at the Factory doing an Internet search, when a *Breaking News* notice scrawled along the top of her laptop's screen.

She clicked on the story and her heart almost stopped. The Associated Press was reporting that a bomb had just gone off in the White House, and that the President of the U.S., along with key members of his staff had been killed.

Quickly reading the story, she clicked on the CBS News website, saw they were confirming the account. The shock of the horrific event made her nauseous, and she took a gulp from the can of Coke on her desk. *How could this happen?* she wondered. *Especially with all the security in D.C., and in particular at the White House.* Being in the CIA, she was fully aware of the sophisticated security measures used by the Secret Service.

As the shocking news spread around the open office space she shared with other operatives, the noise level rose from a low-level hum to a crescendo of voices as the other agents made phone calls to family and other workers.

But Rachel stayed glued to her computer, clicking from one news source to the next, trying to find more details. She went to the CNBC News website, saw that the U.S. stock market had plummeted. The Dow Jones Average of stocks had suffered a thousand point drop because of the tragic news. She switched to the Wall Street Journal site and saw the same thing there.

Swallowing more Coke, she continued reading the growing number of stories, some with conflicting accounts about the deadly explosion.

Chapter 47

Glacier County, Montana

John Smith was alone in the underground study of his estate, a wicked grin on his face. Prism's plan had worked perfectly. He had just made a five hundred million dollar profit on his stock trades in the last hour. Using a technique stock traders called short-selling, Smith had bet against the market right before the shocking news broke. He had expected the DOW Average to drop suddenly, and that's exactly what had happened.

With a self-satisfied smile, he began to turn off his array of video monitors. The stock market was already recovering, but it didn't matter to him now. He had made his money.

Lechenko is a genius, Smith thought. *I'll pay him an extra bonus.*

After turning off his computer, Smith stood and left the room. He wanted to celebrate. Maybe even, have sex with his wife.

Chapter 48

Langley, Virginia

"How in hell could this happen?" Rachel West asked, as she burst into Alex Miller's office.

Miller glanced up from his computer monitor. "Close the door behind you, Rachel."

The agent did so, then sat in one of the chairs fronting her boss's desk.

"I think Prism is behind this," Miller said.

"I figured that, Alex. But how could they hack into the websites of the Associated Press, CBS, CNN, Fox News, the Wall Street Journal, and a bunch of other sites and plant a fake story about a White House bombing?"

"It's incredibly difficult to do, especially when they were all hacked at the same time."

Rachel nodded, still upset about the event. She took a deep breath to calm down. "It's been two hours since the fake story broke, and the news sites are back to normal, all of them reporting the President and his staff are fine. But the short term panic it caused ...."

"That was the point, I think," Miller said, tapping the computer screen on his desk. The monitor showed the Wall Street Journal's website. "The stock market's is recovering now, but it took a huge hit. This event could have been a way to profit from the panic."

Rachel thought about this a moment. "You think this is connected to the electric grid going down in Texas a few weeks back, and the Internet blackout in Europe a month ago?"

"I do, Rachel. The three events are all computer related. And we know Prism has been actively purchasing tech companies, many of them in the computer router business. Routers are used to connect computer networks together. I'm convinced all of this is part of their plan."

Rachel leaned forward in her chair, an uneasy feeling settling over her. "Any progress on finding the right John Smith?"

"We're still running through the thousands of names, but so far we haven't located any possible suspects."

Rachel frowned. "So Prism could repeat what they did today, or hit the U.S. in some other way, at anytime ...."

"I'm afraid so," Miller said, his voice no more than a whisper.

Chapter 49

Langley, Virginia

Rachel West parked her Kawasaki in the underground lot of her apartment building and turned off the motorcycle. Climbing off, she removed her helmet, unclipped her duffel from the bike and made her way up to her floor. Letting herself into the apartment soon after, she did a quick security sweep, and headed to the kitchen.

Rachel was exhausted and in a sour mood from all the fifteen-hour days at the office, with nothing to show for it. They were no closer to finding Smith than when she'd returned from Russia.

She prepared a simple dinner of scrambled eggs, ham, and toast, and after washing it down with iced tea, went to the bathroom. Stripping off her clothes, she checked the assorted bruises on her body and the wound on her shoulder, which was mostly healed. *That's good*, she thought. She was confident she'd be able to talk the doc into clearing her for full duty in a matter of days. She was eager to get back in the field.

After showering and putting on night clothes, Rachel went to her bedroom. Placing the Glock on her bedside table, she lay down on her bed and was asleep in minutes.

***

A scraping noise woke Rachel hours later.

Immediately she grabbed the pistol and listened for the sound again. But she heard nothing. *Had she been dreaming?* Her sleep had been fitful and full of nightmares.

Sitting up, she scanned the dimly-lit bedroom, saw no one was there. The glowing clock digits showed the time: 3:22 a.m. She waited a moment for her eyes to adjust to the darkness.

After racking the slide on the Glock, she padded out of the bedroom, peered around the door jamb. The hallway was empty, as was the kitchen. Keeping the lights off, she crept out of the room, hugging the wall as she approached the dim living room.

In a crouch, she stepped into the room and peered over the sofa. Holding the gun in front of her, she swept the room, saw nothing.

Then she heard it – receding footfalls coming from the other side of the closed front door. She approached the entrance, squatted to one side of it, and unlocked the deadbolt. Opening the door, she peered into the brightly-lit corridor. It was empty.

Then she studied the door's lock plate. There were several scratches there that hadn't been there before. Someone had tried to pick the lock, she was sure.

Reclosing the door, she went to her bedroom and dressed quickly. Then she searched the apartment building's corridor, the elevators, lobby, and the underground lot. But she found nothing suspicious – whoever had been there was long gone.

Chapter 50

Glacier County, Montana

John Smith was in a bare, concrete walled room that resembled a bunker. It was in an underground part in his estate. He didn't use the room often, only when he didn't want to be disturbed by his staff. Smith had it constructed years ago, to very detailed specifications. Like all the rooms in his home, it was soundproof and only purified air was piped in, but it lacked any of the luxury of the other spaces. However, this room was unique in other ways. Ways the man had intended to use on special occasions. Occasions like today.

There was a knock at the metal door and Smith went to it and opened it. Ivan Petrov stood there, and the American waved him in. "Come in, Ivan, have a seat."

"Thank you, Mr. Smith," the Russian said.

They sat down in opposite metal chairs, the only furniture in the room. Petrov glanced suspiciously around the bare room and said, "What is this place?"

Smith smiled, wanting to put the man at ease. "I use this room for very private conversations. When I want to be guaranteed I can't be eavesdropped by my staff. I only meet people here that I absolutely trust." He paused a moment. "I want to compliment you, Ivan. Lechenko has done excellent work. The operation is going extremely well." Smith smiled again. "He's an exceptional programmer. You did a masterful job finding him."

"Thank you, sir." Petrov returned the smile, obviously pleased by the rare compliment.

Smith leaned forward in his chair. "Lechenko has settled nicely into his new environment. He likes the computer lab we built for him, and appears comfortable in his new living quarters."

"I agree, Mr. Smith. He's very happy here."

"Excellent. That's very important to me. I have big plans for him."

"Yes, sir."

"How about your mistress? How is she adjusting to moving out of Russia?"

Petrov shrugged. "She's fine with it for now. I've assured her it's only temporary. Once the operation is complete, we'll be leaving your estate and moving somewhere else. Someplace warm, maybe the Caribbean."

"I gathered that's where you'd be going. You always did say you hated the harsh winters in your country."

The Russian nodded, but he appeared confused as to where the conversation was going.

Smith smiled. "Well, Ivan, there's a special reason why we're meeting here today. Now that Lechenko is here and settled in, and since Prism is going so well, I thought we'd change the timetable for your payout. I know you're eager to get your share of the profits. And since you've done such a superb job, I see no reason for you to wait any longer. How does that sound?"

Petrov grinned widely. "That's fantastic news. I really appreciate it. As will Nikita."

"I thought you'd agree." Smith pointed to the large metal suitcase that was sitting in a corner of the room. "So I came prepared. In there is what you so richly deserve. As we previously agreed, Bearer Bonds worth one billion U.S. dollars. Would you like it now, Ivan?"

"Of course, sir. The sooner the better."

Smith stood, walked over to the suitcase and stooping, opened the case. Quickly removing the Smith & Wesson .357 Magnum revolver that was in the case, he then turned and pointed the handgun at the other man's chest. The stainless-steel finish of the gun glinted from the fluorescent overhead lights.

"What? What is this?" Petrov uttered, shock on his face.

"I'm afraid I have no choice, Ivan. You know too much about me and the operation. There's no way I can let you live."

"But I've always been a loyal partner!" he screeched, as he stared down the barrel of the gun.

"You made mistakes, Ivan. Serious mistakes. You failed to kill that bitch, the CIA agent. And you've put me in jeopardy. I suspect she learned something about me when you were interrogated. I can't tolerate that."

"But! Please, I beg you –"

Smith fired three rounds, the earsplitting blasts echoing in the room.

Petrov's eyes went wide as he clutched his chest; he staggered and slumped to the concrete floor.

The American approached the body, and careful to avoid the pooling blood, put another bullet in the back of Petrov's head.

Then Smith calmly went to a control panel mounted on the wall. Flicking a switch, he heard a hiss as the gas fired incinerator started up. The large, specially-built furnace, located in an adjacent part of the underground bunker, would reach a temperature of 1,560 degrees Fahrenheit in a matter of minutes. More than enough heat to fully cremate Petrov's corpse. Only ashes would remain.

"From ashes to ashes," Smith uttered, then barked out a harsh laugh.

Chapter 51

Langley, Virginia

"You're sure someone tried to break into your apartment?" Alex Miller asked, as he tapped a pen on his desk.

"No doubt about it," Rachel West replied.

The two people were in Miller's office at the Factory. Weak sunlight streamed in from the room's window – it was a cloudy day.

Miller looked worried. "A random robbery attempt?"

"I don't think so. Somehow this is connected to Prism."

"You're probably right. The CIA mole, whoever he is, has access to our records. Finding out where you live wouldn't be difficult." Miller rubbed his jaw. "You need to watch your back. I'd like to assign you a 24/7 protective detail, but I don't have that kind of manpower available."

Rachel opened her jacket and patted her weapon, which was holstered on her hip. "Don't worry. I can take care of myself."

Miller nodded, but he still looked concerned. "I do have some good news for you, Rachel."

"You located the right John Smith?"

"Not that good, I'm afraid. I talked to our doctor, and he's cleared you for full field duty. He was reluctant at first, but based on the fact you are doing better, and that our staff is stretched thin, he relented. So, congrats. You won't be riding a desk any more."

"That's great." Her mood brightened immediately; she'd dreaded the prospect of being cooped up in the office any longer. Rachel had never understood how people could cope with spending eight or ten hours, doing the same thing, in the same office, day after day. To her it felt like a prison sentence.

Just then there was a knock at the door and it opened partway. Miller's assistant poked his head around the jamb. "Sir," the assistant said, "you need to turn on the news."

The door closed and Miller got up from his desk and turned on the flatscreen TV that was in a corner of the room.

What now? Rachel thought, as she apprehensively watched the screen come to life. The TV was tuned to CNN Headline News and a female reporter was sitting behind a desk.

"We're learning the details now," the blonde reporter said, "of a massive air traffic system outage in California. The FAA is telling us that the computer system that controls airport traffic is down in most of the state." The woman paused, looked off-screen a moment, then faced the camera again. "We've just learned that a mid-air collision has occurred over LAX, Los Angeles's largest airport. A Boeing 747 has crashed into an Airbus wide-body jet. We'll bring you video from the scene as soon as we have it." The reporter's face looked ashen. "Those are both large airplanes, with a combined carrying capacity of close to a thousand passengers – so the number of fatalities could be significant."

"Christ," Rachel whispered, a sick feeling settling in her gut.

"The FAA reports," the announcer continued, "that right now there are literally hundreds of planes circling over airports throughout California. If the air control system is not back online soon, the results could be catastrophic. The airport authorities have tried to activate the backup computer system, but that has also failed." She paused a moment. "We now have a video feed of the mid-air collision."

The screen changed from the reporter to a jerky motion image of a huge fireball against the backdrop of a blue sky. Plumes of smoke extended from the fireball, followed by a cascade of blazing fragments raining down on an airport tarmac. Rachel watched the burning debris as it struck airplanes parked on the tarmac and a nearby terminal building, setting off more fires. She turned away from the screen, sickened by the images.

"This is Prism's work," Rachel said, clenching her hands into fists.

Miller lowered the volume on the TV. "I agree. Their fingerprints are all over it. Another computer problem creating widespread havoc. But why this?"

"Somehow it all goes back to money, Alex. I'm sure Prism is profiting from this disaster in some way."

Miller nodded, a grim look on his face.

***

Rachel parked her Kawasaki in the front lot of the strip mall and turned off the motorcycle. Climbing off, she took off her helmet and strode into the small Chinese restaurant located at one end of the long building.

The restaurant didn't look like much, with its faded neon sign and chipped Formica tables. But the food was good and it was close to her apartment. She frequented the place when she didn't feel like cooking herself dinner, which was often, or when she didn't visit Brad, which nowadays was never. Not wanting to dwell on her sour relationship with him, she pushed the thought away and instead focused on the menu. The distinctive aroma of Asian spices filled the air, making her realize how hungry she was. She had been so preoccupied with the horror of the numerous airplane crashes that had taken place that day, that she'd hadn't eaten anything since breakfast. Luckily, the California air traffic control system was back up, but not before several thousand fatalities had occurred. Rachel was angry at Prism, but just as irritated at herself, for not being able to solve the case in time to prevent the deaths.

As usual, there were few diners at the tables since most of the restaurant's business was takeout. She had taken a booth that overlooked the parking lot. Through the front window she could see the rows of parked cars, her bike, and the avenue just beyond. It was nine in the evening and the streetlights were on, casting a bluish pall over the parking lot. Traffic on the avenue had thinned out, the commuter hour long over.

The waitress, a young Chinese woman, came and took her food order. Instead of her usual wine, Rachel ordered a Tsingtao beer.

The waitress brought the drink a moment later and the agent leaned back in the seat, stared at the night sky. Sipping the beer, her mind flashed back to the mid-air collisions.

During the day she had monitored the Internet for other news events, trying to ascertain the motive behind the computer system failures. The price of airline stocks had taken a huge hit, probably on the expectation of all the lawsuits. This confirmed her previous assumption that it was all about money. Prism was once again profiting from the catastrophe of others.

The waitress brought a heaping platter of Moo-shu-pork and a side order of fried rice. Glancing at the delicious looking food, Rachel ordered a second beer. Then she plowed into the steaming platter, savoring the various flavors. It was a good thing she had a fast metabolism, otherwise her poor eating habits would have kept her from maintaining a trim figure.

Later, satiated from the good food and tasty beer, she leaned back in the booth and drank strong black coffee.

She sensed the danger a split-second before she saw it. A small red laser dot appeared on her chest, and she recognized it instantly. Diving to the floor, she heard the shattering of glass as the window imploded from the first shot.

Her adrenaline pumping, she un-holstered the Glock and rolled left, then ducked under another table, just as more rounds pounded in, shredding the Formica and wood booth. As the splinters flew and the echoes reverberated in the small restaurant, she chanced a glance out the shattered window, trying to determine the location of the sniper.

From her vantage point she couldn't see anything.

She weighed her options – she could go out the front to find him, or out the back, then circle around the building and begin her pursuit. Knowing the sniper could be gone if she went out the back way, she crawled forward and squatted to the side of the glass front door. She gazed up at the two-story building across the street, figuring the perp was there on the roof. Still seeing no one, she quickly opened the door, jumped out, and rolled herself behind a parked Impala.

Peeking over the hood, she spotted something on the roofline. It was no more than a moving shadow, but she was certain it was the sniper.

Cautiously, she made her way toward the street, using the parked cars for cover. She waited for a van to drive past, then raced across the boulevard in a zigzag pattern, fully expecting to hear more shots. But there weren't any, and as soon as she reached the opposite side of the street, she hugged the building's wall to catch her breath.

By the faded signs on the structure's exterior, she realized the place was a shuttered clothing store. Spotting the front entrance, she approached it, and after firing one round at the lock, kicked in the door and rolled inside. Empty clothing racks filled the otherwise vacant room. It was dim and smelled musty, with cobwebs everywhere.

She squinted, trying to find a staircase. It was to her left and she sprinted over the dusty linoleum floor, reaching it a moment later.

Holding the pistol in front of her with both hands, she climbed up and reached the second floor. It too was vacant. She gazed around the dark room, looking for a way up to the roof. Spotting a narrower staircase just ahead, she raced over and made her way up. At the top landing there was a closed door. Approaching it from one side, she tried the knob, but unlike the front door, this one was not locked. Clearly, the sniper had gone up this way.

Taking a deep breath to calm her nerves, she opened the door and stepped out on the flat, tar-covered roof. Crouching, she swept the handgun as she peered into the darkness. She could make out the air-conditioner units, but nothing else. Her heart sank – the sniper was long gone.

By the ledge on the front part of the roof, she noticed a glint of metal reflecting from the moonlight. Cautiously, she made her way there and crouched down.

After another look around to insure she was alone on the roof, she took out a handkerchief and used it to pick up the spent shell casing. She studied it closely. It was a from a high-caliber rifle, and from its heft and quality she could tell it was first-rate. With a sick feeling she realized it was very similar to what black ops agents used. She had used rounds just like it.

Chapter 52

Langley, Virginia

Rachel West walked into Alex Miller's office and placed the cloth wrapped shell casing on his desk.

"What's this?" Miller asked, as he glanced up at her. The man looked tired, no doubt because it was midnight and he was still working.

"Somebody tried to kill me tonight."

His jaw dropped. "You're kidding, right?"

"I wish I were, but no," she replied. She didn't sit down, but rather began to pace the office. She was too wired to sit. "I was having dinner at my regular Chinese place, and a sniper took at least five shots at me." She pointed to the spent shell casing. "This was left on the roof of the building the sniper used. I spent two hours trying to locate him, with no luck."

Miller picked up the casing using the handkerchief and looked at it carefully. He let out a low whistle. "This is top quality, .308 caliber. Very similar to what we use at Central Intelligence."

"I thought the same thing," she said. "The sniper was a pro, no doubt about it. He must have followed me, but I never noticed him." She stopped pacing. "After the shooting, he must have seen me coming his way and fled. Otherwise he would have cleaned up all his brass. I was lucky to get this one."

"I'll get our lab guys working on it tonight. If there's any trace evidence on it, we'll find it."

Rachel slumped on one of the visitor chairs that fronted the desk. She was exhausted and still edgy about tonight. "That's good, Alex. Maybe this will get us closer to finding John Smith."

"I hope so. But in the meantime, I want you wearing body armor from now on, 24/7."

She frowned, not looking forward to the prospect of wearing a bullet-proof vest. "It's hot and uncomfortable, but I guess you're right."

Relief crossed his face. "I know you hate it, but it's for your own good." He paused a moment as if in thought. "In light of everything that's happened, Rachel, I'm going to assign Matt Turner to partner with you, effectively immediately."

Jumping off the chair, she groused, "I don't need a bodyguard!"

"He's a good agent. And I can't afford to lose you now. We've got to find this shadowy Smith, and you're my best chance to locate him."

She was about to protest again, but saw the glare on Miller's face. His mind was made up. "Okay. I guess I have to live with it." Then she planted both hands flat on his desk. "But, I'm the lead agent."

His glare melted, replaced with a slight grin. "Sometimes I get the impression you think you're my boss and not the other way around."

Rachel smiled. "That's not true. I've never disobeyed a direct command." She paused a moment. "Well, maybe a few times, but it was unavoidable."

"All right, you can be the lead agent." He pointed to his office door. "Now get out of here. I've got work to do."

She gave him a mock salute. "You got it, boss."

"And put on the body armor!"

"Yes, sir!"

Chapter 53

Glacier County, Montana

John Smith was in the study of his home, feeding the exotic fish in the large aquarium he kept there. He loved the bright colors and odd physical characteristics of the fish. In fact he selected the types to stock in the tank by their physical traits – the more unusual the shape, the better he liked them. It was comforting to him that other living things were deformed, much like himself.

Having completed his daily chore, he stood back and admired the aquarium, which practically covered one wall of the massive room. He loved to stare at the tropical serenity of the fish as they swam languidly in the aquamarine blue water. It was a welcome change from the rapid-fire stock trading that occupied much of his time.

There was a knock at the door of his study. Looking at his watch, he knew who it was. Turning away from the aquarium, he went to the door and opened it. Two people stood there – computer programmer Andrei Lechenko and Petrov's mistress, Nikita Ivanova.

Greeting his two guests, Smith showed them into the room and had them take a seat in front of his desk. Sitting behind it, the American steepled his hands on the desk and studied the two as he contemplated what to say. His two guests were quite a contrast, he thought. Lechenko was the typical cyber geek, with his disheveled hair, sloppy dress, and unshaved face. Nikita was just the opposite. Wearing a low-cut designer dress, and sporting perfect makeup and a stylish hairstyle, the exotic young woman had the looks and bearing of a model. She exuded an erotic allure Smith had found charismatic from the first time they'd met. For a moment he tried to visualize what the Russian woman might look like without clothes. Hopefully one day in the future he would find out. Pushing away the tempting thought, he focused on the matter at hand.

"I want to thank you both," the American began, "for the contributions you've made to my operation. I know it was a hardship for you to leave Russia and resettle here, but as you know, it was unavoidable." He turned to Lenchenko. "Andrei, you've been an incredible asset to my team. Your programming skills are outstanding. Your expertise in orchestrating the recent computer disruptions, including the California air-traffic problems, have been masterful. I'm looking forward to having you implement our next phase."

Lechenko beamed. "Thank you, Mr. Smith."

Smith turned toward the young woman. "I've had many conversations with Ivan Petrov, and I know you've been a real asset to him. And for that I'm grateful. Ivan has been one of my most trusted partners."

Nikita smiled and ran one hand through her hair, a motion he found charming.

The American steepled his hands on the desk again as he gazed at the two people. "I wanted to meet with you both personally, because unfortunately, I have bad news to share. News about my colleague and dear friend, Ivan Petrov."

A look of alarm crossed the faces of his guests.

"But before I share the sad news, I want to tell you something important. I consider you both important assets, and I will insure you are financially secure beyond your wildest dreams."

Nikita and Andrei exchanged questioning glances, then turned back to Smith.

"What's going on?" Nikita asked nervously.

"I guess there's no easy way," Smith continued, "to break this to you, so I'll just come out and say it." He paused a moment and lowered his voice for emphasis. "Ivan Petrov has left us."

"What do you mean?" Lechenko asked, a confused look on his face.

"As you probably know," Smith said, "Ivan and I have had a financial arrengement that we both agreed to sometime ago. He was a key partner in my Prism operation, and in return I agreed to pay him a very large sum of money, once the objectives of the operation were met. Things have been going so well, that yesterday I decided to pay Ivan his share. After I did so, he informed me that he wished to leave my estate immediately. He also told me he wished to leave alone. Frankly, I was shocked by this, as he had always said how fond he was of both of you."

Smith paused a moment to let the news sink in. "So after I paid Ivan his share, he requested transportation to an international airport, and I complied. I had my chauffer drive him to Billings, Montana, where, I assume, he took a flight to another country."

"He left without me?" Nikita screeched. "That son-of-a-bitch!"

Lechenko grimaced. "He didn't even say goodbye ...."

"I knew this would be difficult for both of you to accept," Smith replied, doing his best to sound reassuring. "And I agree, it's a brutal thing to hear that someone you trusted turns his back on you. However, as I mentioned before, I will make sure you both are financially secure." He waved a hand in the air. "My home is your home. You are both welcome to live here as long as you wish. And I've prepared financial agreements for you, which I think you will find quite generous."

The American opened a desk drawer and took out two manila folders, one labeled Andrei and the other Nikita. He slid them across his desk; his guests picked them up, opened them and began reading.

"As you can see," Smith continued, "they are financial contracts lasting for a term of one year. Each of you would continue to be a part of my organization for that time, and for that you will be paid an extremely large sum of money. More money than you can probably spend in a lifetime."

When his guests finished reading the agreements, they both stared at Smith, a look of amazement on their faces.

"This is very generous," Lechenko exclaimed. "I accept!"

"I agree," Nikita said, "it is a lot of money. An incredible amount." She paused a moment. "But I do have a question. I can understand why you'd want Andrei to stay on, as he's a computer genius." She appeared confused. "But why me? I have no technical expertise. What would be my role in all this?"

Smith gave her a piercing stare. "My dear Nikita, I'm a man of my word. When I agreed to having all of you locate to the U.S. and to my home, I accepted total responsibility for your health and welfare. That's why I'm making sure you and Andrei are financially secure." He leaned forward in the chair. "From my perspective, you appear to be a woman of many talents. As we come to know each other better, you may be willing to share some of those talents with me."

Nikita gave him a knowing look. "But aren't you married?"

"I am. However, I have a very understanding wife."

The young woman nodded as a suggestive smile spread on her lips.

Chapter 54

Langley, Virginia

Rachel West was sleeping in her apartment when her cell phone rang, waking her. She sat up on the bed, grabbed the phone and held it to her ear. "Hello?"

"Hi Rachel. It's Alex."

Glancing at the clock on her nightstand, she read the time: 2:37 a.m. "Jesus. Don't you ever sleep?"

She heard her boss chuckle. "Listen, Rachel. I think we caught a break on the case."

Rachel stood up and turned on the bedside lamp, now fully alert. "That's the best news I've heard in weeks. Tell me."

"The shell casing you gave me the other day. The lab guys have been working on it and were able to pull a partial print. It took a while, but they found a match."

"Who is it, Alex?"

"A former CIA operative by the name of Ted Cavanaugh. He left the agency five years ago. Since then he's had no steady job; my sources tell me they suspect he does contract hits for the mob, or whoever else is hiring."

"Where does he live?"

"Frederick, Virginia, a town northwest of D.C. He has a house there."

"I know where Frederick is. It's not far from here. Give me the address."

Miller told her, then said, "Are you heading there now?"

"Yes."

"I want you to call Matt Turner – I don't want you doing this on your own."

"Of course, Alex."

"Good. And wear the body armor."

"Please. Give me some credit," she replied, trying to control her irritation.

"Okay. Call me afterwards."

"You got it boss," she replied testily, then hung up. *He sounds like a mother hen*, she thought. *Jesus Christ! I'm a fucking Federal agent, not a Girl Scout.*

She dressed quickly in black jeans and a black polo shirt. After holstering her Glock and strapping on the bullet-proof vest, she donned a leather jacket. *The hell with calling Turner*, she thought. *I don't have time for that crap.*

Soon after Rachel was on her Kawasaki, headed northwest toward Frederick. Since it was the middle of the night, traffic was light on Interstate 270.

Spotting the sign for the town, she down-shifted the motorcycle and took the next exit. She cruised for the next fifteen minutes trying to locate the right address, and when she found it, drove past the house and parked the bike two blocks away.

It was a well maintained middle-class neighborhood, the houses sitting on large lots. Most were unlit save for a few porch lights. She strode toward Cavanaugh's house and studied the layout from across the street. It was a single-story, with an attached garage. Like the other homes around it, it was dark. The only illumination came from the moonlight and a streetlamp.

Crossing the street, she crouched behind a parked car. As far as she could tell, there was no activity at Cavanaugh's place. Listening for sounds, all she heard were some dogs barking in the distance, the drone of air conditioners, and the hum of cicadas.

She crept around the side of the house and found a back porch. Like the front, this area was in shadows. She crouched by the back door and peered through the window into the dim interior. The kitchen appeared unoccupied.

After putting on latex gloves, she pulled her Glock. Trying the door, she was surprised to find it was unlocked.

She took a deep breath to calm her nerves, then stepped cautiously inside, sweeping the kitchen with her pistol. Verifying it was indeed vacant, she moved down a dim corridor toward the front, passing a living room and a dining room, both unoccupied. She listened closely, but only heard the ticking of a clock and the hum of an air conditioner.

Following another hallway, she slowly stepped into the one of the bedrooms and found it empty. She surmised the master bedroom was at the end of the corridor and after searching another empty room, headed there.

Rachel smelled the blood before she saw it.

Going into the master bedroom, she found a man's inert nude body on the queen size bed. His throat had been slashed and the back of his head bashed in. There was blood everywhere – on the corpse, the linens, the carpet. The acrid stench from the gore almost made her retch.

After searching the bathroom, she went back to the body. As she expected, there was no pulse. But the man's skin wasn't stiff, signifying rigor hadn't set in – he had been murdered less than four hours ago.

Opening a drawer in the nightstand, she found keys and a wallet. Pulling out the driver's license, she studied the photo and confirmed the corpse was Cavanaugh.

Cavanaugh was the sniper and now he's dead, she thought. *Was Prism covering its tracks again?* She was sure of it. But not all was lost – even if she couldn't interrogate the man, there might be something in the house that could lead her to them.

Pulling a penlight from her pocket, she began to search the house. She found nothing useful until she opened a storage closet in the back bedroom. Inside were a break-apart sniper's rifle, a sound suppressor, a scope, and other weapons and ammunition. But she didn't find a computer.

Doing a more thorough search of the other rooms, she found a built-in desktop inside a wooden armoire in an alcove by the kitchen. Most likely Cavanaugh used it to do paperwork. Scanning some of the documents, she saw several promising items. She was elated to find the information, but realized there was no way she could go through all of it now. Locating a large manila envelope, she stuffed it with his check register, bills, and assorted paperwork. She had to get the hell out of there ASAP, before the cops showed up. A corpse was always hard to explain.

Turning off the penlight, Rachel quickly left the house and sprinted back to her motorcycle. She drove quietly out of the neighborhood, but when she reached I-270 she twisted the throttle on the powerful Kawasaki. The engine roared, the wide rear tire squealed, and the bike leapt forward, reaching 100 mph in six seconds. A wide grin spread across her face, something that happened frequently when driving at high speed. Realizing she was well over the limit, she backed off the throttle and continued home.

Chapter 55

Langley, Virginia

Alex Miller glared at her. "You disobeyed a direct order!" he shouted, his voice full of anger.

Rachel West had just stepped into his office, and surprised by his outburst, didn't sit down but instead remained standing. "I've got good news on the case, Alex."

He raised a palm. "Later!"

Miller stood, came around his desk and faced her, the grimace not leaving his face. "I gave you an order. You were to take Turner with you. I just talked with him and he tells me you never called him."

"I can explain," Rachel said with a smile, but saw Miller was in no mood for levity. Rarely had she seen her boss so angry.

He pointed to the visitor's chair. "Sit down, Rachel, and shut up."

She complied and waited for the man to return to his desk and sit down.

"Do you know why I hired you two years ago to work at the Factory?"

She was about to answer but didn't reply when she realized it was a rhetorical question.

"I hired you, Rachel, because you're a self-confident, highly-intelligent, aggressive agent. I hired you against the objections of my supervisor, who thought women should never be field operatives. But I hired you anyway, because I believed in you. I saw the potential a smart woman like you could bring to this job."

"And here I thought you hired me because I was a pretty, blue-eyed blonde."

Miller glared at her again – it was clear the humor hadn't gone over well. He pointed a finger at her. "That's exactly what I'm talking about. You're not taking my authority seriously. But this time you're not going to be able to sweet talk me out of it. This time you're going to face consequences for disobeying orders."

Suddenly she knew her boss was deadly serious. "What do you mean by that?"

"If we weren't in the middle of such a critical operation, I'd suspend you for a month with no pay. Fortunately for you, you're vital to our success in the Prism case." He stabbed the air at her again. "So I'm doing the next best thing. I'm docking your pay for two weeks, and I fully expect you to work your ass off during that time. Is that clear?"

Rachel nodded. "Crystal."

She had disobeyed him, there was no denying that, and she had to take her medicine. "I'm sorry, Alex. It won't happen again."

The stern look on his face melted a fraction. "Bullshit. You're incorrigible. But next time you do it, you'll know there'll be a cost."

"Yes, sir."

She tried a smile. "Are we good, sir?"

Miller tried to keep a straight face but after a moment he returned the smile. He shook his head slowly. "Damn it, Rachel, you're one of my best agents, but you're also a big pain in the ass."

She laughed. "Admit it. I am your *best* agent."

"Maybe." He rubbed his bloodshot eyes. It was seven in the morning and it looked like the man had been working in his office all night long. "Now. Back to the case. Tell me what you wanted to tell me before."

Her enthusiasm returned, and she placed the thick manila envelope she had been carrying on his desk. "Like I told you on the phone earlier, I found Cavanaugh at his house, dead, obviously murdered. I didn't find his computer, but I found a stack of paperwork. It's all in here. Most of it is innocuous, but a few items stood out. He flew to Montana last week, and when he came back he deposited a total of $100,000 split up among a bunch of local banks. All of the deposits were in cash, and each one was less than $10,000, the legal limit for cash deposit reporting."

"Good work, Rachel. Where did he go in Montana?"

"He flew into Billings and rented a car. After that there's no record – Cavanaugh must have paid cash from then on."

Miller nodded. "So. Whoever hired him to kill you probably lives in Montana. That'll help in narrowing down the right John Smith."

"That's what I thought too. And maybe the tech guys can analyze the other documents and uncover additional leads."

Her boss picked up the envelope and stood. "I'll get this to the lab right away."

Just then there was a knock on the office door. It opened and Miller's assistant poked his head around the jamb. "Sir, something's happening. It's on the news."

Miller's shoulders slumped. "Damn. What *else* could go wrong?" His assistant closed the door and Miller went to the TV in his office and turned it on.

The set was tuned to Fox News and Miller raised the volume.

A reporter, a gray haired man wearing a dark suit, was on the screen. "Our local affiliate in Denver, Colorado," the man said, "is reporting that ...."

Rachel listened closely to the TV newscaster as he continued. When she heard the tragic news, a sick feeling settled in the pit of her stomach.

Chapter 56

Glacier County, Montana

Things were going so well, John Smith almost had to pinch himself to make sure it was real. This ran through his mind as he stared out the panoramic windows of his den. Prism was in full gear, every phase of the operation falling into place like clockwork. The latest 'mishap' they had engineered, the collision of two chemical tanker railcars in Denver, had caused the death of forty-five people. And even better, the massive explosion had disrupted rail yard traffic in that whole area. That disruption would continue for weeks. The railroad company's stock had plummeted, resulting in a huge financial gain for Smith. He grinned at the thought.

Ever since Andrei Lechenko moved into Smith's estate, the operation had improved. Having the computer expert close by made everything easier; with every passing day, the American's confidence grew. There was nothing that could stop him now, he realized.

It's a perfect September day, he thought, as he looked out the den's windows. The snow-capped mountain range north of his property jutted up into a stunning cobalt blue sky. He saw no clouds for miles. The temperature outside was an idyllic seventy degrees.

If only he could overcome his fear of the outdoors.

He rarely ventured outside. Preferred staying indoors, breathing the purified air in his home. It complicated his life, even his business dealings. In fact, all of the Prism meetings had taken place inside his jet, as it sat on the runway at Petrov's house in Finland.

And it was getting worse, the older he got. He had become a total recluse, almost a prisoner of his own making. He knew he was being irrational. But overcoming his fear of the outdoors was something he found extremely difficult to do. No matter how hard he tried.

But today he would make a rare exception and venture outside.

He'd promised to meet Nikita on the terrace behind his home. The beautiful young woman loved to sit outdoors and read her high fashion magazines. Besides watching television and reading magazines, there wasn't much for her to do at his remote estate. Last week she wanted to visit the nearest town, which was twenty miles away, but he refused. It might endanger the operation – there was no telling whom she'd meet. Although he trusted her to keep quiet about Prism, she didn't strike him as very intelligent. She could be tricked into talking, or more likely, she would inadvertently say something to jeopardize the operation.

Earlier today Nikita had asked him to join her on the terrace. He'd reluctantly agreed, if only to show her that he wasn't afraid to go outside. He sensed she was testing him in some way.

Although he'd suggested several times during her stay that they become intimate, she had demurred, saying she needed to know him better. It was clear the woman had a domineering personality and used sex to achieve control. Unfortunately, Smith realized, it was working. He lusted after Nikita, to the point where he was ignoring his attractive wife, who he now found boring by comparison.

Turning away from the windows, he left the den and made his way to the back of the massive home. He stopped at the closed French doors and gazed outside to the wide terrace. Flagstone steps led down a few feet to an intricately landscaped terrace, which was flanked by an Olympic size swimming pool. A pool he had never been in.

Nikita was there, reclining on one of the lounge chairs by the pool, reading a magazine. The exotic woman was wearing a very revealing bikini that showed off most of her voluptuous curves. No doubt she had worn it on purpose, he thought, to further tease him.

His libido aroused, he put his hand on the door knob and turned it, but couldn't quite get himself to pull open the door.

Smith stood absolutely still, frozen in place by his irrational fear of the outdoors. Even the sight of the luscious, nearly naked woman couldn't overcome it.

This is insane! his thoughts raged. *Absolutely insane!*

He tried opening the door again, but his heart began to race, and beads of perspiration formed on his forehead. He felt paralyzed. The sheer terror of stepping out onto the terrace made his hand numb.

Smith stood there a long moment, cursing silently at himself.

Feeling defeated, he turned around and walked back to his den.

Chapter 57

Langley, Virginia

Rachel West had just walked into the Factory building when her cell phone buzzed. She pulled the phone out of her pocket and held it to her ear.

"We found him!" she heard Alex Miller shout.

"You found Smith?" she replied, trying to suppress her enthusiasm – she had been close to finding the elusive man before, only to see the leads vanish.

"Yes, Rachel. We finally located the bastard."

"You're sure?"

"Absolutely. Where are you now?"

"I just walked in the building, Alex."

"Meet me in the conference room. Now."

She hung up the phone and sprinted to the stairs, then raced up, two steps at a time.

Moments later she inserted her key card into the reader by the conference room's door. Then she approached the retinal scanner and leaned forward to have her eyes verified. The specially designed conference room was constructed to prevent eavesdropping, with a second level of security beyond the already sophisticated anti-electronic surveillance the rest of the building offered.

The door lock clicked open and she stepped inside. Already sitting there at the long conference table was her boss Alex, and one of the Factory's technical analysts, Robert 'Rob' Brown. A short, bespectacled man in his mid-twenties, Rob was a brilliant analyst, although judging by his baby-faced features you'd swear he wasn't old enough to drive.

Rachel took a seat at the table and turned to Miller. For the first time in weeks, her boss looked cheerful.

"You're sure it's the right guy?" she asked.

Miller nodded. "Yes. You finding Cavanaugh's shell casing and his travel itinerary were the keys we needed."

A feeling of relief coursed through her, and her enthusiasm rose. "Good. Tell me more."

Her boss turned to Rob Brown. "Rob, why don't you take it from here. You have all the details."

"Yes, sir," the analyst said, then faced Rachel. He adjusted his thin black tie, something she'd seen the young man do at other meetings. She surmised it was a nervous habit.

"Don't worry, Rob, I don't bite," she said, trying to put him at ease. It was clear he knew her reputation for toughness.

Brown nodded, "Yes, ma'am."

"And you can drop the ma'am. Call me Rachel."

"Yes, ma'am."

She rolled her eyes. "Go ahead then."

"As Mr. Miller said," Brown began, "the breakthrough came from Cavanaugh's travel records. His flight to Montana and his deposit of the $100,000 when he returned gave us a pretty good indication the right John Smith was located there. Although Cavanaugh paid cash for hotels and other items after he landed in Billings, he still used a credit card to rent a car. We were able to obtain the car's GPS locator records. From those we tracked his travel. He drove to Glen Falls, a city in the northern part of the state. He didn't drive the car for one day, so we suspect a vehicle picked him up and drove him to the final destination."

Brown paused a moment and fiddled with his tie. "From this information, we were able to narrow our search. As you know, ma'am, there are over 45,000 John Smiths in the United States. However there are only 426 of them in Montana. Using computerized analytical tools, we compared the 426 to the other data we had generated previously."

The young man glanced at his notes, then faced Rachel again. "We also searched property records in Montana, and found one large track of land owned by a John B. Smith. The property, which is over 10,000 acres, is located in the northern part of the state, adjacent to the Canadian border."

"Do you have a picture of him?" Rachel asked.

"Unfortunately not," Brown replied. "There's almost no public information about him, and he's pretty much invisible on the Internet. I tried to locate him using all of the web search engines, but found very little. He appears to be an extremely wealthy recluse, a modern day 'Howard Hughes'."

Rachel leaned forward in her chair. "But you're sure he's the right man?"

A grin appeared on Brown's face, the first time she'd seen the young man relax. "Yes. John B. Smith also owns a private jet. And that airplane made several flights to Finland this year."

Rachel smiled back, knowing they had made a real breakthrough. John B. Smith was the right man. "So, Rob, what else can you tell me about him?"

"As I said before, his property is located in northern Montana." Brown pressed a button on the table and a large screen lowered from the ceiling at the front of the room. He clicked on a computer mouse and an image appeared on the screen. It showed a cluster of buildings on a massive parcel of land; the photo was taken from overhead. "This picture is from a CIA surveillance satellite. It shows the property in detail."

"Is that an airplane runway on the property?" Rachel asked.

"That's right. One of those buildings is a plane hangar, which connects to the house with an enclosed walkway. In fact all of the buildings connect with each other that way."

"That's odd," Rachel said, trying to figure out why.

"I agree, ma'am."

"There's another reason we know this is the right Smith," Miller interjected.

Rachel turned to her boss. "What's that?"

"As you know," Miller said, "the National Security Agency keeps records on most of the people in the U.S. And Smith, being a large property owner, has a file at the NSA. But the interesting thing is that it's classified. We couldn't access it."

"So declassify it," Rachel replied testily, "you're Director of Special Operations. That's a big deal at Central Intelligence."

"I wish it were that simple," Miller said. "The file is classified, and it's been sealed by someone in the CIA, above my pay grade. That's why I know for a fact this is the right Smith. It confirms what I've suspected for months – there's a mole at Central Intelligence, and that person is high up."

"Any way of knowing who the mole is, Alex?"

Her boss grimaced. "No. That's the bad news. I've been trying to find out, with no luck."

Chapter 58

Glacier County, Montana

John Smith was in the den of his home, writing in his journal, when he heard a knock at the door. He put the book away in a desk drawer, locked it, and said, "Come in."

The door opened and his chief of security, David Gardner, stepped inside. The tall, muscular man was wearing a business suit which fit him tightly across his broad chest and thick arms. He had a shaved head and piercing black eyes. Before being employed by Smith, he was an intelligence officer in the Russian KGB. Gardner was an alias – his real name was Menshikov. Gardner was one of Smith's key employees. In fact, he was Smith's intermediary for dealing with the CIA mole.

Gardner stood ramrod straight in front of the American's desk. "I thought you should know, sir. Someone just tried to access your NSA file."

Smith's face turned bright red and his hands formed into fists. "What? You're sure?"

"Yes, sir. I verified it with our source at the CIA."

"How's that possible? Only a handful of people even know I exist. Could someone have tried to access it by mistake?"

"That thought occurred to me also, but then I found out who was trying to access the file."

"Who was it, damn it?" Smith yelled, jumping up from his chair.

"The Special Operations division at the CIA."

"That's the department that's conducting the Prism investigation."

"Yes, sir."

The sour taste of bile rose up in Smith's throat. His legs became unsteady and he slumped back down on the chair. "Were they able to read the file?"

"No sir. It's locked up tight. Our source made sure of that."

Smith nodded, feeling somewhat relieved. "That's good. Without the file, they won't be able to find me."

But his mind churned, thinking about the implications of the disturbing news. After a long moment, he said, "Still, I want to be ready in case the inconceivable happens and they find out where I am. Put all of our security forces on high alert. And if any of our men were planning vacations, cancel them. Also, I want our air-defense system completely geared up – if they try flying in, they'll get a rude surprise. I want to be as ready as possible."

"Yes, sir."

Smith glared. "Those bastards at the Factory will never get to me."

Chapter 59

Langley, Virginia

"I've given this a lot of thought," Alex Miller said. "And I've come up with a plan for the assault on Smith's estate." He stared intently at the agents in the room, Rachel West and Matt Turner. The three were sitting around the table in the Factory's conference room.

"From the satellite images," Miller continued, "we know the place is a fortress. The whole property, all ten thousand acres, is enclosed by a ten-foot high chain-link fence topped with barbed wire. We also spotted surveillance cameras along the perimeter, and suspect the area is equipped with motion sensors. Armed guards on Humvees patrol the grounds 24/7. The Humvees are outfitted with .50 caliber machine guns, and probably other weaponry the sat images couldn't pick up."

"Is that it?" Rachel said. "Sounds like it'll be easy for us to get in."

Miller glared at her, irritated by her flippant remark. "This is no time for jokes, Rachel. Your life is on the line, plus Matt's and the rest of the assault team."

"Sorry boss," the attractive woman said.

Matt Turner, who so far had been quiet during the meeting, spoke up, "How do you propose we carry out the assault, Alex?"

"I'll get to that," Miller responded, "but first I want to set up some ground rules. It's imperative that Smith be captured, not killed. We need to interrogate him and find out the total scope of the plan. And if he has other co-conspirators. Just as important, we need to know who the mole is at Central Intelligence."

"I agree," Rachel said. "But I want to set up a ground rule myself."

Miller sighed, suspecting what she was about to say. "What is it?"

Rachel leaned forward in her chair. "I'm glad Matt will be on the assault, but I'll lead the team."

Miller glanced at Turner, saw the man roll his eyes and then shrug. It was clear Turner was used to her forceful personality.

"Okay, Rachel," Miller said, "you'll be the lead agent. But I want you to consult with Matt and get his advice throughout the operation."

The woman gave Miller a mock salute. "You got it, boss."

"Okay," Miller continued, "now that we've got that out of the way, let's talk specifics. Because of the compound's tight security, it's going to be difficult to catch them by surprise if we use ground vehicles. The property is so large that even if we were able to penetrate the perimeter with armored SUVs, they'd know it before we reach the main house." He paused a moment. "So, our best bet is to go in using helicopters and fly over the perimeter defenses."

"Good thinking," Rachel said. "We should do it in the middle of the night and hopefully catch them by surprise."

"I was just about to say that," Miller replied. "So, we're all in agreement so far?"

His two subordinates nodded.

"Okay, then. We'll use four helicopters, specially outfitted Black Hawks. They're whisper quiet and have the same weaponry as used by U.S. Army Delta Force units."

Rachel let out a low whistle. "Where'd you get those? That's not something we have in our inventory."

Miller smiled. "That's a fact. Our budget's so tight, it feels like I have to scrounge around to make sure we have toilet paper in the bathrooms here."

Rachel laughed at his joke.

"The Black Hawks," Miller continued, "are a loan from a friend of mine. He runs a large private security firm."

"Good friend," Turner interjected.

"I've done him some big favors over the years; this is payback," Miller said, placing his hands flat on the table in front of him. "This operation is all-hands-on-deck. I'm assigning all Factory field agents to assist you two with the assault. We've got several agents who are proficient helicopter pilots, and they'll be your flight crew."

Rachel glanced at Turner, then back at Miller. "That'll work. What about weapons?"

"Select everything you need from our armory in the basement," Miller said. "If you need something you can't find there, I'll get it for you."

Miller opened a briefcase that was on the table and took out two folders. He slid them to the agents. "In there are detailed satellite photos, including close-ups of each of the buildings and guard posts. Also in there is all the other information our tech analysts have gathered. Read it, memorize it, and when we're done with the mission, burn the whole file. This assault is taking place on U.S. soil, something the CIA is expressly forbidden to do by its charter. I don't want to leave a paper trail leading back to us. Understood?"

Turner nodded, and Rachel said, "You got it."

"Do you have any questions?"

"I do have one," Rachel said. "It would be helpful if we knew what the bastard looked like."

"I almost forgot," replied Miller. "Inside the folder is a picture of John Smith. The tech guys were able to find it after a lot of work. The man is so reclusive they only found one picture of him. Smith was attending a political fundraiser a few years ago, and someone snapped his photograph."

Both agents searched through the thick files and Rachel found it first. After studying the photo a long moment, she looked at Miller. "Sure this is him, Alex?"

"We're sure."

She tapped the photo. "Smith is physically deformed. His hands and head are too big for his torso. His back is hunched, and his brow is huge. It's a good thing he's rich, because he wouldn't get too far on his looks."

"Forget his looks, Rachel. Just remember that he's a mass killer. A killer who's a master of deception and subterfuge."

"Don't worry," she said, putting the photo aside. "I'll catch the bastard, if it's the last thing I do."

"I'm sure you will," Miller replied, sounding more confident than he felt. He realized with a sick feeling that Rachel, for all of her expertise, might not come back alive. A vision of a black body bag flashed in his mind, but he quickly pushed it away.

Chapter 60

Langley, Virginia

Alex Miller unlocked the heavy metal door to the Factory armory and stepped inside. Rachel, who was right behind him, followed and watched as the man turned on the overhead lights to the room.

Floor-to-ceiling, glass-front cabinets lined the walls of the armory. Each storage compartment contained rows of lethal weapons grouped by type. In one cabinet were handguns, in another were assault rifles. Ammunition, plastic explosives, and other armaments such as knives, shotguns, and grenades were stored in the others. The smell of gun oil hung thick in the air.

Rachel was very familiar with the armory, and in fact it was her second favorite place at the Factory. Her favorite was the shooting range, located in a nearby room.

Miller turned to Rachel. "You've already picked out the weapons you wanted for the assault?"

"Yes. I did that yesterday."

"Good. I have something else I want you to take with you. Follow me." He strode past the glass-front cabinets and stopped in front of a wall safe. He dialed a combination, and when it clicked open, reached inside and took out a wooden box.

Rachel had always been curious about the safe; as far as she knew, no agents had ever opened it. "I always wondered what was in there."

After placing the box on a nearby table, he opened it. "Now you're going to find out." He reached inside and took out a bulky, brushed-chrome pistol and laid it on the table.

Rachel whistled. "Wow. A Desert Eagle. Whose is it?"

"Mine," he replied. "I know you think I'm old enough to be a dinosaur, but I used to be a pretty good field operative back in the day." He picked up the semiautomatic handgun and handed it to her.

The gun felt heavy in her hands, but nevertheless it was a thrill holding such a powerful handgun. The .50 caliber Desert Eagle was legendary. It was the most powerful handgun in the world, packing even more punch than the .44 Magnum Dirty Harry used in the movies.

"I know you're partial to your Glock 42," Miller said. "But I want you to take this with you, in addition to that. Bullets from this penetrate body armor, something you're likely to encounter."

She studied the pistol closely, taking out the clip and checking the sighting. The handgun was the seven round model and had a six inch barrel.

Miller slid the box toward her. "There are extra clips, a holster, and ammunition in here. Ever fired one of these before?"

"No."

"It's got quite a punch. Go to the range, get familiar with it."

"Gladly." She put the Desert Eagle in the box and turned toward the man. "When do we begin the operation?"

"The helicopters are being delivered today to a remote staging area outside of Billings, Montana. I want you and the rest of the team to fly out there tomorrow. You can rehearse the assault when you get there. I want the operation to start in three days, four at the most."

"The sooner the better, Alex."

"I agree. Any questions or concerns?"

A lot of things swirled through her mind. She thought about her ailing mother, her broken relationship with Brad, but most of all she focused on Smith and the mystery of Prism. After a long moment, she simply said, "No. I'm ready to go."

Then he did something quite unexpected. Leaning in, he gave her an awkward hug. When they separated a second later, he said, "Good luck, Rachel."

"Thanks, boss."

She studied his face, saw the concern in his eyes. "Don't worry about me. I'm a big girl; I can take care of myself."

"I know you can," he replied with a smile, but she could tell it was forced.

Chapter 61

Glacier County, Montana

John Smith knocked on the door and, not waiting for an answer, stepped inside Andrei Lechenko's computer lab. The large room was crammed floor-to-ceiling with electronic gear, and he had to step around a row of computer hard drives to reach the cubicle at the back. Smith noticed a cot had been set up in one corner of the room. He had suspected the computer expert rarely left his lab, and now was sure of it.

As usual, he found the tech geek hunched over one of his laptops, typing furiously.

Smith approached him. "Are we ready, Andrei?"

The young man glanced up abruptly, a startled look on his face. "Mr. Smith. I didn't hear you come in."

"No matter. Are we ready for the next phase?"

The man adjusted his black frame glasses. "Soon. I have to finish writing the computer code."

"And after that?"

"I'll test it, and we can be ready to launch in a matter of days."

"That's good, Andrei. Very good."

Smith grinned. This was Prism's most ambitious operation yet, and he couldn't wait to get started.

Chapter 62

Glacier County, Montana

Rachel sat uncomfortably on the hard bench seat of the Sikorsky MH60L Black Hawk helicopter. She was looking out one of the windows, watching the desolate countryside below. They were flying at a cruising speed of 168 mph, and the scene blurred past.

She was wearing night-vision goggles which gave the nighttime scene a ghostly green cast. From her vantage point she could see two of the other choppers as they flew alongside in formation toward Smith's compound. The fourth Black Hawk was on the other side, her view of it blocked by another agent.

As Miller had told them, the modified aircraft was very quiet. The specialized construction of its tail section, with extra blades on the tail rotor, significantly lowered noise levels from that of a conventional UH60 Black Hawk. The wind noise was louder than the main rotors or the twin jet engines.

Besides her, there were four agents in the chopper, plus two pilots. Matt Turner was sitting next to her. All were wearing black fatigues, tactical boots, backpacks, communication headsets, and night-vision goggles. Each carried Heckler & Koch 416 assault rifles. The H&K was a favorite of black ops operators, and in fact it was same type of weapon SEALs had used to kill Osama bin Laden.

In addition to that gear, the twenty person (all male, except for her) assault team and the pilots wore Crye tactical body armor, the same as used by Delta Force operators. She was glad for the high-tech Kevlar, which was light in weight, but like all body armor, still made her perspire. Brushing sweat from her forehead, she adjusted the goggles to get a better look at the ground below.

She glanced at Matt, who had barely said a word during the chopper flight. Obviously he was lost in his own thoughts. Although they had rehearsed the assault several times, and memorized the layout of the compound, operations like these were always a crap shoot – you never knew what could go wrong.

Rachel shifted in her seat and adjusted the heavy backpack. She hated having all the gear, but knew it was unavoidable – they had to carry everything they might need on their backs – once they hit the ground, they were on their own.

"Five minutes to target," she heard the pilot say over her headset. She tensed, knowing it wouldn't be long now.

The Black Hawk's nose dipped and the craft began to bleed altitude; the other choppers followed suit. The plan was to swoop down and fly just above the tree line to avoid detection.

"Get ready," Matt said.

Rachel nodded, gripped the stock of the H&K tighter, and watched as the details of the landscape grew in size. She could now make out individual trees; a meandering river was right below them.

She glanced forward, looked through the front windshield and saw it. A long line of tall, chain-link fencing, stretching for what appeared to be miles.

"Two minutes to target," she heard over the headset.

Just then she spotted a thin plume of white smoke racing toward them, and her heart skipped a beat.

"Incoming missile!" she heard the pilot yell. "Hold on!"

Immediately the Black Hawk veered left, away from the plume, then dropped another twenty feet closer to the ground. The seat harness pressed against her shoulders. Never at ease flying, Rachel felt vertigo as the chopper did another sudden evasive maneuver, this time veering right. The dizziness increased and she watched as more plumes of smoke came their way. *Fuck this!* she thought. *We knew Smith's compound had extensive security, but we never anticipated this.*

Glancing sideways, she saw more plumes fly past, aimed not just at her craft but the others as well.

Rachel saw a bright flash in the nighttime sky and with horror knew instinctively what had happened. The incoming missiles had found a target. One of the Black Hawks, its tail rotor shredded, began spinning wildly out of control and plummeted. A ball of flame erupted on the ground, lighting up the deserted area.

"Agent West," she heard the pilot say into her headset, "should we abort the mission?"

"No!" she yelled back. "Hell no! That's an order!"

"Yes, ma'am!"

"And fly lower, damn it."

"We're already at treetop level, ma'am."

"Fuck that! I said fly lower. I want to clear that fence by inches."

"But –"

"Do it now!" she yelled into her mike. "And tell the other pilots!"

"Yes, ma'am."

Turner turned toward her. "You sure about this?"

"Shut up, Matt," she replied tersely.

Rachel felt the aircraft descend, saw the other choppers do likewise.

The fence ahead grew bigger in size and she heard the clatter of automatic fire, obviously incoming rounds from Smith's armed patrols.

According to the assault plan, once they had lost the element of surprise, the Black Hawk crews were free to return fire. Almost immediately the chopper's four 7.62 mm machineguns blasted away, and she saw its rounds strike a guard post and a nearby Humvee. Two guards collapsed to the ground, and another clutched his arm.

Rachel saw the fence ahead loom larger and realized they would literary clear it by no more than a few inches. She adjusted her shoulder harness even tighter and whispered a quick prayer.

When they flew over the fence she breathed a sigh of relief.

While her chopper and one of the others continued toward the compound, she saw the third Black Hawk circle back and begin strafing with machinegun fire and anti-tank rockets.

The guard post exploded, and black smoke poured out of a nearby Humvee. Then the Black Hawk turned and began following her craft.

"Look there," Matt said, pointing forward.

Glancing out the front windshield she saw it – a group of tiny lights in the far distance – the compound.

"How much time?" she asked into the mike.

"A couple of minutes," the pilot responded.

She mulled this over. "Okay. Wait for the third chopper to catch up to us, then break into the battle plan."

"Roger that, ma'am."

Moments later the three aircraft broke formation, separating from each other as they flew toward the buildings.

Just then the compound's lights went dark, all at the same time. *No coincidence*, she thought. *Smith must have prepared for something like this*. It was a good thing the assault team had brought night-vision and infrared equipment. *What the hell is he going to do now?*

She got her answer seconds later.

More plumes of white smoke raced toward the helicopters, and she heard the pilot yell, "Incoming!"

Once again the Black Hawk lurched abruptly left. Suddenly she felt dizzy and nauseous. *Damn it*, she thought, *I can't get air sick now.* There was a barf bag in a seat-back nearby, but she ignored it, willing herself not to throw up.

Their helicopter began flying in a zigzag pattern toward the compound, while spewing metallic chaff to throw off the surface-to-air missiles.

They were close to the main house now and she spotted a nearby building that, to her, resembled an air-defense installation with stationary and truck-mounted missile launchers. The pilot must have seen it too, because instead of flying toward the house, he veered toward the installation. The helicopter opened fire, strafing the facility. The darkened installation erupted into flames and the Black Hawk continued toward the main house.

Even though there were no lights on in the home, its blurry green image was visible through her night-vision goggles. As the satellite pictures had shown, the house was massive. A three-story structure of ultra modern design, it was constructed all in concrete and glass. She guessed the place was at least 20,000 square feet.

In her mind Rachel reviewed the assault plan again. Since Smith was obviously located in the home, there was no way they could strafe the building. They had to capture the man, not kill him. The plan called for her chopper to be the lead insertion team, while the second Black Hawk would provide air cover, neutralizing the nearby guards posted outside the home. The third chopper would search the vast property to kill the remaining armed patrols roaming on Humvees, preventing them from reinforcing the guards at the home. The fourth Black Hawk was supposed to destroy the airplane hangar and airfield, but since that craft had been shot down, that process would take place later, once the home was secured.

Ahead of them was the entrance to the home, fronted by a circular driveway, empty of cars. Her helicopter hovered ten feet off the ground, the pilot obviously trying to figure out the best place to land.

Just then she saw two Humvees race toward the home and halt in the driveway, blocking access to the front door. The Humvee's crews swung their roof-mounted .50 calibers toward the chopper and began firing. She tensed as the machinegun rounds thudded into the helicopter – the aircraft shuddered a moment, then flew off. Although the Black Hawk had bullet-resistant plating, at this close range the .50 caliber rounds could still do damage. While their chopper gained altitude and circled toward the back of the home, she watched as one the other Black Hawks fired off several rockets at the Humvees. One vehicle exploded, while black smoke poured out of the other one.

Like the front of the home, the back was also unlit. But she could still see a patio area and a large swimming pool, something she remembered from the sat photos. There were no guards visible here.

"Land here!" she yelled into her mike.

"Roger that," the pilot responded.

The chopper put down in a flat, grassy area, and one of the other agents grabbed the door handle and slid it open. The man jumped out, followed by Rachel and Matt. The other agents poured out as well. Then the whole team, their H&K assault rifles at the ready, spread out across the patio area, hiding behind whatever cover they could find.

Rachel, crouched by a low stone wall, observed the rear entrance. She saw no movement or lights anywhere; still, she sensed that Smith's guards were close by. Her adrenaline was pumping and she was edgy, but also relieved to be out of the damn helicopter. It felt good to be on firm ground again.

Although it was quiet in the immediate area, she could hear the loud clatter of automatic weapons from a firefight in the front of the home. She also heard gunfire and explosions in the distance, coming from other parts of the property.

Turner was nearby and she motioned to him. "See anything?" she whispered.

"Negative," he responded.

"Advance," she whispered into her mike, and pointing her H&K forward, she moved cautiously toward the house. Matt and the other agents did likewise.

Suddenly she saw a burst of light and heard the growl of a heavy machinegun. One of the agents staggered and collapsed to the ground.

"Fall back!" she yelled into her mike.

She retreated and took a position behind a fountain. As the men scattered and took cover, small plumes of grass and dirt flew up all around her, the machinegun continuing to strafe the area. Her heart pounding in her chest, she returned fire with the H&K. The others did the same, the din of the firefight deafening.

Rachel strained to see where the machinegun emplacement was located, and after a moment, found it – a narrow opening in the concrete wall by the back entrance.

"Matt," she said into her mike, "it's by the back door. See it?"

"Affirmative," he replied over the headset.

"You're a better shot than me, Matt. Put two RPGs on that damn thing, will you?"

"You got it."

Seconds later the wall by the door exploded and she knew the rocket propelled grenade had found its mark. A second RPG detonated, this time taking out part of the entrance itself.

"Good work, Matt," she said into her mike. Then she said, "Okay, everybody. Pour some lead into the entrance, but no more RPGs. If Smith is nearby, we can't take a chance on getting him killed."

The agents opened up, the torrent of rifle fire shredding the door area. Wood, glass and stone fragments flew as the rounds found their target. The massive door literally disintegrated and pock marks covered the nearby walls.

"Hold your fire," she said. She listened closely and only heard gunfire and explosions in the distance.

"What do you think, Matt?" she said into her mike.

"I say we go in," he replied.

"I agree. Listen up, everybody. Matt and I are going in. The rest of you provide cover fire. Got it?"

There was a chorus of 'yes, ma'am' and she raced forward in a zigzag pattern. Matt followed, while the rest of the team let loose with a barrage of rifle fire.

When she reached the entrance, she hugged the wall to one side of it and waited for Matt to catch up. Glancing through what was left of the door, she peered into the dim interior.

Among the litter of stone and glass fragments, she saw two uniformed guards, their bloody, inert bodies laying on the floor. The scent of gore and cordite hung in the air.

Using hand signals she motioned to Matt, who nodded.

Then, after taking a deep breath to steady her nerves, Rachel crouched and rolled inside the entrance. Her body crunched over the debris and she took cover next to a wooden breakfront. Peering around the cabinet, she surveyed the scene with her night-vision goggles. She was in a large room, a sitting area furnished with plush sofas and teak wood tables. There was no one there, except the two corpses she'd spotted earlier. From her vantage point she could see into a long, wide corridor leading to more rooms.

"Okay, guys," she whispered into her mike. "It looks clear in here. Matt, you come in; the rest of you guys follow him." She pointed the assault rifle toward the corridor and waited for the team. When the group was inside she pointed to herself and Matt and then pointed to the hallway.

The two operatives advanced, making their way slowly into the hallway. She could still hear gunfire from the front of the house, that firefight obviously ongoing.

They encountered no one as they made their way forward along the corridor. Continuing on, they searched two other rooms, which were luxuriously furnished, but deserted.

There was a bend in the hallway ahead and when Rachel reached it, she peered around the wall. A makeshift barricade had been set up – furniture pieces pushed together haphazardly to block the way. She heard whispers from behind the barricade and spotted a rifle barrel. *Could that be Smith?* she thought. *Likely not.* The man had plenty of guards. She guessed the man was in a much more secure place, probably a safe room in another part of the house.

Turning to Matt, she motioned with her head. The man nodded, understanding her meaning.

Rachel rested the assault rifle against the wall, then unclipped a grenade from her vest. Pulling out the pin, she arched her arm and lobbed it full force around the wall. She crouched quickly and covered her ears, and a moment later heard the deafening explosion. Although she was shielded by the wall, she still felt the concussion wave from the detonation.

Grabbing the H&K, she peered around the wall once more – the area was in shambles – shattered furniture pieces everywhere, blood, and splattered body parts. Portions of the walls were coated red.

In a crouch, she advanced, stepping around the bloody debris. Matt was right behind.

They went into a kitchen, unoccupied, then a dining room which was also empty. Adjacent to that was a very large office with a massive desk. That room was also vacant.

Just beyond was another corridor leading to a wide staircase. She listened for sounds, but all was quiet. *Was the firefight by the front entrance over?* she wondered.

They cautiously made their way there and she got her answer. The front foyer was littered with corpses, uniformed guards and several of her agents. She shook her head in grief at finding the dead agents, but didn't have time to dwell on it. Instead she focused on the task at hand.

As she hugged the wall, she peered outside to the front driveway and saw more inert bodies, operatives and guards. Also there were the smoking ruins of the Humvees and beyond that the second Black Hawk. No one was in the helicopter. From this she assumed the men from that assault team were dead. *What about the agents in the third helicopter?* she thought. *Where are they? Are they dead too?* She pushed that thought away, hoping they were still somewhere on the vast property, battling it out. Nevertheless, it was clear the assault would have to continue with four operatives – herself, Matt, and the other two men.

The foyer was filled with smoke from the firefight. She coughed and her eyes began to tear. Her assault rifle at the ready, she crouched by the bottom of the staircase and watched as the rest of her team secured the rooms around the foyer, then approached her when they were done. While two of the men kept watch, Matt kneeled next to her.

"Find anybody?" she asked.

"No," Matt said. "No one alive that is."

She nodded. "Same thing outside."

"So our guys ...." He didn't finish the sentence.

"Afraid so," she replied. "Hopefully the team from the third Black Hawk is still out there. But we can't count on that now."

"I agree."

Rachel pointed up the staircase. "That's next. All we've found so far are the guards, but no civilians. It's a good bet they're up there."

"How do you want to play this, Rachel?"

She thought about this a moment, unsure of their next move. There were bound to be more armed guards, and there were only four agents left. "Any suggestions?"

"We can't split up," he said. "Back there I noticed a staircase leading down to a basement. But that'll have to wait. We need to clear the upper floors first. And all of us have to continue the attack together, so we can provide cover fire."

"I agree." In spite of the fact she liked to work alone, she was glad to have Turner at her side. "Good thinking, Matt."

"I'll take point," she said, "you follow. The other guys can cover us. But let's reload our weapons first." As she changed out the magazine in the H&K, Matt relayed the instructions to the others.

When everyone was ready, she began climbing the wide staircase, her heart pounding in her chest. She kneeled a few feet from the top landing and waited for the others to catch up.

She peered over the top step and only saw a lavishly carpeted corridor leading both ways. Large, modern artwork hung on the walls. The hallway was deserted, but the doors to all of the rooms were closed. They'd have to search one side of the corridor, then start on the other.

Rachel pointed left, and waited a moment for Matt to cover her. Then she advanced warily down the corridor, pointing the assault rifle in front of her.

Just then one of the doors opened and a uniformed man appeared, brandishing a handgun. She pulled the trigger on the rifle and her heart stopped when nothing happened. *The fucking thing's jammed!* her brain screamed.

She heard the loud clatter of automatic fire and the guard dropped to his knees and collapsed to the floor. Turning, she saw Matt approach and going past her, he peered into the room where the guard had emerged. "Clear," he said. By this time the other two agents had taken positions in the corridor, looking both ways.

Her adrenaline pumping, she took a deep breath. "Thanks, Matt."

That's the second time he's saved my life, she realized.

Turner simply nodded.

She dropped the jammed assault rifle and quickly pulled out the Desert Eagle from her holster. The large handgun felt heavy but also reassuring. She had spent an hour at the firing range and had become proficient with the powerful weapon.

Rachel pointed down the hallway. "Let's go, Matt."

They searched the other rooms, and finding no one, they turned back and began searching the other end of the corridor.

Hearing voices from behind one of the doors, she hugged the wall and waited for Matt to cover her before proceeding. Then she slowly turned the knob and found it locked. She fired off one round from her pistol, the heavy gun bucking in her hands. The round disintegrated the lock. She kicked in the door, but instead of entering she stood to one side of it, waiting for return fire. When there was none, she peered in.

There were six people inside, huddled together in a corner of the large room. Three were male, the others female, and all were wearing civilian clothes. None seemed to be armed. Unlike the other rooms they'd encountered so far, this one was well lit.

"Don't shoot!" one of the women screeched.

Rachel pointed the Desert Eagle at the group. "On your knees!" she ordered. "Now! And put your hands behind your head."

The group quickly complied, and she stepped into the room, followed by the other agents. She told Matt to frisk the group, and when that was done, she searched the large walk-in closets and an adjoining bathroom, all vacant.

As Rachel studied the six people, she realized Smith wasn't there. "Where's John Smith?" she demanded.

They all looked nervous and none of them replied.

"We're Federal agents," Rachel stated. "We're after Smith. You tell us where he is and you won't get hurt." She motioned with her pistol. "But I'm not afraid to use this thing, either."

The woman who had spoken out before, said, "I'm sure he's in the safe room in the basement."

"Who are you?"

"I'm his wife."

Rachel studied the woman, an attractive brunette in her forties. "I don't believe you. Why would he leave you here?"

"Because he's a God damn bastard," the woman said. "He doesn't really care about me; he just keeps me around to fuck once or twice a month." A grimace crossed her face. "And now that he has that Russian bitch living here, he doesn't even do that. Bastard!"

From the wife's venomous tirade, Rachel knew she was telling the truth. "How many more guards are up here in the upper floors?"

"A couple," the wife spat out. "I know he left one with his Russian cunt, Nikita."

"Nikita Ivanova?" Rachel asked.

"You know her?"

"Yeah. I met her in Russia. Where is she?"

"Probably in one of the other bedrooms."

Rachel nodded. "Are the other guards with Smith, in the basement?"

"I'm sure of it," the woman said.

Rachel pointed to the other people in the group. "Who are they?"

The wife motioned to the man kneeling next to her. "This is my husband's doctor and over there is his assistant; next to him is the computer programmer. The three women are maids."

"Okay," Rachel replied. She turned to Matt. "Tie them all up. We'll come back for them later."

"You got it," he replied.

When he was done, the four agents continued searching the other bedrooms. Two were empty, but they heard muted voices from behind the last closed door.

Figuring the door was locked, she fired one round, which blasted away not only the lock but also a good chunk of the door. It swung open on its own and she peered inside. All she saw was a king-size bed and other furniture.

"Come out with your hands up!" she shouted.

When there was no reply, she crouched and cautiously made her way inside, followed by the others.

Just then she heard a loud bang, and a hole appeared in the wall above her. Firing blindly, she got off a round, and in the same split-second, felt something massive slam her chest. The blinding pain felt like a sledgehammer had hit her. She tumbled backwards, gasping for breath, and collapsed to the floor. As she lay there on her back, she heard a multitude of shots.

A moment later she saw Matt Turner leaning over her, an anxious look on his face. "You okay, Rachel?"

"I hurt ... like hell," she replied, sucking in air. "What ... happened?"

"Are you okay?"

"I don't ... know ...."

"Lie still," he said, "let me check." After un-strapping her body armor vest, he unbuttoned her fatigue shirt.

"What the hell ... are you doing?" she said weakly. "Quit ... taking my clothes off ..."

He laughed. "Don't worry. It's not what you think. Just checking for wounds. You're lucky – the Kevlar held. You'll be okay."

"I feel ... like shit."

"Your chest is going to feel really sore for awhile," he said, re-buttoning her shirt and strapping on the vest.

She took a couple of deep breaths, then painfully sat up. "That's ... a fact." Seeing her pistol on the floor, she picked it up and re-holstered it.

"Where's ... the guard?" she asked.

"Dead. You blew a hole in him the size of Texas with your big gun."

She almost laughed, but it hurt too much. "Help me up, will you?"

Matt lifted her off the floor.

Frank Wheeling, one of the other agents, came into the room holding a young woman by the arm. "I found her hiding in the bathroom," Wheeling said.

"Nikita Ivanova. We meet again," Rachel said. Nikita was wearing jeans and a polo shirt, but the simple clothes didn't dampen her exotic good looks.

"Who the hell are you?" Nikita asked defiantly, her vibrant green eyes flashing. She had a Russian accent, but her English was good. And it was clear she hadn't recognized Rachel.

"Last time we met," Rachel replied, "it was in St. Petersburg. I wasn't wearing military fatigues then."

A flash of recognition crossed Nikita's face. "You! You tricked me, bitch! You told me you were with Vogue Magazine."

"We're Federal agents," Rachel replied. "That's all you need to know. Where's Smith?"

"Who's that?"

"Give it up, Nikita. Don't make me angry."

"I don't know who you're talking about."

Rachel glared. "I don't have time for games."

She pulled out the Desert Eagle, crossed the room and pressed the muzzle of the gun to Nikita's forehead. "Where's John Smith?"

Nikita's eyes went wide. "*Da.* I'll tell you."

"Now!"

"He's probably in the basement," the Russian woman said. "He spends a lot of time there."

This corroborated what the wife had said. "Who's with him?"

"His goons – the guards and his head of security."

"Who's that?"

"His name is David Gardner; he's a big, muscular man."

"Okay. Where in the basement?"

"I heard Smith talk about a 'safe room' one time. Probably there. Can you please point that gun away from me?"

Rachel pulled the pistol an inch away from Nikita's head. "What do you know about Prism?"

"Not much. It's some crazy plan to make money. I don't know the details. My fiancé, Ivan Petrov and the programmer worked with Smith on it."

"Where's Petrov now?"

A pout crossed her face. "He left me. He took the money and left me."

"How sad for you, honey," Rachel replied. She pressed the gun against Nikita's head again. "What else do you know about Smith?"

"I told you everything I know!" she screeched.

"You must know more. You were fucking him, weren't you?"

"No! Not yet! He wanted to. But I was being coy about it." Even though the girl was nervous, she flashed a smile. "I was waiting until I had him under my control, then I'd spread my legs for him."

Rachel shook her head slowly. "You lost your sugar daddy Petrov, so you were replacing him with Smith, huh?"

Nikita smiled but said nothing.

"Some women," Rachel uttered with disgust. "Still, you must know more. Talk!"

"I swear! I don't." She thought a long moment. "Wait. I do know something. He kept a journal. I caught him writing notes in it several times."

"A journal? Like a diary?"

"Yes!"

"That's something. Where did he keep it?"

"I don't know. I swear!"

She appeared to be telling the truth. Rachel re-holstered the pistol and turned to Matt. "Tie her up; after we find Smith, we'll question her some more."

"What's going to happen to me?" Nikita asked nervously.

Rachel gave her a hard look. "Let's just say that where you'll be going, you won't need makeup or fancy clothes. You'll be wearing a baggy orange jumpsuit."

After Matt tied up the young woman, Rachel faced him. "You ready to go to the basement?"

"About that," Matt replied. "I've got an idea."

"What is it?"

"You're lucky to be alive, Rachel. You may not want to admit it, but you're probably sore as hell. You ought to let one of us take point from now on."

She realized he was right. The pain in her chest was intense; still, she hated the idea of not taking point. After a moment, she grudgingly said, "You're right, Matt. Frank, you go first."

Frank nodded and left the room, followed by Rachel and the others.

Chapter 63

Glacier County, Montana

John Smith paced the underground safe room like a caged tiger. Ever since the assault began several hours ago, Smith had been manic, his frenzied thoughts tortured by the idea that Prism, his goal for years, was now in real jeopardy. He stopped pacing a moment and looked over at David Gardner, who was sitting at a desk hunched over a computer monitor.

"What's happening now?" Smith demanded.

Gardner pointed to the computer screen. "The security cameras just picked up the Factory team again. They're on the second level, heading down the main staircase."

"You think they're coming to the basement?"

"That would be my guess, sir."

"I pay you for results, you fucking idiot!" Smith yelled. "Not to guess!"

Gardner's face turned red. "Yes, sir. Since they just left Nikita's room, I suspect she told them you were in the safe room."

"That Russian bitch!" Smith ranted. "I should have killed her the same time I killed Petrov. If I hadn't wanted to –" He caught himself before admitting to his security chief that he'd allowed her sexual allure to cloud his judgment. "No matter. I'm sure West and her crew would have found out about the safe room from the others."

Gardner nodded. "Yes, sir."

"Have you heard back from any of our guards on the property?" Smith asked, rubbing his temples in an attempt to calm his nerves.

"Negative, sir. We have to assume they're all dead."

Smith scowled. "How many men do we have left?"

"Besides me, we have four guards outside this room."

Not a large force, Smith thought, *considering the havoc the assault team had already inflicted.* "Have you heard back from our CIA source at Langley?"

"No sir. I've left several high-priority messages for him, but he hasn't gotten back to me."

"Damn!" Smith shouted, his rage at a fever pitch. "Call him again! We need help. Now!" *What the hell is going on?* he thought. *Was their source getting cold feet?* Smith's hands formed into fists as he thought of all the money he'd paid the man. A fortune.

As Gardner got on the phone, Smith went back to pacing, hoping to calm his nerves.

"Sir," his security chief said, after putting down the receiver. "I have bad news."

"What now? You can't reach him?"

"It's worse than that, sir."

"Spit it out, damn you!"

"He's blocking my calls."

Smith felt like someone had punched him in the stomach. He slumped on a chair. "How's that possible?"

"I'm sorry," Gardner replied. "Looks like he's cutting us off. Things must be getting hot in Langley, and he's trying to save his own ass."

Smith nodded, realizing they were on their own. There would be no reinforcements. He sat there for a long moment, saying nothing.

Smith had faced adversity many times before. His severely deformed appearance had seen to that. It had made his childhood unbearable, and even later as an adult caused him numerous hardships. But in the end, he'd always been able to come out on top. He couldn't give up now. He was too close to making his dream come true. *Prism will succeed*, he told himself.

A feeling of optimism surged through him. "Where are they now?" Smith asked.

Gardner glanced down at the computer screen. "They're in the main hallway on the first floor. Close to the basement door."

"Are the underground security measures in place?"

"Yes, sir."

"Good," Smith said with a cold smile. "Let's see if that bitch West can get past *that*."

Chapter 64

Glacier County, Montana

Frank Wheeling stood by the basement door and glanced back at Rachel West, waiting for the go signal. The four agent team, their weapons at the ready, was in the main corridor on the mansion's first floor.

Rachel tensed, and after tightening her grip on the Desert Eagle, nodded.

Wheeling turned the knob and opened the door. The lights were on in the staircase leading down. According to their prearranged plan, he flicked them off. Up to now the team had not encountered guards with night-vision equipment; Rachel had decided to continue using obscurity to their advantage.

Wheeling began to carefully descend the stairs, followed by Carlos Gonzales, Matt Turner, and then herself. She hated bringing up the rear, but had swallowed her pride. Her chest still felt like it was on fire from the impact of the gunshot, and she knew she'd be black and blue for weeks. But she also knew she had been extremely lucky the round hadn't penetrated the body armor – she'd been shot at close range with a high-powered weapon.

Wheeling reached the bottom of the stairs and quickly turned off the lights in the basement corridor. She adjusted her goggles to get a better view and continued down the stairs.

The group spread out once they all reached the basement hallway, their eyes focused on the dim corridor to their left. Crouching, Rachel noticed three closed doors ahead – two on the opposite sides of the long hallway and a door at the very end.

Wheeling, still on point, turned toward her and she waved him forward. The man advanced and the rest of the team followed. He stopped at the first door on the right. After crouching to one side of it, he turned the knob and kicked it open. Gonzales covered him as Wheeling went inside; he came out a moment later, shaking his head, signaling it was unoccupied.

They followed the same procedure with the door to their left, with the same result. That meant Smith and his men were all in the room at the very end of the long corridor.

Wheeling advanced slowly in that direction, as did the others including Rachel. But she had an uneasy feeling – why hadn't Smith posted guards outside the room? Earlier they had encountered guards behind a barricade. Why now here?

Twenty feet from the door she heard a click, then an ear-splitting blast. Immediately she was lifted off her feet and thrown backward, where she crashed against a wall and collapsed to the floor.

Dazed and with her ears ringing from the explosion, she sat up on the floor and scanned ahead. The bloody scene turned her stomach. Wheeling, or what remained of him, lay in a gory mess. Blood and body part fragments coated the walls. Clearly the blast had come from a mine, triggered by a pressure plate on the floor. It was obvious the bomb had been installed some time back, probably when the home was constructed. Like with the missiles earlier, Smith had planned for the unexpected.

Luckily it appeared that neither Gonzales or Turner had been seriously hurt, as both men were now back on their feet, training their assault rifles toward the door, which remained closed.

Rachel had only suffered cuts and bruises on her face, but her backpack had been damaged so she took it off. After wiping blood from her forehead, she got on her feet and advanced toward the two men.

"What now?" Matt asked, turning toward her.

Could there be more explosives on the door itself? she wondered. *Probably.*

"We have to take down the door from here," she replied. "There's no other way."

Matt nodded in agreement. "RPG or grenade?"

"Grenade," she replied, unclipping one of the explosive devices from her vest. "Take cover. And afterwards, I'm back on point." *No way will I bring up the rear from now on,* she thought. Frank Wheeling was a good agent with a large family – she couldn't bear the idea that he was gone, and she was still alive.

As Turner and Gonzales crouched down, she pulled the pin and rolled the grenade across the floor. The device came to a stop moments later, outside the entrance. She crouched quickly, facing away from the imminent blast.

She heard the roar of the explosion and felt the concussion wave at the same time. Looking toward the entrance again, she gazed through the smoky haze – only fragments of the wood door remained, and just beyond she could make out a well-lit room. Furniture pieces had been pushed together into a haphazard barricade; she couldn't see around it, but was sure Smith's men were on the other side.

Wasting no time, she sprinted toward the entrance, and once there hugged the wall to one side, waiting for the others to catch up.

She peered around the jagged opening into the room's interior, trying to asses the situation. It appeared to be a large office, and at the back of it was another closed door, this one constructed of heavy metal. *The safe room?* she wondered. *Most likely.*

Matt, who was next to her, whispered, "See anything?"

"They set up a barricade about ten feet in," she whispered back. "And there's a closed metal door at the far end of the room. That's probably the safe room. I'm sure Smith's holed up in there. That's going to make things easier – we don't have to worry about injuring him."

"What's the plan?" he asked.

Chapter 65

Glacier County, Montana

"What the hell's going on?" John Smith growled.

He was looking over David Garner's shoulder as the man clicked on the mouse, trying to get an image on the computer screen. Both men were inside the basement's safe room.

"The mine I set off," Gardner replied. "The explosion must have taken out the surveillance cameras in the corridor. That's why the screen is black."

"So we don't know if we killed them?"

Gardner shook his head. "No sir. I'll call the guards in the outer room, see if they can tell." He picked up the walkie-talkie on the desk and spoke into it a moment. "Sorry, Mr. Smith. Some of the CIA team must have survived, because they're still trying to penetrate the area."

"Damn it all!" Smith barked.

"Don't worry, sir, we'll get them."

Smith glared at him, hoping the man was right. But just in case, he began formulating a backup plan.

Chapter 66

Glacier County, Montana

Rachel West peered into the room again, weighing their options. Settling on one, she turned to Matt Turner and whispered, "Put an RPG on the barricade."

She glanced at Carlos Gonzales, who was on the other side of the entrance. Speaking into her mike, she said. "Okay, Carlos. Lay down cover fire for Matt."

While Matt got into position to fire the rocket propelled grenade, Gonzales crouched by the entrance and let loose with a barrage of rifle fire. The rounds thudded into the stacked furniture, sending splinters flying. Rachel heard the clatter of return fire as Matt shot the RPG into the room.

Hearing the loud explosion, she signaled to Matt for another.

With the second RPG blast still ringing in her ears, she peered into the now smoky, dim room. The barricade was gone, replaced by a jumbled, bloody mess of wood, plastic, metal, and body parts.

As the ringing in her ears died down, she heard other sounds from the room – an agonizing cry for help, and labored breathing – some of the guards were still alive, but wounded.

"Cover me," she said to Gonzales, who was now replacing the clip in his H&K. "Matt, you follow me in."

As soon as the cover fire started, Rachel rolled into the room, hid behind what was left of a desk and a bookcase. Matt joined her seconds later, as did Gonzales.

"Cover me," she whispered, getting ready to move.

Matt grabbed her by the shoulder. "Let me."

"Bullshit, Matt. I said cover me."

Both men fired off three-round bursts over the ruined desk. With her heart pounding in her chest, she crawled further into the room, moving over the gore and the debris. She found a mangled corpse a moment later and a second one soon after.

Hearing labored breathing from behind another shattered desk, she quickly rolled left and saw the wounded guard. He was holding a pistol with one hand, while clutching his abdomen with the other. She fired off two rounds, head shots, and the man's skull exploded like a watermelon. She was so close to him that his brain matter splattered on her face.

Rachel felt sick to her stomach for killing him, but knew she had no choice. Wiping the mess off her face, she continued crawling forward. *How many guards are left?* she wondered. Listening, all she heard was the continuing cover fire as it blazed over her head and thudded into the far wall.

Just then she heard a groan from the corner of the room – glancing over she spotted a pool of blood seeping from underneath an overturned bookcase. She tightened her grip on the pistol and crawled forward.

Stopping five feet from the bookcase, she shouted, "Throw your weapon out!"

A revolver slid out on the floor from behind the cabinet, and she heard a man's labored voice, "Don't ... shoot ...."

Rachel pointed the Desert Eagle with both hands. "Come out from behind there, arms up!"

"I can't," the man responded, gasping for breath, "I'm wounded ...."

Matt came up from behind and crouched alongside her. "I got this," he said.

She nodded, and Matt went forward while she covered him.

"Clear!" Matt yelled a moment later, and she joined him behind the bookcase.

The wounded guard was sprawled on his back and there was blood everywhere – on his torso, legs, and face. It was obvious he had been near one of the RPG explosions. Matt was pointing his assault rifle at him. She squatted next to the wounded man.

"How many guards were in this room?" she asked the man.

The guard was glassy eyed, and it took him a moment to answer. "Four," he said, blood seeping from his lips. She'd encountered three of the others, and all of them were now dead.

She pointed toward the metal door at the back of the room. "Is that the safe room?"

The guard nodded.

"Smith in there?"

"Yes ...." he whispered, as more blood trickled out of his mouth.

"How many others are with him?"

The man's eyes lost focus again, and he coughed up blood. He groaned, his body shuddered, and he closed his eyes. She knew he didn't have much time left.

"How many others?" Rachel asked again.

The guard blinked a few times. "Just one ... Gardner."

"Okay. What else can you tell me?"

The man's eyes went glassy and a moment later his head slumped to one side. She felt for a pulse, found none. He was dead.

She stood and turned to Matt. "Let's go check out the door."

Gonzales joined them and the three of them approached the entrance of the safe room.

Rachel studied the large, heavy metal door and the metal frame that bordered it, trying to figure out the best way to get in. Knowing Smith was on the other side, they had to be careful.

"We can't blow it with an RPG, or a grenade," she said.

Matt nodded. "I've got an idea, Rachel."

"What's that?"

"I've got a laser torch in my backpack – we can use that."

"Good thinking," she replied, glad once again Turner was on the mission. "How'd you know to bring that along, Matt?"

"Always prepared."

She smiled. "You're such a Boy Scout."

"Yeah. But it pays off, doesn't it?"

"That it does. Okay, let's get to work, Matt."

While Gonzales stood guard, Rachel helped Turner assemble the torch. Minutes later Turner crouched by the entrance and began cutting through the heavy metal door.

The door was constructed of an extremely high-grade of steel, and it was slow going.

Rachel realized it would take some time to cut through.

Chapter 67

Glacier County, Montana

John Smith stared at the darkened image on the computer screen. "What the hell is happening now?" he demanded, looking over David Gardner's shoulder. Both men were in the safe room.

Gardner glanced up from the screen. "I don't know, sir. The bombs the CIA team set off in the outer room must have blown out the cameras there."

"Damn it man, find out!"

Gardner picked up the walkie-talkie and spoke into it.

He tried calling each of the four guards, but none answered; he kept at it for several more minutes, but eventually put down the device and looked up at Smith. "I'm sorry, sir. I can't reach any of them. All I'm getting is static."

Chapter 68

Glacier County, Montana

The acrid smell of burning metal filled the outer room.

Rachel watched as Matt continued using the torch to cut through the heavy door, the red laser light leaving a charred wavy line on the metal as it moved. He had already cut through three sides – the top, bottom, and left side. He was now working on the right hand side. *It won't be long now*, she thought.

"Stop," she said, putting her hand on Matt's shoulder.

The man looked at her and turned off the laser.

"Let's get in position," she said to him and Gonzales, who was standing off to one side.

Rachel again reviewed the plan in her mind. They would cut through most of the door using the laser, and then set off a small C-4 charge on the lock plate, blasting the mechanism open. Then they'd kick down the door and toss in a stun grenade. Simple and effective. Smith wouldn't be injured, and the stun grenade would incapacitate everyone in the safe room.

While Matt and Rachel prepared the C-4, Gonzales stood near the safe room door, keeping a watchful eye on it, his H&K assault rifle at the ready.

Just then Rachel heard a clicking noise from the door and quickly realized it was being unlocked from the inside. Before she could warn Gonzales to stand clear, the door began toppling forward. The men in the safe room were pushing the door from the inside. Since there were no hinges to hold it in place, the door toppled forward, toward Gonzales.

In horror she watched as Gonzales tried to get out of the way of the foot-thick metal door. He screamed, fired off a burst of gunfire, then fell under the massive weight.

She tried to figure out what had just happened. Then she knew. Smith and Gardner, feeling trapped from seeing their only protection gone, must have decided to go on offense.

Rachel unclipped a stun grenade from her vest, pulled the pin and tossed it inside the safe room. The flash-bang device detonated a second later, its brilliant light spewing out of the entrance, almost blinding her.

Holding the Desert Eagle with both hands, she stood next to the door area and peered in the safe room. She waited for the smoke inside to subside. A moment later the details became visible. From what she could see, there was no one inside the small, concrete-walled room. There was a desk with a computer on it, and several chairs, but nothing else. There was a corridor that led off at the back of the safe room, but she couldn't see into it. *Where the hell are they?* she thought. *Is this another damn trap?*

Matt, standing next to her, whispered, "See them?"

She shook her head.

"I'm going in," she said, and he nodded.

Rachel waited for Matt to cover her. Then she crouched and rolled inside the safe room, coming to a stop by the desk. She trained her pistol forward and waited for Matt to catch up.

Seeing blood splatter on the floor close by, her heart sank. *Had Smith been killed inadvertently? I need the bastard alive!*

She noticed bloody footprints leading toward the corridor at the back of the room. A blood-stained assault rifle lay nearby on the floor.

"They must be hiding in that corridor," she said to Matt, who by this time was crouching next to her.

"Okay," he replied, "I'll cover you."

They advanced cautiously toward the back of the safe room, and once there, Rachel peered around the wall. Sprawled on the floor of the hallway was the inert body of a muscular man in a business suit. Blood was oozing from his abdomen. She had memorized what Smith looked like, and this guy wasn't him. Rachel checked the scene beyond and saw it was an unoccupied kitchen. Through an open door, she could see into a bathroom, also vacant.

She turned to Matt, who was crouching next to her. "I don't see Smith," she said. "There's a corpse on the floor; probably Gardner. I'm guessing Gonzales's shots got him."

Matt grimaced. "Where's Smith?"

She was thinking the same thing. *Where the hell was he?*

She thought about setting off another flash-bang before going in, but realized they didn't need it. She motioned with her head and both agents advanced into the corridor. While Matt went to check on Gardner, Rachel searched the kitchen area and the bathroom, finding nothing.

She came back into the hallway a moment later.

"I checked the dead guy's ID," Matt said. "His name is, or was, David Gardner; he was Smith's chief of security. Anything back there?"

"Nothing," she said, with disgust.

She scanned the corridor, the kitchen and the bathroom again, trying to figure out where John Smith could have gone. It was a small area, with no exits. "Let's search every inch of this place, Matt. He's got to be here somewhere."

The two agents split up and spent the next fifteen minutes methodically looking into every square inch of the safe room. But they found nothing.

Standing in the kitchen area, her anger boiled over. *Did he get away?* she thought, gritting her teeth. They had searched everywhere. *Where is he?*

Smith was a master planner, she knew. Could he have foreseen an assault like this and planned for it?

Her hands clenched into fists and she yelled, "Damn it, Smith, where the hell are you?"

Chapter 69

Glacier County, Montana

John Smith crawled forward on his hands and knees along the narrow, dim tunnel.

He was guided only by the beam of the flashlight he was holding. Never thinking he would have to use this passageway, he had not put in any modern conveniences, like lights or good ventilation. Now he wished he'd planned better. The tunnel should have been larger, more comfortable, and with some type of automated transport to shuttle him to the other end. *Minor details*, he thought. *The important thing is I'm alive, and I got away from West and her team.*

He'd had a contractor build the tunnel in secret many years ago. No one on his staff knew about it, not even his chief of security. *It was a shame I had to kill Gardner at the very end*, Smith thought. *But it was unavoidable. I couldn't leave him behind alive. He knew way too much about me.* And there was another reason Smith had killed him. The security measures Gardner had put in place were penetrated by the assault. Gardner had failed him.

As Smith continued crawling forward, he realized keeping the tunnel a secret had been a very good idea, in light of what had just happened with his source at the CIA. You never knew who would turn their back on you when things got difficult.

Smith stopped crawling a moment to catch his breath.

He was not physically fit and any type of exertion wore him out quickly. The tunnel was not high either, and his hunched back kept bumping up against the roof as he crawled along. He also despised getting his hands dirty from the dusty floor, and breathing the stale, unpurified air. *No, I didn't plan this tunnel as well as I should have.*

Pushing those thoughts aside, he began crawling forward once again. He estimated he only had another hundred feet or so before he reached the end of the tunnel, which led up to a remote part of his property. Freedom was so close, he could practically taste it.

Chapter 70

Glacier County, Montana

"Take a look at this," Matt said. He was peering into an open cabinet located underneath the kitchen counter.

Rachel was nearby, searching the safe room's kitchen area for the third time. She walked over and gazed into the interior of the cabinet. Not seeing anything besides food supplies, she said, "I don't see anything."

He pointed. "Right there. There's a tiny seam in the wood panel at the back."

"You may be right, Matt."

After pushing aside the supplies, she reached in with her hand and felt the panel. "Yeah, there's definitely a seam here. I never saw it before because it was so small." Her enthusiasm surged. "There may be a hidden exit here. Give me a crowbar and a flashlight."

Matt took off his backpack, removed the items, and handed them to her.

She inspected the seam carefully, then using the crowbar pried off the inset wooden panel. The panel had covered a hole. She shined the light into the hole, revealing a concrete tunnel, similar to a sewer pipe. "I'll be damned. So this is how the bastard got away."

How long of a head start does Smith have? she thought. *No use worrying about that.* The important thing was to catch him before he reached the end of the passageway and escaped. They'd have to move fast.

She turned to Matt. "We'll split up. You go outside and hunt for Smith. My guess is this tunnel leads to a remote part of his property; we have to locate him before he gets away. Use whatever vehicle you can find and start looking."

"On it. How about you, Rachel?"

She flashed the light into the tunnel again. "I'll go this way."

"The passageway may be booby-trapped," he said.

She hadn't thought of that possibility, and a feeling of dread settled in the pit of her stomach. Hopefully Smith hadn't planned that well ahead. In any case, she had no choice. "It's a chance I'll have to take."

She got on her knees and began crawling forward into the tunnel.

Chapter 71

Glacier County, Montana

John Smith was totally exhausted.

He had just reached the end of the tunnel and he flashed the light on the metal steps leading up. He still had to climb a distance of fifty feet. *I'll never make it*, he thought. *I'm just not strong enough.* All of his flabby muscles screamed in pain. He was so physically drained that he was gasping for breath.

Then Smith visualized images of being locked up in prison for the rest of his life. *I can't handle that. I'll never survive it.*

It was the motivation he needed. Sucking in another gulp of stale air, he grabbed the handrail, pulled himself up and climbed the first step.

Reaching the top of the stairs much later, Smith shined the flashlight on the locking wheel over his head. All he had to do now was to turn the wheel and push the cover plate off. Then he'd be free. Putting the flashlight in his pocket, he turned the metal wheel and with great difficulty pushed against the cover plate. It didn't open at first, but after another minute, the cover plate popped open, and he felt the rush of fresh, cool air. He gulped it in, then climbed out of the hole.

Smith surveyed the scene to make sure no one was around. He was in a desolate, lightly wooded part of his property, out of sight from his estate. It was early morning now, the sun rising on an azure blue, cloudless sky. His legs, arms, and back ached, and he tried stretching to alleviate the pain.

Close to the tunnel exit was a garage and he limped toward it.

By the garage door was a keypad where he punched in his security code. He pressed another button next to the keypad and the wide door rolled up. Going inside, he flicked on the lights.

In the garage was a Chevy Suburban, just as he had left it some time ago. In the vehicle's cargo area was a suitcase full of cash, credit cards, fake IDs, and passports.

With a smile, he climbed into the SUV and started it up. After backing out of the garage, he drove off, already gloating over his escape.

Chapter 72

Glacier County, Montana

Rachel was crawling so fast that the concrete surface of the tunnel had worn away the knee patches on her pants legs. She could feel the rough cement scrape the skin off, but she kept moving forward as rapidly as possible, ignoring the pain.

After what seemed like an eternity, she saw a tiny light in the distance. The light emanated from what she assumed was the end of the long, dark passageway. She redoubled her efforts and sped up.

Eventually she reached the end and looked up toward the circular opening above. Bright sunshine flooded in. Wasting no time, she grabbed the hand rail and raced up the steps. Reaching the opening moments later, she peered over the edge. She was in a wooded area with a small building nearby. There was no one around.

After climbing out, she quickly pulled her pistol and began her search. Carefully approaching the nearby building, she noticed it was a garage with the door open. Glancing in, she saw it was empty. She entered the garage and recognized the scent right away. The area smelled of fresh gasoline, as if the engine had been gunned only minutes ago.

Rachel clenched her jaw in anger and frustration.

Smith is gone. The bastard escaped!

Then she did something she hadn't done in a long time. She started crying.

***

Rachel had been following the fresh tire tracks for what felt like hours, but in reality she knew had only been thirty minutes. The tracks led south across the rough, lightly wooded terrain. She guessed the nearest airport was in that direction. As she jogged, she listened closely for sounds of a vehicle engine, but all she heard was the call of birds flying overhead, and the rustle of tree branches. She realized her chase was a long shot – Smith was probably in another county by now.

It was a cool, mid-September day with a light breeze blowing. If she hadn't been so focused on her hunt, she would have appreciated the natural beauty of her surroundings. At her back rose majestic snow-covered mountains and the rolling landscape was a patchwork of brilliant, multi-shades of green.

Just then she heard a whispering sound in the distance. She stopped jogging and listened closely. It wasn't a car engine, something different.

As the sounds grew nearer and more distinct, she finally recognized it. A helicopter.

Then she saw it, coming over the horizon, a black dot growing in size as it came closer. She jogged toward a clearing to get a better look, and her enthusiasm surged. It wasn't just any helicopter, it was a Black Hawk. Now she knew – the third chopper and at least part of its team had survived the assault.

Excitedly, she waved her arms in the air. The chopper must have spotted her because it diverted course and came her way.

Minutes later the Black Hawk landed and its rotor blades began to slow down.

Matt Turner jumped out of the helicopter and ran towards her, a wide smile on his face.

"We got him!" he yelled.

Rachel couldn't believe it. "You found Smith?"

"Yeah," he said when he reached her. "He was headed south in an SUV – he tried to outrace us, but that was pointless."

"Where's he now?"

"We have him in the chopper, in handcuffs."

"Good work, Matt. I'm glad to see our third team made it. How many did we lose in the attack?"

He grimaced. "Two guys. I found the rest of the team on the second floor of the mansion – they were securing the prisoners."

Rachel nodded, saddened by the news of the two additional casualties. "I need to interrogate Smith right away; I can't wait until we get back to Langley. Let's head back to the house – I'll do it there."

The two agents turned and headed back to the waiting helicopter.

Chapter 73

Glacier County, Montana

"Tell me about Prism," Rachel demanded, staring down at John Smith.

Smith was sitting in a chair with his hands cuffed behind his back. Matt stood nearby, his pistol drawn. The three people were in an office on the first floor of the mansion.

"I don't know what you're talking about," Smith replied, his expression full of hate.

She studied him closely, not quite believing he was a criminal mastermind capable of implementing a worldwide plot. His grotesque physical features belied his intelligence, she realized. It was clear he had been born severely deformed.

She crossed her arms. "Don't bullshit me, Smith. I've been tracking your operation for months. I know all about Deng, and Petrov, and Sincore Technologies."

"If you know so much," he spat out angrily, "why ask me anything?"

"I know all the pieces – I just can't figure out what the hell you're trying to do. Is it about money? Is that why you're disrupting the Internet?" She shook her head slowly. "And in the process you've killed a lot of innocent people. Some of those people were fellow agents, good friends of mine."

"Those people are nothing; less than nothing. Prism will vastly improve our country –" Smith stopped in midsentence, as if he realized he'd said too much.

"So – you admit Prism is your plan."

He flashed a cold smile, but didn't reply.

She paced slowly in front of him. "I need to know three things, Smith. First, I need to know the full scope of Prism. Second, if you have any co-conspirators left." She stopped and faced him again. "Third, the name of your mole at the CIA."

Smith's head bent back in laughter.

When he finished laughing, he said, "Why should I tell you anything? I know my rights. I want my attorney present before I say another word."

"That may be true once we get back to Langley." She waved a hand in the air. "But we're out here, in the middle of nowhere Montana. Now talk, before you really piss me off."

"I know my rights," Smith repeated. "I want my attorney."

Her anger surged. "I guess you want to do this the hard way."

"What does that mean, West?"

"You'll see soon enough." She turned to Matt. "I need you to leave the room."

A puzzled expression formed on Matt's face. "Why?"

"It may get ugly in here," she replied. "I want plausible deniability. You won't see anything and it'll be Smith's word against mine."

Matt nodded. "I'll be right outside if you need me." He turned and left the room, closing the door behind him.

Rachel smiled. "Now it's just the two of us, Smith."

"I'll repeat what I said before," Smith stated. "I'm invoking my rights and I'm refusing to talk until my lawyer gets here."

"Now that Matt's gone, I don't have to play nice. Now you're going to find out what kind of heartless bitch I really am."

A worried look crossed the man's face, but he stayed silent.

She un-holstered the Desert Eagle and placed it on top of the nearby desk. Then she took a switchblade out of her pocket, and after flicking it open, laid it next to the pistol. She studied the two weapons. "What shall I use? The gun is more efficient – I can shoot you in the leg and watch you slowly bleed to death." She paused for effect. "Or I could use the knife. Messier, but sometimes more effective. I learned a certain technique while interrogating prisoners in Afghanistan. It involves cutting off your gonads, very, very slowly, then stuffing them down your throat."

She hoped it would never get that far, and that the man would break at the mere threat. Her stomach was queasy from even thinking about the actions she was describing.

She turned toward Smith. "What do think, John? Gun or knife? I hope you're not offended I called you by your first name. Call me Rachel. I think it's appropriate, now that we're going to be close, personal friends."

Smith's face showed true terror. He scrunched his shoulders, trying to move away from her. Her act appeared to be working on him.

"What's it going to be, John? The gun or the knife? It's your choice, my friend."

"You can't do this!" he screamed.

"I can. And I will." She smiled. "Unless you tell me everything I want to know."

His eyes went wide and his grimace deepened. "Please ... don't ... I'm begging you."

"If I wasn't a heartless bitch, I'd fall for that. But the problem is, I am. And I have been my whole life." She went quiet, wanting to let the futility of his situation sink in. "So, what's it going to be. It's a simple question really. Talk. Gun. Or knife. Which one do you want?"

"Please," he pleaded. "I just want my lawyer."

She gave him a hard look. "That's not one of your options. All right, since you can't decide, I'll choose for you." She picked up the knife and held the long, razor-sharp blade in the air. The blade's bright silver finish shimmered from the overhead lights. "I think I'm going with the knife. A little messier, but I think it creates an aura of raw fear that pistols don't have. Wouldn't you agree, John?"

His terrified eyes darted between the blade and Rachel several times.

She smiled a cold, calculating smile and stepped closer to him.

Chapter 74

Glacier County, Montana

John Smith stared in terror at the beautiful blonde woman, who by her actions, showed she was totally insane. He'd never met a law enforcement agent who had such disregard for a person's legal rights.

Holding the knife in her hand, she moved closer to him.

"Stop!" he shouted, his voice breaking. "Please stop."

She paused and her piercing blue eyes bore into him. "You'll talk, John?"

He didn't respond, his mind churning over his very limited options. Escape was impossible. Talking meant life in prison or even death by lethal injection. And not talking – that option was the worst of all. He could visualize the sharp blade cutting into his skin and organs. He shuddered at the thought.

"You're not saying anything, John. Are you ready to tell me about Prism? Or do I have to start cutting off your balls?"

A menacing smile spread on her lips. It was difficult to believe someone so attractive could be so heartless.

"I'm ... thinking ..." he replied.

She glanced at her watch. "I don't have all day. Here's what I'll do. I'll give you exactly 60 seconds to decide. I start cutting when the count reaches zero. I think that's more than fair, don't you, John? 60... 59 ... 58 ..."

His heart thudded in his chest. He had one other option. An option he didn't want to contemplate. But he wanted no one to know the true scope of Prism. If he died, he wanted his plan to die with him. He swallowed hard and thought about his final option, as he listened to her counting down.

"... 45 ... 44 ... 43 ...."

Chapter 75

Glacier County, Montana

"... 3 ... 2 ... 1 ... zero," Rachel said, a hard edge to her voice. "Are you going to talk, John? Or do I use my knife? Time's up."

She stared at the man, waiting for his answer.

After another moment Smith's facial expression changed from terror to a strange calmness.

"Fuck you, bitch," he said. Then something happened she hadn't expected – he smiled.

She watched as he clenched his jaw and ground his teeth.

Suddenly he grimaced, his eyes went wide, and his lips parted, a frothy substance seeping out. His body convulsed, and a second later his eyes rolled white as his head sagged on his chest.

"What the hell?" she blurted, rushing over and checking his pulse.

The man was dead.

She stared at his lifeless eyes, and then pried his jaw open. More of the frothy substance spewed out. Peering into his mouth, she inspected his back molars, and realized what had happened. It was a tactic KGB agents used in the old days. They'd surgically implant a fake molar filled with cyanide. Death was instantaneous.

She pushed his head away in disgust.

"Damn you, Smith!" she screamed. "You bastard. Now I'll never figure out what Prism is all about."

Chapter 76

Glacier County, Montana

Matt Turner rushed into the room. "What's going on, Rachel? I heard screaming." Then he saw Smith's inert body. "What happened?"

Rachel, feeling completely dejected, slumped on a chair. "Smith committed suicide. He had a cyanide capsule in one of his teeth."

"Did he tell you anything?" Matt asked.

She shook her head. "No."

"Christ. So we still don't know what he was planning or who else was involved."

"Thanks, Matt," she said testily, "for telling me the obvious."

"Calm down, will you?" He approached her and placed a hand on her shoulder. "We still have the computer programmer, the wife, and the other people upstairs – they probably know something."

She glanced up at him, his comment making her feel a bit better. "You're right."

Then Matt's face lit up with a smile. "I just remembered. There's one other thing."

"What?"

"The diary," he said. "Nikita told us Smith kept a diary. I'd bet there's quite a bit of info in there."

Rachel's optimism surged. "You're right! I'd forgotten all about that." She got up from the chair and gave him a big hug.

Pulling away from him, she said, "Thanks, Matt. We just have to find the diary."

"We'll find it."

***

Rachel, Matt, and the rest of the agents spent the next several hours searching the mansion top to bottom. They looked in all of the numerous rooms and storage areas, and closely inspected every piece of furniture and appliance. But they found nothing.

Crestfallen, Rachel questioned each of Smith's associates again, trying to ascertain if they knew where the diary was hidden. All of these people, realizing they were detainees possibly facing many years in prison, were nervous and very cooperative. Unfortunately none of them knew the location of the journal. Rachel did learn something interesting from the wife, the fact that Smith spent a majority of his time in his den. Based on this, the agent decided to once again search that room.

***

Rachel stepped into the massive den and glanced around.

In her previous search of the room, she had focused on the huge desk that was the focal point of the space. She had inspected every drawer and every surface of the desk, and only found typical office paperwork and supplies, but no diary.

She strode toward the desk now, and once again methodically searched the drawers and surfaces, looking for hidden panels, and once again came up empty.

She gazed out the floor-to-ceiling window that encompassed an entire wall of the room. The window looked out over a vast stretch of property – foothills, and beyond that, snow-peaked mountain ranges in the far distance. No wonder Smith had spent so much time in here, she thought, with a vista like that.

Turning back to the room, she carefully examined each of the furniture pieces, even cutting into the sofa and chair cushions and taking out the stuffing. Afterward she searched the large closet and the adjoining bathroom.

Not finding the book, she then ran her hands over the wall surfaces, checking for hidden seams. Next she closely examined the areas behind the paintings and other wall decorations, looking for wall safes.

After an hour of painstaking scrutiny, she slumped on a couch, discouraged by her lack of progress. *Where the hell is it?* she wondered. She was sure he would have kept it here, the room where he spent so much time.

Glancing around the room once more, her gaze fell on the large aquarium that practically covered one wall. She walked over and again examined the tank, which was filled with exotic fish swimming in shimmering aquamarine water. She was mesmerized by the serene beauty – it was clear Smith had spent a small fortune designing the intricate aquatic environment and stocking it with the striking-looking fish.

The aquarium rested on a teak wood pedestal that was decorated with elaborate curlicues and fanciful flourishes engraved into the wood. As she ran her hands over the pedestal's curlicues, she noticed something interesting. There seemed to be more wear on one of the engraved designs on the left side of the pedestal. Inspecting that area more closely, she found a hairline seam in the wood. *Is this a hidden panel?*

Removing the switchblade from her pocket, Rachel inserted the tip of the blade into the tiny seam. Then she jabbed the knife deeper into the wood and twisted. Nothing happened. She plunged the blade even deeper into the crevice and began prying out chunks of wood. She heard a metal cracking noise as if a lock had broken, and a section of the panel popped out of the pedestal. *It was a hidden panel!*

Obviously Smith had spent quite a bit of time designing the secret storage area. He had shrewdly avoided using an external lock or keypad that would attract attention. Instead, she realized, he had devised another way to access the storage compartment, probably by pressing several of the wood curlicues in a certain sequence.

She removed the panel and pulled out a large drawer, which was filled with leather bound books. Grabbing the book on top, she quickly leafed through the pages. It was full of handwritten notes, with specific details including names and events. Her heart began to pound when she found several references to Prism. Flipping to the end of the journal, she looked at the handwritten date. It was dated very recently.

Elated, Rachel smiled.

She knew she had found the diary.

Chapter 77

Langley, Virginia

Rachel West walked into Alex Miller's office, a wide grin on her face.

Miller got up from behind his desk and extended his hand. "Congratulations, Rachel."

"Thanks, boss," she said, as they shook hands and then sat down opposite each other.

"Good job on the operation," he said, "and on finding Smith's diaries. Without them ...." He didn't finish the sentence but the implication was clear to Rachel. Without the journals they wouldn't have discovered the full extent of Prism.

He steepled his hands on the desk. "Where are the books now?"

"I locked them up in the evidence room downstairs. They'll be secure there."

"Excellent. I'll have the tech guys go through them with a fine-tooth comb, get any information you may have missed. On the phone you said you'd had a chance to examine most of them?"

"That's right, Alex. I spent hours at the mansion reading the diaries and then on the flight back, so I was able to piece together Smith's operation. I also interrogated the computer programmer, Andrei Lechenko. He corroborated a lot of what's in the books."

"When you write your report, I want it as detailed as you can make it. Cover everything."

"Yes, sir."

He leaned back in his chair. "You look tired."

She was exhausted, but the excitement of closing out the operation hadn't worn off – she felt like she could do a hundred pushups and go on a 10K race. "I guess I am, a little."

Miller smiled. "After you complete your debriefing and you get checked out by the medical team, I want you to take a two week vacation."

She was about to protest, but a stern look crossed his face.

"That's an order."

"Yes, sir."

"Let's start. On the phone you gave me some info, but I want to go through the details."

"You got it, boss. Prism was much bigger than we suspected. Although we knew Smith was involved in hacking into Internet web sites in order to create havoc, we never understood his real motivation. From his journals I was able to piece together his objective, and it turns out Prism was multi-faceted. First of all, he bought the tech companies in order to control the router technology that enables computer networks to communicate with one another. Once he had that, he had access to information flow on a worldwide scale. He was able to control data on the Internet, at least for short periods of time."

"So Smith's objective was to control the worldwide Internet. That's a terrifying thought."

"Yes it is, Alex. After each of the disasters he caused, the authorities eventually figured out the intrusion and regained control, but that took days or even weeks."

"How did Smith profit from it, Rachel?"

"He was an expert at trading in the stock market. Smith did what's called short-selling – in effect betting that a stock would go down in price. He would short-sell large blocks of stocks in a particular industry. Then he would create havoc in that industry, thereby causing the stock prices of those companies to plummet while he made a fortune. Since Smith knew when the disaster would take place before it happened, he would short-sell right before the catastrophe, and profit from his trades after the event."

Miller laid his hands flat on the desk. "So his motive was to make money."

"Yes. But Prism was much bigger than that."

"How so?"

"It turns out he wasn't just interested in creating chaos to turn a profit, as if that wasn't bad enough." She paused a moment and leaned forward in her chair. "Smith's ultimate goal was to convert the United States from a democracy to a totalitarian state, much like Russia."

A shocked expression came over Miller's face. "What are you talking about?"

"Just what I said – he was planning, over time, to eliminate the Constitution, Congress, and the Supreme Court, and replace it with a dictatorial, completely powerful President."

"That's insane."

"I agree, Alex. It is insane. But that was Prism's ultimate goal."

"How was he planning on doing all this? It sounds far-fetched."

"That's what I thought too at first, but the more of his notes I read, the more convinced I am he could have done it. Prism was a way to generate almost unlimited amounts of money. And with that money he was going to fund politicians who had similar ideas as himself. I'm sure you've heard of Alison Blakely?"

Miller nodded. "Sure. She's the current Governor of Massachusetts."

"That's right. From his notes it's clear Blakely shares his views, although from her public speeches you'd never know it. You've probably heard that she's planning on running for President of the United States. Well, it turns out that Smith had already made massive donations to her campaign, in secret of course. And she wasn't the only politician he was backing – the diaries mention several other like-minded people he was funding for other high-level elected positions."

"So. Smith would be the power behind the throne?"

"Yes, Alex. He was a very reclusive man – he never wanted the spotlight. He only wanted the power."

"I still don't understand how he was planning on turning America into a totalitarian country."

"Once Blakely and the other politicians he backed were in power," Rachel continued, "Smith would pass very restrictive gun control laws. He figured that once firearms were only available to law enforcement personnel, U.S. citizens couldn't fight back, even if things like the Constitution or Congress were eliminated. It's a pattern we've seen before in communist countries like Russia, Cuba, North Korea, and others. When the citizens are powerless to resist, a totalitarian state can exist."

Miller nodded. "And since Smith in effect controlled information flow on the Internet, he had access to all of the private data of every American. Emails, web searches, Facebook posts, credit card info, health records, phone texts – all of it is online now. Was Smith planning on using this info also? With it he could blackmail or intimidate everyone, including politicians, elected leaders, and other Americans he couldn't buy off. Was that part of Smith's plan also?"

"Yes it was, Alex. He has notes about that in the diaries."

"But why did Smith want to turn the U.S. into a communist-like country? For the power and control he would wield?"

"That and more. This is where it gets even more sinister. As we suspected, John Smith was an alias that he had been using. And from his diaries I learned he'd gone by several different names throughout his life. But you'll never believe his true background."

"Tell me."

Rachel leaned forward in her chair. "John Smith's parents were from Russia. They were Russian KGB agents, moles planted in the U.S. a long time ago to spy for their country. The couple had only one son, 'John', who was born here in the U.S. The couple planned to have him grow up and follow in their footsteps as spies. But there was a big problem with that. 'John' was born severely deformed. There was no way he could blend in easily in order to become a spy. So, over time, his parents came to resent their repulsive-looking child. As he went from childhood into his teen years, that resentment grew into shame and outright hatred. Smith was psychologically damaged and never recovered. It was clear from Smith's notes that he spent his whole life trying to get his parents to accept him and love him. In order to please them, he sought to become a better Communist than they were, studying Marxist and Leninist ideology. His devotion to Communist ideals comes through strongly in the diaries. In fact Prism, his plan to turn the U.S into a totalitarian country, was a way for him to prove to his parents that he was worthy of their love."

"That's amazing, Rachel. Where are the parents now?"

"From his notes it appears they died a few years ago in a car accident."

Miller nodded. "Ironic, isn't it?"

"What's that?"

"If Smith had succeeded, his parents would have never known about it."

"You're right, Alex."

Miller smiled. "It's a good thing we were able to stop Smith. At first, I was disappointed he didn't live. I wanted to interrogate him myself. But now learning how sinister his plan was, and how close he was to implementing it, I'm glad he's dead."

"Me too, boss. My only regret is we still don't know who the mole is at CIA."

"I agree. But after the tech guys pore over the books, maybe we'll get additional leads."

Rachel leaned back in the chair. "Where are the prisoners now?"

"Matt Turner put them in a cell downstairs – he's questioning them for additional information about Prism. I told him to focus on the computer programmer – he's probably the best source. Once we're done with the group, I'll turn them over to HQ."

A disturbing thought struck Rachel. "What about the politicians Smith was backing? They received huge amounts of money. And the secret aim of their campaigns is to overthrow democracy in the U.S. What do we do about them?"

"I'll take care of that end," Miller said. "I'll leak their secret intentions to the press. It will create a media firestorm. We have enough specific information from the diaries that it'll be clear to the country what those politicians were planning. I'll be *very* surprised if their campaigns survive."

Rachel grinned. "Good thinking, boss."

"See, for an old man, I can still be useful."

"I never said you were old."

Miller laughed. "I guess not. But I'm sure you've thought it. By the way, after your two week vacation, I've got another assignment for you." He reached in a drawer, pulled out a thick folder and held it in the air. "And I think you're going to like this one."

"Let me see," she replied eagerly.

He put the folder back in the drawer. "Not now. Now I want you to write your report, and then see the doc to get checked out." He pointed to his office door. "After that you're going home. I want you to take that well-earned vacation."

"Yes, sir," Rachel said with a smile. She stood and left the office.

But in the back of her mind, she was already thinking about the next case. *I wonder what that's about?*

END

***

Lee Gimenez is the author of 10 novels. Several of his books became bestsellers, including *The Washington Ultimatum* and *Blacksnow Zero.*

Lee's books are available at Amazon, Barnes & Noble, Books-A-Million, Apple, and many other retailers in the U.S. and around the world.

He invites you to visit him at his website, www.LeeGimenez.com.

You can also join him on Twitter, Facebook, Goodreads, Google Plus, and LinkedIn.

Other novels by Lee Gimenez

The Washington Ultimatum
Blacksnow Zero
The Sigma Conspiracy
The Nanotech Murders
Death on Zanath
Virtual Thoughtstream
Azul 7
Terralus 4
The Tomorrow Solution

Lightning Source UK Ltd.
Milton Keynes UK
UKHW012227121021
392097UK00001B/62

9 780692 245873